THE MELLOW MADAM

MICHAEL ARDITTI

THE MELLOW MADAM

AND OTHER STORIES

SALT
MODERN
STORIES

S
SALT

CROMER

PUBLISHED BY SALT PUBLISHING 2025

2 4 6 8 10 9 7 5 3 1

First published in Great Britain in 2025 by
Salt Publishing Ltd
12 Norwich Road, Cromer, Norfolk NR27 0AX United Kingdom

GPSR representative
Matt Parsons matt.parsons@upi2mbooks.hr
UPI-2M PLUS d.o.o., Medulićeva 20, 1,0000 Zagreb, Croatia

www.saltpublishing.com

Salt Publishing Limited Reg. No. 5293401

A CIP catalogue record for this book is available from the British Library

ISBN 978 1 78463 297 7 (Paperback edition)
ISBN 978 1 78463 298 4 (Electronic edition)

Typeset in Granjon by Salt Publishing

Printed and bound in Great Britain by Clays Ltd, Elcograf S.p.A

For Miranda Seymour and Sian Phillips

Contents

As Seen on TV

JEAN LED THE repairman to the door. She dreaded his visits even more than those of the district nurse and Social Services. He always told her the same thing: the set was fifteen years old, and a new one would save her money in the long run as well as providing her with a better picture. Last time, he'd left a leaflet on the settee about 'the next generation of televisions': LEDs, LCDs and plasma screens, but she made it a rule never to buy anything with initials, while plasma put her in mind of hospitals. He called them *smart* sets, which made her laugh since hers was a smarter set than he would ever know. It was a super-smart set; she thought of it as the Mavis Trimble of televisions, Mavis having been the first girl from her school to go to university. It was a set in which the people on screen didn't just talk to one another, they talked to her.

The repairman wasn't the only person to leave leaflets. Taisha, her case manager, had brought several about the activities the council ran for *super adults*: *super*, to Jean's surprise, meant *old*. Taisha made pronouncements like 'No one should be lonely in Lewisham' and 'Seventy is the new fifty', which was all well and good, but Jean was eighty-nine and, however Taisha might twist the figures, she couldn't imagine taking part in Boogie Nights, Drag Bingo or Low Impact Aerobics. Besides, keeping to herself didn't mean that she was on her own. Over the years, she had befriended the casts of many TV serials. She'd shared their births and bereavements, loves and adulteries, windfalls and bankruptcies, promotions, redundancies, illnesses and prison sentences and, latterly, even their abortions and same-sex affairs, of which she didn't approve. But like Marcia, the matriarch of *Waverley Square*, who'd weathered storms ranging from her husband's conviction for fraud to her daughter's heroin addiction, while never succumbing to self-pity or wearing the same dress twice, she was of the opinion that 'It takes all sorts to make a world.'

Jean had known tragedy, albeit not on the scale of Marcia's. Her father had been killed in the Blitz, along with her Aunty Rose, when a bomb hit the house in Spicer Street. Her mother claimed that he'd gone there to do some odd jobs while Uncle Bill was in the desert fighting Rommel, but Olive, Jean's older sister, told her that the fire-watchers found them in each other's arms, neither of them wearing a stitch. Desolate, her mother took to her bed, where she remained for the next twenty years. Olive and Jean, who was nine at the time, had run the house between them, until Olive moved away to train as a nurse ('After all, I've had enough bleeding practice!'), leaving Jean to take care of Mother.

On quitting school, Jean worked at the Robertson's jam factory until it closed in 1970, when she started charring. Olive married and had two sons: grown men now, most likely married with children and even grandchildren of their own, but Jean had never met them. Olive, Bernie and the boys had emigrated to Australia. Over time, communication had dwindled to an annual Christmas card. Then Olive died of throat cancer (Mother blamed the climate) and the cards stopped. After more than sixty years, Jean had to look at a photograph to picture her face. The last time she'd seen her was when she waved her off at Tilbury in 1958. She remembered because it was the year that they rented their first television.

It sat on the chest of drawers in Mother's room. Uncle Mark and Cousin Geoff hauled an armchair up the stairs, so that Jean could watch in comfort. She worried aloud that moving it would make it harder to invite the family round on a Sunday afternoon, at which Mother looked at her blankly, before they both burst out laughing. They took to eating their teas on trays in front of the early evening programmes. Even Saturday night's *Six-Five Special* was better than sitting in silence since, with Mother confined to the house all day and Jean busy on the shop floor bottling Golden Shred, conversation was limited.

There'd been nothing smart about that set and Jean rarely chatted to it, knowing that Mother disapproved. 'You're as daft as a brush and not half as useful,' she would say, when she was watching *The Grove Family* or *Emergency Ward 10*. 'Carry on like that and men in white coats will come and take you away.'

Mother died in 1963, the winter of the big freeze. Having scarcely left her bedroom in months, she'd taken herself downstairs and built a snowman in the yard. The mystery of it consumed Jean more than the grief. The funeral was delayed for five weeks because the gravediggers were unable to break up the ground. It was a small affair, with only Uncle Mark and his family, Uncle Bill and his new wife, Mrs Thurston who'd worked with Mother at the dairy during the War, and Mrs Bridgewater from Number 23, who went to every local funeral, counting the mourners as eagerly as a programme controller monitoring the ratings.

It made sense for Jean to move into Mother's room, rather than risk carrying the set into her own or, more perilously, down the stairs. At the suggestion of the man from Radio Rentals, who called her his favourite customer, she upgraded to colour in time for the Queen's Silver Jubilee. Then when Mrs Henshaw, for whom she'd cleaned for fourteen years, died in 1985 and left her £500, she bought a set of her own. The salesman pointed out its unique features, but it wasn't until it was installed that she discovered quite how unique it was. In the past, no matter what she said to them, her on-screen friends acknowledged her only on special occasions, like when the Ogdens in *Coronation Street* won a second honeymoon at the Savoy Hotel and raised their champagne glasses to her as well as to each other (she'd grabbed her tooth mug to join in the toast). Now she found that she could talk to anyone she wished at the end of a programme and they would reply. So she was heartbroken when the set was damaged during her move to Marcus Garvey House. Miraculously, the replacement enabled her to conduct the private conversations as before. But there was no guarantee that a third set would do the same, which was why, whatever Taisha and the repairman might say, she was determined to stick with the one she had.

Several of Jean's neighbours had protested against the Council's decision to redevelop Leveret Terrace. Miss Parkin, who'd never given any of them the time of day, posted flyers condemning the destruction of the community, and Jill Lewis, who was studying politics at night school, alleged that it was gerrymandering, which put Jean in mind of the Blitz. The upheaval apart, she hadn't been overly exercised by the move. While most of the residents of Marcus Garvey House were not her sort (although she didn't like to say so in case she sounded prejudiced), they were perfectly friendly. Her flat was airy and snug, and Taisha assured her that the black mould above the bath was harmless. Number 16 was on the third floor, and she was still steady enough on her pins to use the stairs when the lift was broken, but most weeks she only went out on pension day to do her shopping. Mr Jampa, who ran the Mandala Market, always had a few words for her, even when he had a queue of customers.

Although the heavy work had become too much for her, she carried on charring until she was seventy-four. She gave up after a stay in hospital for what the surgeon, who wore a polka dot bow tie, called a 'minor procedure to tidy up your bits and bobs.' Mrs Wentworth (Monday and Thursday mornings) tried to arrange a retirement party with her other ladies, but it proved to be impossible to find a date to suit them all. Instead, they gave her some lovely presents: an electric foot massager, a bottle of scent, a quilted housecoat and a Wedgwood vase exactly like the one she'd broken.

It was during her two-month recuperation that she started keeping the television on all day. She overheard complaints in the post office and the Mandela Market that there was 'nothing to watch', or else that there were too many quiz or property shows, but that was nonsense. The range of choice, even in the early afternoons, was one reason that she didn't want any extra channels (the other was the fiddly remote control). The questions on quiz shows were an education in themselves, and property shows provided a glimpse into other people's lives, not just their houses. She found something of interest in everything, apart from the wildlife programmes, which used Nature as an excuse for cruelty. But what she most enjoyed were the dramas: not the single plays or even the mini-series which ended before she'd had a chance to get to know the characters, but the long-running serials. She never called them *soaps*, which made them sound frothy, and they were far too important for that.

The characters were her friends. Over time – she wouldn't say how long, because people on television were touchy about their ages – they'd all shared their secrets with her. She took care not to pry and they, in turn, valued her discretion. Although her own life was even less eventful than that of Beryl Flanagan, the eighty-year-old lollipop lady in *Wellington Towers*, they never made her feel that it was trivial or dull. Indeed, as Lou Beale, a pillar of *EastEnders*, said to her shortly before she passed. 'I envy you, Jean. You've got things sorted. Not like the rest of us, never knowing what's going to hit us from one episode to the next.'

Jean tried not to play favourites, but her resolve crumbled when it came to *Boardroom*. Set in Bridgetown on Teesside, a part of the country she'd never previously visited or even considered of interest, it featured the Fishburnes, a family with a property empire extending from a tower block (not unlike Marcus Garvey House) and a shopping centre to an amusement arcade and a country club. At its head was Sir Douglas, whose recent knighthood for services to charity was doubly unmerited, given that his crooked accountant, Brian Dixon, had ensured that not a penny came out of his own pocket. For the past eight years, almost as long as *Boardroom* had been on air, he'd topped the poll of *Best TV Villains*. To Jean's dismay, he'd also twice been voted *Sexiest Man on Television*, his shock of silver hair and gap-toothed grin proving as seductive off-screen as on.

As he confessed at intervals to his downtrodden wife Angela, he'd carved out a career in crime long before the serial began. As a boy, he blinded Nanny Walters in an 'accident' with baking soda and vinegar, after she ordered him upstairs to remake his bed. In his youth, he ruined his sister Mabel's fiancé, Toby, freeing her to marry the wheelchair-bound landowner, Lord Matterdon. The loveless match had driven her to drink and a string of affairs with men young enough to be her sons, were her husband not impotent. Finally, and crucial to the storyline, he'd engineered the disappearance of his older brother, Ned, whose whereabouts remained unknown and whom Jean prayed would one day return to take revenge. Perhaps that would be the fateful confrontation that viewers were promised for the forthcoming 1,000th episode?

Aided by Dixon, Sir Douglas bribed, blackmailed and back-stabbed his way to ever-greater wealth and power. The sole check to his ambitions was his nephew, Rory, who'd inherited Ned's stake in the company. Having plotted against him for years, Sir Douglas had now determined to dispose of him once and for all. To that end, he'd invited Rory and his wife Deborah to a hunting lodge in the Dales to celebrate their tenth wedding anniversary, in the course of which he was to meet with a shooting accident. Meanwhile, 'unable to help myself,' as he put it to Dixon, he planned to 'comfort' the soon-to-be-grieving widow.

Although some viewers, who, it had to be said, didn't share her inside knowledge, accused Rory of being holier-than-thou, Jean thought him almost perfect. His one fault was that he was too trusting. No matter how many people, not least Jean herself, warned him of Sir Douglas's intrigues, he refused to take heed. 'It's just Douglas's manner,' he remarked regularly to Deborah, along with 'Family always comes first for the Fishburnes,' which, in his uncle's case, was patently untrue. Given that he'd studied in Oxford, the home of *Brideshead Revisited* and *Inspector Morse*, Rory could be surprisingly naïve.

On the other hand, his open-heartedness was one of his most attractive qualities. He was warm and generous, a devoted husband to Deborah and a doting father to Fliss and Ginny. He was the voice of reason in the board meetings that gave the serial its name, and of decency when he spoke up for the tenants and shopkeepers, whose rents Sir Douglas wanted to raise. In an act that had endeared him to Jean forever, he personally broke up the concrete that his uncle's henchmen had poured into the drain of an elderly widow they were trying to evict. The work was so gruelling that he'd had to remove his shirt.

Jean had never bothered with bodies. The only one apart from her mother's and her own) that she'd touched since leaving school, was Bert Steele's in a moment of weakness after the factory's summer outing – even then, he hadn't removed his vest. But Rory's was another matter: so firm and brown (but in an English way). Seeing him gave her the same guilty pleasure as eating a layer of Dairy Box in a single go.

Rory had stayed to chat to her after the very first episode, when she was still struggling to memorise everyone's name. Unlike the characters in other serials, he was the only one in *Boardroom* who did. 'I'm greedy, Jean,' he told her, in a voice that made her tingle, 'I want you all to myself.' When she questioned why such a handsome young man should be interested in her, he replied, with a dimpled smile, that 'It's what's on the inside that counts.' He never let her down. At first twice and now three times a week, except when he took Deborah and the girls on holiday, he lingered behind after the credits. They discussed the day's events on *Boardroom* and, despite dismissing her concerns about Sir Douglas, he sought her advice on various matters, including his marriage. Although she'd remained single, Jean had observed enough on-screen couples to be considered something of an expert.

In recent weeks, Rory had been preoccupied, preparing for the hour-long 1,000th episode but, although it had now been filmed, he was sworn to secrecy and forbidden so much as to hint at what it contained. With all the principal characters converging on the hunting lodge, the potential for conflict was huge. The anticipation kept Jean awake at night and, with only one episode left before all was revealed, she switched the television to BBC One at 7 p.m., a full hour before it was due to start. Even though *The One Show* and *Road Rescue* were among her least favourite programmes, she could not run the risk of her increasingly arthritic fingers fumbling with the remote, causing her to miss a single moment of *Boardroom*.

Clutching her chicken cup-a-soup and a wedge of what her mother had called 'mousetrap' (a purpose it had indeed served in Leveret Terrace), she sat and waited for the familiar theme tune, which, even if there were no mourners, she wanted played at her funeral. After opening in Bridgetown, where Penny, Sir Douglas's secretary and one-time mistress, was threatened by an ex-boyfriend (either a taxi driver or a taxidermist with a thick brogue), and moving to Matterdon Manor, where Mabel drunkenly dangled a vodka bottle just out of her husband's reach, the scene shifted to the hunting lodge, where a conscience-stricken keeper confessed to Rory that Sir Douglas had paid him to tamper with his gun. It had taken 999 episodes, but Rory's eyes were finally opened to his uncle's treachery. He stormed through the lodge, finding him in the library, playing chess with himself.

'I know,' he said, gulping for breath.

'You know what?' Sir Douglas asked, with a telltale twitch.

'Everything. The anniversary present you've picked out for me. Just the latest in your fiendish schemes. But this time I intend to make you pay.'

He headed into the hall and picked up one of the guns laid out for the morning's shoot, fingering the barrel as the credits rolled.

Jean watched frantically. There was no question that Sir Douglas deserved to die, but not at Rory's hands. 'No!' she shouted at the screen: 'You're young. You're sure to get caught. You'll spend the rest your life behind bars. It's not worth it.'

He turned and looked her straight in the eye. 'You were

right all along, Jean. Can you forgive me for doubting you?'

'Of course. You know I'm always on your side. I've no love for your uncle. But there has to be a better way. Put the gun down!'

'He's the mould on your bathroom wall.'

Jean started. She had no recollection of ever mentioning it to Rory.

'The stain on your dentures.'

She clapped her hand over her mouth.

'Why didn't I listen to you?'

'You mustn't blame yourself. You weren't able to see what he was plotting with Dixon the way I was.'

'Brian Dixon, he's in on it too?'

'From the word go.'

'I should have listened to Deborah and bugged his office.'

'It would have gone against your nature. You're too noble.'

'I suppose I am, aren't I?' His sad smile melted her insides. 'But that doesn't make me weak. I'll prove myself to Deborah. I'll prove myself to you all.'

'But your little girls—'

'Not so little these days, Jean.'

'Which is why they need you more than ever. You haven't thought it through.'

'There's never enough time at the end of an episode.'

'We have time now.'

'You're right. Who knows what it would do to them to have a murderer as a father?'

'Indeed,' Jean replied. 'So you must find somebody else for the job.' She didn't like to say *shoot* or *kill*, but *waste*, *whack* and *rub out*, routine in London serials, might not mean the same on Teesside. 'Somebody older, with less to lose.'

'You, Jean?'

She trembled. She hadn't dared to suggest it but, as ever, he'd read her mind. 'Me, Rory.'

'But how? You live so far away. Your pension won't cover the train fare.'

'I'm not clever like you, Rory. I know you'll come up with a plan.'

'Wait! I've got it. You live in Lewisham, don't you?'

'That's right. And you're always welcome at Number 16, Marcus Garvey House.' She reminded herself to buy some more biscuits.

'One day, Jean, just as soon as I can get away. First things first. Sir Douglas is making a personal appearance in the shopping centre on Friday.'

'Yes, he's opening the supermarket. It was in the local paper. I picked up a copy at the bins.' She wished she hadn't mentioned that. 'Funny, I never usually read it.'

They'd given him a second name – an alias – alongside *TV's Douglas Fishburne*, but it was without doubt him.

'There's your chance. You can bump him off.' *Bump off*: why hadn't she thought of that one?

'But how?' She looked dubiously at the weapon in Rory's hands. 'I don't have a gun.'

'No, no gun. It would be too conspicuous. Let me think! What about the knife your mother used for carving the brisket?'

Jean felt her eyes well with tears. Fancy Rory knowing that! It showed that he took as much interest in her life as she did in his. 'I haven't had brisket since Mother died.'

'But you've kept the knife, haven't you?'

'In the top drawer next to the sink.'

'When all this is over, I'm going to see you have brisket every week. Now, you mustn't leave anything to chance. Check what time he'll be cutting the ribbon. You'll need to be there well in advance to make sure you get a good position. Sir Douglas is very popular, especially with the ladies. Remember that he's twice been voted *Sexiest Man on Television*.'

'It should have been you, Rory.'

'Oh no, Jean. I scorn such tawdry accol . . . titles. I just want to be loved by the people close to me: Deborah and the girls and you.' Jean's tears streaked her cheeks. 'And take care to keep the knife well hidden. The plan will be foiled if somebody spots it. Then, when he's stiff . . . kaput . . . brown bread—' Rory appeared to be having as much trouble finding the right word as she had – 'come and tell me about it after the next episode.'

'The thousandth.'

'Yes, the thousandth. Goodbye, Jean. Good luck and God bless.'

He fizzled out like the picture on an old-fashioned set, leaving Jean staring at a celebrity wine tasting, one of the many programmes that Rory used as camouflage. She pressed the Off switch on the remote, as she always did after their private conversations, but she had more to mull over than usual. She'd agreed to rid the world of a notorious villain (eight years topping the poll was a record), which would earn her the gratitude of millions, yet she'd never stabbed anyone, even by accident. How easy would

it be? Was her wrist strong enough to wield the knife?
No matter what happened, she would never betray Rory.
They could keep her in solitary confinement, feeding her
on bread and water, and she would still swear that she'd
acted alone.

After another sleepless night, she took the bus to the shopping centre, mingling with the crowds, like Emma when
she'd kidnapped the baby in *Waverley Square*. She had no
difficulty locating the supermarket, which had replaced
the old sportswear shop at the far end of the mall. Posters plastered over huge plate glass windows announced
the Grand Opening at 11 a.m. on Friday. Turning away
from Sir Douglas's grinning face and the criss-crossing
stickers offering various deals and discounts, she peered
at the bustle inside. Assistants scurried to and fro, some
wiping shelves and others stocking them. A cleaner pushed
a heavy-duty polisher around the floor, bobbing her head
to the music pouring through her earphones. She felt a
twinge of remorse that all their hard work would be over-
shadowed by Sir Douglas's death, until she remembered
that they were the ones who'd invited him. They might not
be blessed with a television like hers, but they'd had plenty
of chance every Monday, Wednesday and Friday evening
to learn the truth about their so-called Guest of Honour.

She returned home and took her best dress out of the
wardrobe to air. She'd bought it for Mrs Wentworth's party
and never worn it. The police would be sure to treat her
with greater respect if she looked smart. In the morning,
she sellotaped the knife to her arm, which was uncomfortable but not painful, put on the dress, which hung more

loosely on her than she'd expected, forced herself to eat a slice of toast and sat, thinking of Rory, until it was time to leave.

The overcast sky threatened rain and, for one agonizing moment, she feared that the event would be cancelled, before recalling that the mall was under cover. She reached the store, where the posters and stickers had been replaced by red, white and blue bunting, as if Sir Douglas were royalty. A crowd of thirty or so fans had gathered, some clutching autograph books, which she hoped, for their sakes, he would sign on arrival. She edged her way forward, prompting a young man to hiss 'Go on then, love, age before beauty,' and a woman with tattoos to grab her arm. Thankfully, it was the left and not the right, to which she'd sellotaped the knife. So far she'd managed to hold it straight, suffering only two slight pricks. She smiled at the thought that, like a magician, she had something up her sleeve.

Abracadabra, and out it would come! She chuckled, breaking off abruptly for fear of drawing attention to herself. A ripple of applause ran through the crowd as a town crier, straight out of *Poldark*, led a group of five men and one woman towards the store. They were too far away for Jean to identify them, although the woman's blonde hair ruled out Angela. Seconds later, Sir Douglas himself walked up, as close as if he were in her front room. She was thankful to see him sign several autographs, sparing the fans a wasted journey. It was odd, but as he chatted and joked with them, his face looked kinder than it did on the screen. She reminded herself that it was a pretence and carefully loosened the Sellotape on the knife.

It was a tricky manoeuvre, trying to avoid being both cut and seen, particularly by the security guard, who stood with the staff at the store entrance. To her relief, he turned to face a small man with a bald head, gleaming like a banister, who read out a speech welcoming Sir Douglas to Lewisham.

Sir Douglas, word-perfect, replied that he'd opened various buildings during his time on *Boardroom*, usually with bodies buried beneath. It was a blatant confession and Jean looked to the security guard to arrest him, but like everyone else, he was laughing. She had to act before Sir Douglas won them over completely. Her heart began to race and her mouth tasted like salt as, knife in hand, she sneaked up on him. Meanwhile, the bald man passed him a pair of scissors, the size of shears, and he moved to cut the ceremonial ribbon. Her mind went blank and her body seemed to float, as she lunged forward and stabbed him in the chest.

She was surprised at the solidity of his flesh. She had used all her strength and the knife barely penetrated. For a moment, she wondered whether he was wearing a bullet-proof vest, but then he clutched his chest and his body folded. She felt a rush of relief, which vanished when somebody grabbed her from behind, knocking away the knife and wrenching her arms behind her back. Didn't he know that old bones were brittle? Somebody else pulled her hair as though to check if it were a wig. Her vision was obscured by the crowd and her senses scrambled by the pain shooting through her arms, but she made out a cluster of people around Sir Douglas, with the blonde woman kneeling by his side, cradling his head. Elsewhere, a mother thrust her hand over her screaming daughter's eyes, while she herself stared at the scene, transfixed. Several people talked on their phones and others held them up to take photographs. A woman spat in Jean's face and, with her arms pinioned, she was unable to wipe it. This was not what was supposed to happen. Didn't these people know what kind of man Sir Douglas was? Didn't they watch *Boardroom*? If not, why were they here?

She felt a trickle in her pants and feared that she would disgrace herself. Her body sagged like a dressmaker's dummy. 'I'm eighty-nine,' she shouted to the man who had hold of her, but he took no notice. She watched as two ambulance men rushed up to tend to Sir Douglas. Moments later, there was a stir behind her; her arms were released and she pitched forward against a policeman, who spoke to her, but she couldn't hear him above the din. Clasping her shoulder, he swept her through the crowd, leaving his colleague to question her captor. She felt bruised, and not just where she'd been grabbed. She was not used to people touching her. They assumed that, because she was old and alone, she must be dirty. Whereas she kept herself as spotless as her screen.

The policeman led her towards the store entrance and, as she glimpsed Sir Douglas's statue-white face, she felt an unexpected pang of guilt. Once indoors, she sensed the staff watching her more intently than anyone since Jim Dodds, the foreman at Robinson's. Somebody brought her a chair and somebody else a paper cone full of water, which she grasped, splashing her dress. The policeman asked her questions, but the volume appeared to be switched off, and she could only shake her head. Eventually, he stopped

and stood beside her, gazing through the window as Sir
Douglas was wheeled away on a stretcher. Three more
officers arrived, two talking to witnesses and one replacing
the red ribbon with yellow-and-black crime scene tape.
A woman police officer, looking like DCI Tennison in
Prime Suspect, entered the store and asked her further
inaudible questions. Instinct, however, alerted her when
she was uttering the stock phrase: *You do not have to say
anything. But it may harm your defence if you do not mention
when questioned something which you later rely on in court.
Anything you do say may be given in evidence*. Midway, she
joined in, to the officer's visible surprise.

They drove her to the police station, where procedures
had barely changed since *Dixon of Dock Green*. She gave
her details to the custody sergeant, who asked if she had a
solicitor, which made her laugh. He informed her of her
right to legal advice, as well as to a phone call to a family
member, friend or carer (he emphasised the last) to let them
know where she was. But there was only one person she
wanted to call and she didn't have his number. For the
first time, she would be separated from Rory by something
other than a power cut. He was more important to her now
than ever: not just her friend but her key defence witness.
Boardroom attracted four million viewers each week, but
what if the judge and jury weren't among them? How
would they know the truth about Sir Douglas?

She was taken to a cell and offered a cup of tea, which,
reassured by the stainless-steel toilet, she accepted. An
aching tiredness overwhelmed her and she lay back on
the bunk, the meagre mattress more comfortable than it
looked. She must have dozed off since, before she knew

it, the custody sergeant came to lead her to the interview room. To her surprise, Taisha was sitting opposite the *Prime Suspect* officer, but her greeting lacked its usual ebullience: a quick nod as if she suspected that the officer was making notes. As she sat down beside her, Jean spotted a male officer standing in the corner, even though there were two empty chairs. The female officer switched on a tape recorder, identifying herself as Detective Inspector Helen Arthur and her colleague as Detective Constable Hugh Larkin. She explained the interview process and read Jean her rights in words that were once again familiar, although this time she chose not to repeat them. She said nothing until the inspector accused her of wounding Samuel Wearing, which had been Sir Douglas's alias in the paper.

'Wounding?' she asked. 'Isn't he dead?'

'Jean precious, please,' Taisha said.

'No, thankfully,' the inspector said. 'Why, were you hoping for a murder charge? Believe me, *Grievous Bodily Harm with Intent* still carries a life sentence.'

'He looked dead to me.'

'He might well have been if the incision had been a few millimetres higher. Your knife struck a rib.'

'The Lord be praised!' said Taisha, who sang in her church choir.

'So he wasn't wearing a bullet-proof vest?'

'He's an actor!' the inspector said.

'She lives in a fantasy world,' Taisha said, patting Jean's hand, which made her wince.

'Can you give me any idea of what was going through your mind . . . why you did it?' the inspector asked, in the same tone as the doctor's when he questioned her about her bowels.

'I did it for Rory.'

'Rory who?'

'Rory's one of the characters in *Boardroom* . . . the TV programme,' Taisha interposed.

'He's like a son to me. Sir Douglas was trying to kill him.'

'Do you have any family of your own?'

'Only Rory and Deborah.'

'Deborah?'

'Rory's wife. And Fliss and Ginny, their two little girls.'

'I see.'

'Do you? No! You think I'm just a lonely old woman. Like she does.' She turned to Taisha, who smiled bleakly. 'Rory's chosen me. I don't know why. There's nothing special about me, except for my television. He stays behind after every episode. He never misses a chance to chat.'

'And these voices you hear—'

'I see him too. And all the rest of them.'

'Yes, of course. Do they tell you to do things?'

'Like what?'

'Kill Mr Wearing.'

'Sir Douglas,' Taisha said.

'Oh no, absolutely not. It was all my own idea. Rory never knew a thing. You have to believe me.'

'I do,' the inspector said, more gently now she realised that Jean had Rory on her side.

'You promise you won't arrest him?'

'I promise. But it's what we're to do with you that concerns me. You won't be able to go home. For one thing, there's a horde of photographers camped outside who'd follow you back.'

'They can't come in. I don't have any biscuits.'

'Don't worry. You'll stay here tonight. We'll make you as comfortable as we can. Then you'll go before the magistrates in the morning and, with Taisha's help, we'll find you a bed in a secure hos . . . in a unit where you're able to talk to people who understand these matters better than we do.'

'Talk? What about?'

'To tell them your story, precious,' Taisha interposed.

'But I've already told you,' Jean said. 'It was my idea, not Rory's.'

'Yes, we've ascertained that,' the inspector said. 'Now DC Larkin will take you back to the cell, and I'll see you again tomorrow.'

'Oh no! I can't. What's the time?'

'Almost half-past six. You'll be wanting something to eat.'

'I have to go home. *Boardroom*'s on at eight. I can't miss it. I've watched every episode since it began.'

'I'm sorry. But you must appreciate that after what you've done—'

'Please! I have to.' Jean started to cry, tears and mucus streaming down her face. She turned to Taisha, her words muffled by sobs. 'You must explain. I have to watch. I can't miss it. I can't!'

'Is there any way that she can watch it here?' Taisha asked. 'A television in the station?'

'I'm afraid that's impossible.'

'Boss, if I might have a word,' the constable said, moving forward and whispering in her ear.

'DC Larkin has kindly offered to stay behind and let you watch it on his tablet.'

'I don't want any tablets.'

'The tablet is a screen, precious,' Taisha said. 'A bit smaller than yours. But you'll still be able to watch your programme, which is what counts.'

'No, it has to be my television. Or how will he know where to find me?'

'Just this once he may not,' Taisha said. 'But you'll be able to catch up with him soon, I promise. Now you take care, and I'll see you at the court in the morning.'

The constable escorted Jean back to the cell. Another officer brought her tea on a white plastic tray, like in hospital, but her stomach was too tight to eat anything. She'd seen too many police series to trust the constable to keep his word.

She lost track of time and began to despair until, with a cheery shout of 'It's about to start,' he entered the cell. He sat down next to her on the narrow bunk and produced the smallest, thinnest portable television she'd ever seen. He switched it on and, to her intense relief, she recognised *Out of the Mouths*, a programme where children commented on the week's events, which preceded Friday's episode of *Boardroom*. He held the screen between them like a hymn book.

'Can you see clearly? Would you like me to turn up the sound?'

She shushed him, as *Out of the Mouths* ended and the continuity announcer introduced the 'milestone' 1,000th episode of *Boardroom*, followed by the unmistakable theme tune and opening montage of bridges, hills, mansions and tower blocks, intercut with shots of the principal characters as they stepped out of cars.

The episode opened with Sir Douglas and Angela in bed.

'No,' Jean said, gulping. 'It's all wrong. I stabbed him. You . . . she said he was in hospital. How can he be out already?'

'Um . . . the show must go on?'

Sir Douglas stood up, slipping off his pyjama jacket to reveal a pale chest with a patch of hair and no sign of any injury.

'Not a scratch!' Jean said. 'Look at his chest!'

'Not in bad shape for a man his age,' the constable said.

'But the cut!' Jean said, fighting for breath. 'Where has it gone?'

'Make-up?' the constable suggested. 'What am I . . . ? I'm going mad!' He looked at Jean as though it were her fault. 'They'll have recorded the episode weeks, maybe months in advance.'

'Of course,' Jean replied. 'That's what Rory told me. Shush!'

Reassured, she watched the ensuing scenes, in which Mabel arrived at the lodge, accompanied by a swarthy young Romanian called Cezar; Deborah's mother, Jill, was bitten by horseflies at the lake; and in an unwelcome distraction from the family drama, Brian Dickson conspired with the contractor of a new development to use cheaper insulating material than the council had specified.

Back at the lodge, Rory rehearsed his daughters in the poem that they were to recite for Deborah at the anniversary dinner.

'That's him,' she said to the constable, gripping the screen, even though her arm was throbbing.

'Is he talking to you now?' he asked.

'Of course not. Not on your television. Besides, he waits until the end of the programme or it wouldn't be fair to the other viewers. He'll be worried when he doesn't see me, but I'll explain next time.'

She turned back as the girls, in matching pink frocks, spoke the last lines of the poem in front of the dinner guests. When the applause died down, Sir Douglas opened a bottle of champagne and toasted the happy couple. The tension between him and Rory, who'd resolved not to ruin Deborah's evening by exposing his uncle's wickedness, simmered throughout the meal.

Both men went up to bed, wondering what the other had planned for the morning's shoot. In the early hours, Rory was woken by a phone call from the keeper, warning him that Sir Douglas had fitted his gun with explosive cartridges and urging him to replace them at once. As the keeper put down the phone, a masked man was seen to be holding a knife to his throat. Jean's suspicions that it was Sir Douglas were confounded when he turned out to be back at the lodge, fixing a tripwire across the top of the stairs. Moments later, she watched in horror as Rory crept out of his room in the semi-darkness and tumbled over it. Quick as a wink, Sir Douglas rushed up and wrenched the wire free, shutting his bedroom door just as Cezar, clasping a pair of antlers like a shield, came out to investigate. Spotting Rory spawled on the flagstones, he ran down and pressed his fingertips to his neck. Looking aghast, he yelled for help.

Deborah, Sir Douglas, Angela, Mabel, Fliss, Ginny and Jill appeared on the landing in quick succession. Hearing Deborah scream, Jill grabbed the girls and swept them back into their room.

'Is dead,' the boyfriend said, the words shockingly clear despite his accent.

'No!' Deborah screamed again, as Sir Douglas sidled across the landing towards her, the final shots being first of his gap-toothed grin, more sinister than ever in the half-light, and then of Rory, lying face down, with blood matting his hair.

'No!' Jean's scream echoed Deborah's as the theme tune played. 'It's not possible. I warned him. He knew what to do.'

'It isn't real,' the constable said.

'It's my life,' she replied, letting go of the screen.

'Perhaps it's a counterplot. He knew what Sir Douglas was up to. And he faked the fall. What if he's in league with the old woman's boyfriend to make it look like he's dead, so he can hit back at Sir Douglas without anyone suspecting?'

'It's possible,' she replied doubtfully. 'Rory's so clever. He went to Oxford university.' She reflected for a moment. 'But all that blood in his hair . . . on the floor . . . everywhere.' She put her hand over her mouth and hobbled to the toilet, where, despite having eaten nothing since breakfast, she was sick.

'I'm sorry. If I'd known how it would upset you, I'd never have suggested watching it.'

'Rory . . .' She cried, with hot, dry eyes.

'Sometimes an actor asks to be written out of a programme, so he can go on to better things.'

'What could be better than *Boardroom*?'

'In that case, I'm sure he'll stay. Didn't you say this was a special 1,000th episode? Remember, he was killed at night. What if it's shown to have been a dream?'

'What do you mean?' she asked in bewilderment.

'One of the characters – Rory . . . anyone – wakes up to find that everything is exactly as it was when he fell asleep.'

'Do you think so?'

'They've done it before.'

'Yes, of course. I should have known. All this will be just a bad dream.'

Post-Mortem

A T BREAKFAST ON his sixteenth birthday, Matt proudly informed me of some of the things he was now entitled to do.

'I can have sex and get married.'

'Anyone particular in mind?'

'I can order a glass of beer or wine in a restaurant, as long as I'm with a responsible adult.'

'That rules me out then.'

'I can enlist in the armed forces if I get my parents' consent.'

'Over my dead body!'

'I can change my name by deed poll.'

'Now that I can live with . . . how about Jemima Puddle-Duck?'

One thing that didn't feature on his teenage bucket list was to overdose on Ecstasy and die.

He'd told me he was spending the evening with his friend Mandy. Not having heard her name before, I teasingly asked if he were hoping to exercise the first of his new entitlements. With a look of filial disdain, he declared that I was 'nasty', adding with an inscrutable smirk that, in fact, Mandy was more Tyler's friend than his. He went out, promising to be home by 11:30, and since Lucy, his younger sister, was visiting their father in Bristol, I made dinner for Rupert, my colleague, confidant and, on occasion, lifeline (sometimes words come back to punch you in the face). After the meal we shared a joint, my buzz laced with nostalgia, and over the next hour, we solved the problems of our careers (both of us to quit teaching: me to focus on my art, him to compile crosswords), our love lives (me to meet Mr Right, him to meet fewer Mr Wrongs), and the government (me to campaign for more women MPs, him to topple the Tories).

'I don't know whether youth is wasted on the young, but Purple Haze most definitely is,' Rupert said, as he handed me the roach.

I was wrenched from my mild euphoria by a pounding on the door. Swallowing a telltale giggle, I went to open it. The sight of Matt, slung between two of his friends, instantly cleared my head.

'Darling, what is it?' I asked, but he didn't look up.

'He passed out,' Jenny piped up from behind the boys.

'He was sick and then he started – like – fitting,' Trevor said.

'So we brought him home to sleep it off,' Peter said.

'Sleep? Christ!' I raised Matt's chin. His face was caked in sweat and his eyes were rolling. 'No! Darling! Bring him inside. Give him to me. Rupert . . . Rupert, call 999!'

I clasped Matt's arm, draped over Trevor's shoulder, as he and Peter dragged him into the lounge, his willowy body now a dead weight (more words to pummel me later). Rupert, suddenly sober, shouted 'Ambulance,' into his phone.

The two boys laid Matt on the sofa and stepped back, as I crouched beside him, cradling his head. 'Matt, darling, what is it? Tell me,' I asked as, somewhere far off, I heard Rupert speaking to the operator.

'What did he take?' Rupert demanded of the friends. 'Quickly!'

Tongue-tied and terrified, Trevor stammered, 'He was bumping.'

'Heroin?' The horror in Rupert's voice wafted over me.

'Es. Ecstasy. We told him to pace himself, but he wouldn't listen.'

Ignoring Trevor's evasions, Rupert relayed the information to the operator. 'The ambulance is on its way. Help me get him on the floor,' he said to me. I blindly obeyed and watched as he began CPR, counting and kissing, counting and kissing, until there was another rap at the door and Peter, closest to the hall, escaped to answer it.

The paramedics lifted Matt's inert body on to a stretcher and into the van. I followed them, as Rupert called out that he'd take the children home and meet me at the hospital. Shock and fear and the remnants of the joint rendered the journey a daze. I sat, strapped into my seat, as the paramedic worked swiftly, attaching a defibrillator to Matt's chest, injecting his thigh, and placing one ice pack under his neck and two more in his armpits.

'Is he breathing?' I asked.

'For a moment. We're doing all we can. We'll soon be there.'

I prayed to a God in whom I didn't believe, promising that I would believe . . . that I'd devote the rest of my life to helping others believe. But all I could see was my own face staring back at me, oozing scorn.

At the hospital, he was rushed into the emergency department, surrounded by a team of medics. It was Saturday night, but in spite – or because – of that, I reasoned that they must have several of their best staff on duty. Surely a sixteen-year-old boy with his whole life ahead of him was worthier of their attention than a middle-aged drunk or an elderly stroke victim or . . . ? I stopped before I scorned myself even more. I sat in the corridor, looking desperately at everyone who came through the door, but no one would meet my gaze. I walked to the nurses' station and asked an auxiliary, who looked barely older than Matt, to convey the message that I wanted him to be resuscitated at all costs. 'No matter if he's paralysed or . . . or brain-damaged, as long as he's alive.' She offered to make me a cup of tea.

Rupert arrived. Two hours earlier, he'd been making up puerile names for the principal; now he looked as though he'd witnessed a school shooting. He sat down next to me and took my hand, which I withdrew as soon as it felt polite.

'I'm sure he'll be fine. I spoke to the kids on the way back. It was hard to get much out of them; they're convinced they're in serious trouble. That's why they brought him home instead of dialling 999.'

'Oh God! If anything happens . . . if he could have been . . .'

'Don't! They swear he only took two pills. Apparently, he'd been for a McDonald's before the rave—'

'Rave?'

'Party. So the first E was slow to kick in, and he took a second. Everyone agrees that that's all he had. They'll just have to pump his stomach . . . get it out of his system.'

'Please shut up,' I said, 'before I start to hate you.'

We sat in silence for an indeterminate time, until a doctor came and escorted us into a small office.

'You're Matthew's parents?' she asked, as we took the designated seats.

'I'm his mother and Rupert's his godfather.'

'Of course,' she said. 'I'm very sorry to have to tell you that Matthew didn't make it.'

I felt both the doctor's and Rupert's eyes bore into me, as I tried to make sense of words which were as jumbled as the magnets Matt shuffled daily on the fridge.

'Do you mean he's dead?'

'I'm very sorry.'

'But he only took two pills.' I turned to Rupert. 'Two! You told me: two!'

'We'll know more after the post-mortem. We did everything we could. By the time he got here, his temperature was 44.2 and his heart was racing at 250 beats a minute. He suffered cardiac arrest and multiple organ failure.'

I vomited. 'Oh God, I'm sorry.'

'Please don't worry.'

'But the carpet.'

'It's nothing. Would you like some water?'

'For the carpet?'

'For you.'

'I just want to see him. Can I see him?'

'Of course.'

I watched Rupert take my arm, but I couldn't feel it. That was good. I knew that provided I remained numb, I'd be able to go on living. The doctor led us into the casualty room, where Matt lay, electrode patches on his frail chest, hooked up to tubes and drips and machines, which, in a few hours, would be used on another patient . . . perhaps one who survived.

'Take all the time you need.'

'How about forever?'

The doctor gave me an awkward smile and went out. Rupert stood at the side of the room, choking back his tears. He loved Matt, but there was a hierarchy of grief and he knew his place in it. I pulled a stool up to the bed and took Matt's hand, which still held the warmth that had killed him. I stroked his cheeks and felt the gentle stubble of which he was both embarrassed and proud. It was years since I'd walked freely into his bedroom and watched him sleep. It was almost as long since he'd last allowed me to sketch him, and I'd studied the flat forehead, high cheekbones and full lips, which, though it pained me to admit, he'd inherited from his father. His russet hair was the one trait he'd had from me.

'Do you have any scissors?' I asked Rupert. 'Or a knife?'

'What?'

'A penknife. I want to keep a lock of his hair. Do you think they'll permit it?'

'Yes, I'm sure if you want.' He sounded bemused. 'I don't have either on me, but I can ask.'

'Thank you.'

I heard him leave, but I kept my eyes fixed on Matt. It was only yesterday that we'd discussed his getting a haircut . . . No, we'd *argued*; there would be equivocations soon enough. Now we would never argue and he would never go to a barber again. Nothing had ever felt so final. *The curtain has come down* . . . but it could be lifted. *The lights have gone out* . . . but they could be switched back on. This, however, defied metaphor. There wasn't even the fleeting hope of a life support machine, which it would be my decision to turn off. That would be the last thing I'd ever do for him – and the hardest thing I'd ever do for him, but at least, as I agonised over it, he would still be alive.

Or was I despairing too quickly? Might he be a medical miracle, reviving after being pronounced clinically dead, with a story of floating through darkness towards a bright white light, or even days later, tapping on his coffin as it was lowered into the grave? Only a couple of years ago, he'd made me promise to bury him with a bell and an air tube, after an over-literal reading of Edgar Allan Poe.

'It'll be the other way round,' I'd said lightly. 'Sons outlive their mothers. You're the one who'll be burying me.'

Rupert returned with the doctor, who glanced at me uneasily and suggested that she be the one to cut off the lock. As she leant over him, a thought struck me.

'His organs! You haven't asked about harvesting his organs.'

'You don't need to do this, Bea,' Rupert interjected.

'But I do. He registered as a blood donor straight after turning sixteen. He said it was the socially responsible thing to do. He'd want to donate his organs.'

'That's a kind thought,' the doctor said. 'But time isn't on our side. Given the post-mortem, all we could use are his corneas and some connective tissue.'

'No! Look at him, so beautiful, so perfect, so healthy. And all you can take are his corneas?'

'Which will restore someone's sight,' Rupert said.

'And his connective tissue,' the doctor said. 'Blood, fat, cartilage, bone.'

That was when I passed out.

◊

Philip, Matt's father, brought Lucy home a few hours later. Rupert had put me to bed, and I dreamt of watching help- lessly as Matt clung to an out-of-control merry-go-round, screaming at me to rescue him. I was woken by Lucy flinging herself on top of me, her tears soaking my neck, as mine did the crown of her head.

'It isn't true,' she whimpered.

'He loved you so much,' I said. 'You were like twins.'

'He was my older brother.'

'Only fifteen months.'

'Dad said that someone spiked his drink. Who would do that?'

'We don't know precisely what happened,' I replied, furious with Philip for trying to absolve Matt from unwar- ranted guilt. Did he think that the truth wouldn't come out? 'There'll have to be a post . . . inquest.'

'I can't believe . . . how will . . . ?'

'We will. For Matt's sake.' Even as I spoke, I knew that, for Lucy's sake, I had to curb my grief, my pain and my anger. She must never feel that she had to compensate. She must be able to live life to the full, making her own choices, however foolish – just as long as they weren't fatal. 'I must go and speak to your father. There are people to tell . . . so much to do.'

'I don't want to speak to anyone.'

'You don't have to. Do only what feels right for you.'

Lucy went to lie down in her room. I splashed cold water on my face and, not bothering to change clothes, went downstairs, where I heard Philip talking to Rupert.

'It's freezing in here,' I said, entering the lounge. 'Why did you open the French doors?'

'It smelt a bit fusty,' Rupert replied.

With a stab to my heart, I realised that he'd been dispersing the lingering fumes of the pot.

I turned to Philip, whose face betrayed a raw anguish that I'd not expected. I felt a rush of . . . not love, not even affection, but gratitude: gratitude for his having made Matt with me. In the nine years since I'd left him, weary of his relentless brashness, I'd avoided being in the same room as him, let alone touching him, but now I wanted nothing more than to bury my head in his chest, acknowledging the weight of our shared loss. He must have felt something similar, since he gathered me in a fumbling embrace. Then as abruptly as it had arisen, the moment passed. We each retreated to an armchair, where Rupert brought us coffee.

'How did he even get the drugs?' Philip asked. 'This is Gloucester, not Soho.'

'There are drugs everywhere,' I said. 'You know that.'

'He'd have been safe at Malvern. But oh no, you didn't want him to go away to school. What you meant was you didn't want him to turn out like me.'

'Matt would hate you to quarrel,' Rupert interjected. 'The police said they'd send round a liaison officer this morning. You'll be able to ask them anything. But for me, the one consolation is that he spent his final hours with friends at a party. He was happy.'

'How do you know?' Philip asked sharply. 'Were you there?'

'No, but I spoke to some of the kids afterwards. Peter, the host, had set up strobe lights in the bathroom. They were taking turns under the shower, switching it from hot to cold. Matt told them he could feel every single drop of water on his skin.'

'Taking showers together? What was it: an orgy?' Philip shook his head in disgust, and glared at my male nudes.

'No, not at all.' Rupert looked wounded. 'Peter's parents were away for the weekend, and he organised a house party.'

'It wasn't Peter who asked him,' I said. 'Matt told me distinctly. It was a new friend, Mandy.'

'Oh darling,' Rupert said. 'Mandy is the street name for Ecstasy. He was pulling your leg.'

'What?' I struggled to make sense of it and started to laugh.

'Stop it!' Philip said. 'You're hysterical.'

'On the contrary, I'm glad. At least I was, just for a moment. To think how triumphant Matt must have felt, having put one over on me.'

'I don't understand you. I really don't.'

'No, but we both discovered that years ago.'

We sat in a scratchy silence, which Rupert, whom Philip had always distrusted, made futile attempts to fill with memories of Matt. Eventually, there was a knock at the door. 'Why don't you get a bell?' Philip asked, as Rupert moved to answer it. 'Or would that be too suburban?'

The officer's arrival was almost a relief. We effected introductions, and she stared at my paintings as if they were part of a crime scene. She outlined her role and gave us a notional timetable: the toxicology report within six to eight weeks; the inquest within six months.

'Must we wait that long to bury him?' I asked, horrified.

'Absolutely not. I expect the coroner's office to release

the body later today. In the meantime, I'd recommend issuing a press statement to ward off the worst intrusion.'

'Is there a danger of that?' I asked.

'I'm afraid so. There's been an epidemic of drug-related deaths in the city.'

'Why?' Philip asked.

'I'm no expert,' she replied, sounding surprised, 'but overdoses, allergies, adulterated supplies.'

'No, I mean why haven't the police done something about it? Why are you sitting on your backsides rather than out there, catching the criminals?'

'I assure you, sir, we're doing everything in our power to bring them to justice.'

'Yes, and then what happens? A slap on the wrist! So my son's just another statistic?'

'Not now, Philip,' I said.

'I understand your distress, sir, and you're welcome to call me at any time to discuss your concerns. I would urge you to be patient.'

Patience didn't come naturally to the only man I'd ever known to wear out a car horn, but his son's death had crushed him. After a desultory exchange, he accompanied the officer to the morgue to view Matt's body. Rupert, who'd been up all night, asked if there were anything else he could do.

'Yes, go home and rest. Come back later, if you're up to it. My brother's bringing my parents. I'll need all the help I can get.'

'Can't you put them off till tomorrow?'

'They adored Matt. They'll think they're supporting me, but I can already hear their unspoken rebukes. Why didn't I vet his friends more carefully? Why didn't I set a better example? Why was I such an all-round crap mother?' He led me back to the chair and passed me a box of tissues. 'I'm sorry,' I sobbed. 'This isn't fair on you.'

'I'm fine, don't worry.'

'It was so much easier for them. They could say *Just Say No* without being accused of hypocrisy.'

'They were teenagers in the '60s.'

'It might as well have been the 1860s! Both kids knew I'd done drugs. All I could do was warn them that the pills were three times as potent as the ones we took . . . that skunk was way stronger than the weed we smoked – hell, that we were smoking last night. At exactly the same time as he . . . Ring Philip! Tell him that I'm the one who should be locked up.'

'I'm not leaving you in this state.'

'Why didn't I let him send Matt to Malvern? So what if it offended my principles? He'd still be alive.'

'Do you really think there are no drugs in public schools?'

'But his mother wouldn't have been on the staff. He wouldn't have had to work so hard to be cool.'

'You made him cool. What other teacher had a green streak in her hair or two-page spreads of her exhibitions in the local press?'

'Yes, my male nudes. My bursting seeds. My flowering vaginas. What adolescent boy could ask for more? I embarrassed him.'

'Every mother embarrasses her children. You made Matt proud.'

For all the officer's talk of an epidemic, Matt's death rocked the local community. I received more flowers than I could fit into vases; more food than I could cram in the fridge. Only the postman appeared to be oblivious to the news, delivering a sackful of cards with a cheery 'Somebody's birthday?' The school held a memorial assembly, which neither Lucy nor I attended. The chaplain told me that, at times of great grief, God could be a comfort. I replied that I preferred Nina Simone.

I was grateful that friends had such fond memories of Matt but afraid of their diminishing mine. As we conversed, I felt that I was wading through treacle, not just from the sentiment but from the effort it took to put one word in front of another. Sleep was the only time that I had him to myself. I dreamt of him constantly and, while I never forgot that he was dead, it didn't distress me until I reached out to touch him, and he faded away. I had violent arguments with inanimate objects and invisible people. Yet in company I remained composed, to a degree that some found disturbing. Rupert insisted that I see a doctor ('for Matt's sake', which I feared would become a routine formula). She prescribed two sets of pills, but I couldn't take either. I couldn't take so much as an aspirin for my nagging headache without thinking . . . the reason was clear.

I threw myself into the preparations for Matt's funeral. I may not have been able to donate his organs, but I could give him the eco-friendly burial I'd planned for myself. To my surprise, Philip agreed. The objections came from our parents, who longed for the solace and, I had no doubt, the respectability of a church service. To set the seal on her disapproval, my mother mistook my mention of a wicker casket for a Wiccan ceremony. In any other circumstance, I would have laughed.

The day of the funeral was mild, but heavy rain earlier in the week left two hundred of us tramping through a muddy meadow. Linking arms with Lucy, I tried in vain to make her smile at the sight of Philip's cousin, Sarah, one hand clutching her husband's shoulder, tottering across the turf in two-inch heels. We held the wake in the school cricket pavilion, where Matt had spent many of his sunniest summer afternoons. I'd always been baffled by how the chief mourners were required to double as party hosts, and it felt even more perverse now that I was one of them. I did my best, so much so that at some point I greeted my old college friend Lauren Godden, who'd driven down from York, with 'How lovely to see you! It's been too long.'

Lucy and I slipped away before the end, returning to a house which, for the first time since Matt's death, was free of well-wishers. 'It's just the two of us now, darling,' I said.

'No, there'll always be three,' she replied, hugging me. 'You look worn out, Mum. Did you eat anything at the pavilion? I can warm up one of those lasagnes or the cottage pie.'

'No, leave it. I'll do it.' I was appalled at the thought that someone had told her to take care of me, when it was for me to care of her. I was about to head into the kitchen when there was a call on Matt's mobile, which we'd kept reverently on the mantelpiece. Feeling queasy, I picked it up.

'Hi, Matthew.'

'Who is this?'

'Malik from Eastgate Games. Who am I speaking to?'

'His mother.'

'Will you tell him that *Zombie Apocalypse 2* is ready for him?'

'I'm afraid I can't. He's dead.'

'Are you sure?'

It was Tyler who'd supplied the pills. Had I been thinking straight, I'd have figured it out for myself long before the liaison officer told me. Why else hadn't he called round or even sent a card? Despite everything, I couldn't bring myself to hate him. I tried, not least because everyone expected it of me. It wasn't that I was naturally charitable or forgiving . . . quite the opposite. Anyone who'd ever driven with me or sat next to me at a concert could vouch for my towering rage towards people who stole my parking space or forgot to turn off their phones. But all I felt for Tyler was pity, knowing that, under different circumstances, it might have been Matt who'd proposed to 'sort out' his friends.

I'd met him on Matt's first day at his new primary school: a sad-eyed seven-year-old, waiting at the gates for his chronically late mother. I offered to drive him home; he took one look at my clapped-out, candy-striped VW and jumped inside. Although his mother was angry at his accepting a ride from a stranger (and, I suspect, embarrassed by the rank, chaotic flat through which a naked toddler was carrying a potty), she came to see me as an ally, if only because, despite my 'stuck-up voice and ideas', I was another single parent. But whereas Philip, for all his faults, was a generous and attentive father, Jacey's partner (her marital status was never defined) had walked out shortly

after the birth of Tyler's younger brother, Brett, leaving her
with nothing but a bitter hatred of men, which she poured
out on her sons.

Nine years on, Tyler who, for all her carping, remained
her one hope of a better future, had been charged with
possession and intent to supply. He was released on condi-
tional bail with a night-time curfew, but Rupert, who
visited him at home, reported that he rarely ventured out at
any hour, preferring to lounge around in his shorts, smoking and watching television, alongside his equally listless
mother. He'd planned to take maths, physics and chemistry
A levels, prior to a degree in engineering. Rupert, who
taught him maths, and three of his colleagues had designed
a study programme for him, but he ignored it. 'Can't you
teach me something useful, sir, like boxing? I'm looking
at being sent down for seven years.'

The procedural delay was hard for us all, but especially
for Tyler. First, we had to wait for the toxicology report.
It confirmed that the pills had been adulterated with a
substance called PMA, or para-Methoxyamphetamine,
which, in a phrase forever etched on my brain, had raised
Matt's *body temperature so high that he effectively boiled to
death* (sometimes I wonder how I've stayed sane). Next,
we had to wait two months for the inquest, which was
promptly adjourned pending criminal proceedings. We
had to wait a further eight months for the trial itself, during
which, as I later learnt, Tyler slit his wrists. I wanted to see
him, but his bail conditions prohibited contact with any of
Matt's family. All I could do was send him a message of
support through Rupert, which he refused to believe was
genuine. He would discover the truth in court.

On the first day of proceedings, Philip drove up from Bristol, joining Lucy, Rupert and me outside the court. He explained that he'd booked a room at the Mercure, to avoid travelling back and forth during the estimated three-day trial. Ten minutes before we were due to go in, the CPS lawyer told us that Tyler had changed his plea to guilty.

'I suppose now he'll get some Mickey Mouse sentence,' Philip said furiously.

'It will be a mitigating factor, of course. But rest assured, we'll press for the maximum penalty. First, because there was a death involved, and second, to serve as a deterrent.'

Lucy, Rupert and I exchanged looks. From the corner of my eye, I watched the usher inform Matt's friends that they would no longer be required to give evidence. One of them let out a whoop of relief, cut short when another grabbed his arm and pointed at us.

They hurried out, as we made our way into the court-room where, after the judge's entrance, Tyler was led into the dock. With his head bowed and shoulders slumped, he looked as if he'd stepped straight out of Doré's *Newgate Exercise Yard*. The judge accepted his guilty plea and called on both the prosecution and defence counsel to make statements before sentencing. The prosecution challenged Tyler's claim that he'd merely been helping out his friends, emphasising that by buying forty pills for £100 and selling them at £5 each, he'd made a sizeable profit, his tone that of a man whose mother had never sent him to school hungry or in unwashed clothes. The defence acknowledged Tyler's role in supplying the pills but insisted that, even though he'd been unaware of the contamination, he'd warned Matt not to take more than one: a warning Matt had ignored.

He was filled with remorse and had already attempted suicide. Whatever sentence the court imposed, he'd bear the burden of having facilitated his best friend's death for the rest of his life.

'There's little doubt in my view that a substantial part of that should be spent behind bars,' the judge said. 'But before I pass sentence, the victim's mother wishes to make a personal impact statement.'

As I walked to the witness box, I saw Lucy edge towards a mystified Philip, slipping her arm through his, as if to allay his concerns. Despite my nervousness, I was glad that I'd refused the liaison officer's offer to read the statement on my behalf. Whether or not it swayed the judge, it would convince Tyler of my good faith.

'The world was never the same for me after Matthew was born, and it can never be the same now that he's dead. He was radiant, charming, a loving son, brother and grandson, a loyal friend . . . and, yes, a bit of a rogue. He was an A-grade student and a first-class cricketer, with artistic talent (although the last person he'd have admitted that to was me). He was inquisitive, and fearless, always open to new experience. There was no way that he could be coerced into doing anything against his will (believe me, I tried!). I'm quite sure that he'd have been the first to encourage Tyler to procure the pills.

'The events of the 4th of May last year will haunt my family and myself for the rest of our lives, as they will Tyler, the other party guests, and their wider circle of friends. Tyler will have Matthew – Matt's – death on his conscience; I don't wish to have Tyler's wasted life on mine. He's a young man, who has grown up with few advantages but whose teachers are confident that, given the chance, he will excel in his chosen field of engineering. So I entreat Your Honour not to send him to prison but to permit him to complete his education, to fulfil his promise and become a credit to us all and, especially to Matt who, from the first day they met, counted him his closest friend.'

The judge ordered a thirty-minute adjournment to deliberate on her ruling. Tyler was led away; the rest of us filed out into the vestibule.

'You certainly bowled a googly, as Matt would have put it,' Philip said.

'I should have warned you, I know. But it's what Matt would have wanted.'

'Not if he were my age, with a son he'll never see again.'

'But he was my age,' Lucy said. 'Or near enough. Trust me, Tyler's one of the good guys. Please don't do anything to make things harder for him.'

'All right, princess. For your sake.'

'I love you, Dad.' Lucy hugged him.

'I love you more.'

The usher summoned us back into court, where the judge addressed Tyler. 'I had been minded to impose a custodial sentence, but after reflecting on Ms Meercroft's statement, I find that it would ill behove me to show less clemency than a mother whose son has been so cruelly taken from her. I therefore sentence you to eighteen months in a young offender institution, suspended for two years, during which time you will be required to complete 250 hours of community service. It is my hope that you will appreciate the leniency that the court has afforded you and prove yourself worthy of it.'

As the judge left and the court cleared, Tyler, who I suspect had been bewildered by the language and thought that he was being imprisoned for eighteen months, looked dazed. He sank into a chair, until the guard helped him to his feet and conducted him out of the dock. Our group returned to the vestibule, where Philip took Lucy off for lunch. Rupert and I stayed to see Tyler, who appeared ten minutes later, flanked by his mother and an equally bedraggled woman in a plastic rain hat. Tyler stopped short, but Jacey made straight for me.

'You showed them,' she said. 'This whole case was a set-up, that's what it was. My Tyler ought never to gone through it. I wept for your Matthew, and that's a fact. But it's the manufacturers who should be on trial. You never know what's in half the pills they give you these days. It's criminal!'

I asked Rupert to fetch Tyler, who watched in dismay as Jacey jabbered on about his wasted year, heedless of the fact that, were it not for me, he'd have had to waste another two or three in far tougher surroundings. Tyler was more reserved, hanging back even once Rupert brought him over, pain stamped on his pimply but handsome face.

'I'm sorry . . . so sorry. I'm sorry,' he repeated, starting to cry.

'Don't make a spectacle of yourself,' his mother snapped. 'Just say your piece to Mrs Meercroft. I'll be waiting for you outside. With all this stress, I need a ciggy. Come on Audrey!' Beckoning her rain-hatted friend, she walked away.

'I think of Matt every day,' Tyler said softly.

'So do I.'

'I never stop thinking about him. I'd give anything to get him back.'

'I know. But we both have to accept that it isn't possible. What you have to do is get your own life back.'

'Back on track,' Rupert interjected.

'I meant what I said in my statement.'

'Thank you. Thank you so much. I can never . . . '

'Perhaps you can print out a copy for Tyler,' Rupert asked. 'So he can keep it to remind himself.'

'Yes, please,' Tyler said. 'And if there's anything – anything at all – I can do. Things that Matt used to do . . . I don't know, like mowing the lawn or washing the car.'

I laughed at the thought of Matt's having done either, breaking off abruptly in case Tyler supposed that I was laughing at him. 'You've got your hours of community service. That's how you "pay your debt to society". The only way to pay your debt to us is by living your best life. And, yes, by coming to see us from time to time. I know that Lucy would like that too.'

I never expected that reports of the trial, posted later that day on local news websites, would be picked up by the national media. Before the week was out, I found myself giving interviews to the *Guardian* and the *Today* programme, as well as appearing on BBC South West's *Spotlight* and ITV's *This Morning*. My defence of Tyler had struck a chord, and I was compared to Gordon Wilson, who forgave the IRA murderers of his daughter at Enniskillen, which I dimly remembered from childhood. In a sermon at the cathedral, the Dean of Gloucester praised me as an exemplar of Christian charity, which was all the more incongruous given that I'd lost my faith irrevocably at the

age of nine, when a neighbour ran over my dog. But at least
it made my mother happy.

While I was admired, Tyler was reviled. Having turned
eighteen two months before the trial, he was fair game for
the tabloids. Much of the coverage, harping on his dual
heritage, was borderline racist. But he seemed as impervi-
ous to the venom as to the taunts and sneers he endured at
school, where he'd entered the sixth form a year behind his
peers. He struggled to find a quiet place to study, since his
mother's relief at his reprieve didn't extend to lowering the
volume on her television or curbing Brett's boisterousness.
He visited the public library, but the librarians constantly
monitored him, 'like they think I'm trying to get the winos
who hang out there hooked on Es.' So I invited him to use
Matt's room which, it went without saying, stood empty.
I'd left it unchanged, taking comfort from sitting there
and evoking his presence. But I didn't want it to become
a shrine.

Lucy endorsed the invitation. Although she'd bristled
when Matt joked that she had a crush on him, she'd always
liked Tyler and their lost contact over the past year had
compounded the greater loss of her brother. Despite pressure from her classmates to take the lead, she refused to join
in the widespread demonisation of Tyler. She made a point
of waiting for him after school, so that they could walk
home together. They worked diligently in their respective
rooms, and the knowledge that the house was full again
invigorated me. For months, friends had been urging me
to resume painting, as if it were a form of therapy; for the
first time since Matt's death, it felt like making art.

With Tyler using the room most afternoons, I had less

opportunity to be alone there with Matt, but one Saturday, when both Tyler and Lucy were taking part in the school's World Ocean Day run, I ventured upstairs, opened Matt's wardrobe and looked for his favourite bomber jacket, which I sometimes wore in private. Failing to find it, I assumed that Tyler had taken it. I felt faint and longed to ring Rupert, but besides confirming his doubts about my letting Tyler get too close, I'd have had to explain why I wanted the jacket, which even to a sympathetic friend would sound pitiful.

I sat brooding until Lucy returned, elated at having raised £268 to tackle plastics pollution. I asked casually whether she knew what had happened to the jacket.

'Yep. I kind of told Tyler he could have it,' she replied cagily.

'You did what?'

'He didn't have a coat and his school jacket was soaked.'

'So you lent it to him?' I felt relieved.

'No, I told him he could keep it. What's the big deal? It was just hanging there. No use to anyone.'

It was of use to me, I wanted to shout but, instead, I asked if she hadn't thought to clear it with me first.

'No, I didn't. Sorry. End of, OK?'

'No, it's not OK. You'll have to tell Tyler it was a mistake and get it back. I'll buy him a jacket if he needs one.'

'What the fuck, Mum!'

'I beg your pardon.'

'He's not some Afghan refugee.'

'It's a piece of Matt, don't you understand?'

'No, sorry, I don't. Anyhow, you gave away pieces of Matt. His eyes, his skin, his bone tissue.'

'Stop it!'

'Yet you won't give away one lousy jacket.'

'I don't want anyone else wearing it.'

'Anyone at all or just Tyler?'

'Anyone.'

'I don't believe you. You let everyone think you're some sort of Mother Teresa. Only not a nun. But I know the truth. You invite him here – you give him Matt's room – but it's all so he can never forget what he did. It's not a helping hand, it's a punishment. Well, I won't let you. Tyler's my friend.'

'That's fine. He's mine too.'

'He's my boyfriend.'

'What?'

'I didn't tell you because I knew you'd be weird about it,' she said, her face crumpling before hardening. 'I'm sixteen now. Remember that list Matt made on his sixteenth birthday? He could have sex.'

'You're sleeping with him?'

'It's none of your business.'

'Of course it is. You're my daughter. This is my house.'

'I can move in with Tyler.'

'Don't be absurd! You mean every afternoon, when I thought you were both busy with homework . . . ?'

'Not every afternoon, no! You've got a sick mind.'

'How the hell did you manage to keep so quiet?'

This time I didn't hesitate to ring Rupert.

'I feel shocked and angry and betrayed,' I said. 'Don't tell me it's irrational, I know! But he's overstepped the mark.'

'You're the one who said you wanted him to feel like one of the family.'

'Feel like one, yes. Not become one.'

'She's sleeping with him, not planning to marry him! They are being careful?'

'Apparently she's on the pill. That's another thing I didn't know.'

'Well then, I don't see the problem. Better it's under your own roof than somewhere unsafe or sordid.'

'It's bringing up so much that I thought I'd dealt with. Was he just trying to help his friends have a good time or out to make a handsome profit? He's penniless, so how come he had a Bitcoin account? What else was he up to on the dark web? Is he still taking drugs? Lucy says not. But what if she's lying? What if he's supplying them to her?'

'Whoa there! Promise me you won't fly off the handle. I think you've done brilliantly these last eighteen months. I'm in awe of how you've carried on . . . without *carrying on*, if you get my drift. But perhaps you need some support. As you say, there are things you may have buried.'

'I've buried my son.'

'Which is why you need support.'

'I've got support: you, first and foremost. Or has it all become too much?'

'Not at all. I'll always be here for you. But I'm not a trained counsellor.'

'I saw one after I left Philip. Bent her ear. Scrunched her tissues. Thumped her cushions.'

'Then how about a bereavement support group: talking to others who are going through the same thing?'

'You mean mothers whose daughters are dating their dead sons' dealers?'

'If you're determined to twist everything I say . . .'

'I'm not. I'm sorry.'

'Then listen. There are specific groups for bereaved parents.'

'Yes: cot deaths, childhood cancers, accidents, suicides. Let's give a warm welcome to Bea, whose son overdosed on Ecstasy.'

'Remember Fabio?'

She gave him a puzzled look. 'Of course.' How could she ever forget the love of her best friend's life?

'No, I mean remember how he was hailed as a hero when he jumped into the Severn to save Janet Prynne? Until it came out that he had HIV. Then what was his courage worth, since he was on the brink of death anyway? Then the parents at Janet's primary school insisted she be tested, in case his kiss of life had had the opposite effect. Then the smears and the slurs and the hate mail that made him so depressed that . . . I won't go on, even though I could. Every life is of value. There's no scale of tragedy. And if there were, Matt's – like Fabio's – would be right at the top.'

Galvanised by Rupert, I googled the support groups and, after some preliminary calls to Millie, the convenor of HeartHelp, drove to Cheltenham for one of the bi-monthly meetings she held at her home. She greeted me with a smile as chintzy as her chairs, along with a plate of vol-au-vents. There were six others present: two couples (Ruth and William, and Elaine and Paul), a single man (Luke), and Millie's husband (Brian).

'I keep a low profile at these events,' Brian said. 'I'm not a parent.'

'You're my rock,' Millie said. 'Without Brian . . .' She left the sentence unfinished. 'You may be interested to hear how we met.'

'Of course,' I said politely.

'My first husband and two daughters were killed in a crash on the M5.' My commiserative look was compromised by a mouthful of pastry. 'Some months later, my laptop packed up. I took it to Brian to repair.'

'I'm *PC Fixit*.'

'He's *PC Fixit*. He saw that I'd been visiting suicide sites and questioned me about it so sensitively that I ended up telling him what had happened, and how I didn't feel able to go on living.'

'But you'd taken your computer in for repair.'

'Makes no sense, I know. Unless, of course, you believe in a higher power (I'll leave it at that). Brian asked me out. We "clicked", as they say. And the rest is history.'

'But not search history,' Brian interjected, and Millie beamed at him.

'This isn't a religious group, but you'll understand why I see God's hand at work.'

I ached to ask where that hand had been during the car crash, but instead I gave her a guarded nod. I was grateful when, having established her credentials, Millie moved on to chat to Ruth and William, before summoning us all to our seats. She welcomed me formally to the group, and I offered a brief account of Matt's death. Their quiet sympathy showed how wrong I'd been to worry that my loss would be belittled, let alone besmirched. Listening to the others tell their stories, I realised that my grief wasn't exceptional – unique, yes, but not exceptional. Ruth, who clasped William's hand the entire evening, described how hard she was finding it to accept that their dead daughter's fiancé had a new girlfriend. Elaine and Paul, who regularly finished each other's sentences, spoke of their fears for their surviving son who, consumed with guilt over his estranged brother's death, was throwing his own life away. Millie reported on her battle with the Highways Agency to replace the 121 miles of motorway lights they'd extinguished, 'putting saving the planet before saving lives.'

The story that most moved me was Luke's. 'Thelma sends her apologies,' he said, 'but she's staying at home with our daughter, Becky. She's been struggling at school, and we were devastated to hear from her teacher that she felt she'd not only lost her sister but her parents. We'd been so caught up in ourselves, so absorbed by our own pain, that we'd forgotten – no, of course we hadn't . . . we'd ignored the fact – that we had a wonderful, wounded younger child, who needed us more than ever.'

His words felt as if they were being pricked on my skin by an amateur tattooist. I knew that I too needed to make amends to my daughter: Lucy, who'd lost her brother far too young; Lucy, whose presence had sustained me every day since he died; Lucy, who'd hidden her relationship with Tyler, because she'd gauged the limits of my compassion more clearly than I had myself.

'If you'll excuse me,' I said, as Millie drew the discussion to a close, 'I have to leave.'

'So soon?' she asked. 'There are plenty more nibbles. And Ruth's made a lemon drizzle cake.'

'My daughter's expecting me home.'

'But you'll come again?' Brian asked.

'Definitely.'

I drove back as fast as I could, for once sharing Matt's disdain for my 'Stone Age car.' Returning to a house plunged in darkness, I called up the stairs to Lucy.

'Mum! You're back earlier than you said,' she replied accusingly.

'I wanted to see you, my darling.'

'Are you drunk?'

'Of course not, I've been driving. Have you eaten?'

'Not yet. Tyler's here. We've been doing some maths.'

'Really?'

'He's prepping me for my mocks.'

'I'll make something for you both. All that studying must have given you an appetite,' I said skittishly.

'Mum!'

Tyler appeared alongside her. Any signs of hasty dressing were well concealed.

'Good evening, Tyler,' I said.

'Hi Beatrice.' I'd finally persuaded him to drop 'Mrs Meercroft', but he still resisted Bea.

'We'll eat in fifteen minutes. And Tyler, if all the hard work ever leaves you too tired to go home, you're welcome to stay the night.'

'In Matt's room?' Lucy asked.

'No, darling. I don't want anybody else to sleep there. In yours.'

Break a Leg!

'BREAK A LEG!' Brian called, as Laura fussed in front of the cloakroom mirror.

'I'll do my best,' she replied, wincing at the relish with which he'd embraced theatrical idiom. She wondered how he'd cope were she to be laid up with her leg in plaster, unable to cook his meals, launder his clothes or run his house, let alone entertain his clients. Then again, such speculation was reckless, since an injury would keep her off the stage and it was her proud boast that she had appeared (let others say *starred*!) in every Stationhouse Players production since the society's inception sixteen years ago.

Brian joked routinely that if he were to sue for divorce, citing the four months each year she dedicated to the Players' spring and autumn productions, there was no court in the land that would rule against him. Laura knew that this was a coded way of admitting that, were she so inclined, she could cite more conventional co-respondents. His acceptance of her extramural activities was outweighed by hers of his extramarital ones. But, while eager that he recognise the balance of obligation, she was content with the status quo. For everyday affection, she had her pugs, Anton and Henrik, who confined their slobber to her hands.

Acting was Laura's lifeblood. It had long been acknowledged, not least by successive critics of the *East Cheshire*

Chronicle, that she would have graced any professional stage. But, as she'd explained in interviews with both the *Chronicle* and the *Knutsford Guardian*, she'd chosen to devote herself to her family, supporting Brian as he built Crawford Harding into one of the foremost property developers in the North West and watching her two sons, Peregrine and Gawain, grow up and take their seats on the board. There were times when, like any mother, she felt underappreciated, but, unlike her friend Gillian who'd chastened her children by showing them videos of their births, all that she needed for Perry and Gawain to see what she'd sacrificed was to invite them to her opening nights.

She would be the first to allow that a quiet life had its compensations. Brian's success which, as he'd affirmed on numerous occasions he could never have achieved without her, had made them rich. Twelve years into their marriage, they bought Marston Hall, a Georgian millowner's house, which, after Laura's loving restoration, had been featured in both *Cheshire Life* and *The World of Interiors*. Although the unease she'd felt during the second verse of 'Jerusalem' was only part of the reason for her short-lived membership of the Lower Marston WI, she consoled herself with the thought that Joseph Bridgeport, who founded the mill, had been a model employer, building the cottages in which many of the villagers still lived.

Even Brian's PR manager would have struggled to cast him as a philanthropist but, at Laura's instigation, he'd bought the former stationhouse, which had lain empty since Dr Beeching axed the Macclesfield to Marple railway line in 1970, and transformed it into a community arts centre, with a hall for films, exhibitions and, crucially, plays. There had been calls to name it after the donors, which Laura persuaded Brian to resist, in favour of a marble plaque in the foyer attesting to their generosity. Nevertheless, she'd insisted that the fusty Marston Mummers be rebranded as the Stationhouse Players. She'd accepted the lifetime presidency, only to relinquish it eight years later, when Derek Ackroyd, the Players' regular director, alerted her to talk of nepotism.

She'd tried to avoid using the Range Rover for short trips, ever since Perry's wife, Gaynor, dubbed it a 'gas guzzler'; a term that her two elder granddaughters then gleefully transferred to her, without a word of reproach from their father. This evening, however, she needed to arrive daisy-fresh for the audition. Like any serious artist, she suffered from nerves, which her wealth of experience had done little to assuage. Driving through the village, she relaxed by recollecting past triumphs. Although it was poor taste to quote one's own reviews (even to oneself), she could hardly be blamed if words such as *'sparkling,' 'majestic'* and *'as beautifully spoken as she is dressed'* had lodged in her mind.

She longed to essay a dramatic role and had begged Derek to cast her as Hedda in *Hedda Gabler*, reluctantly accepting his verdict that, even had Lower Marston been ready for Ibsen, there was too small a pool of talent to do justice to either the play or her. Having reconciled herself to a diet of crowd-pleasing comedies and thrillers, she was willing to grant that J.B. Priestley's *When We Are Married*, the Players' spring choice, was superior middlebrow entertainment.

The plot centred on the discovery by three smugly

respectable Yorkshire couples, each celebrating their silver wedding, that the minister who married them had not been officially licensed and they'd therefore been living in sin. The question for Laura was which of the three roughly equivalent female roles she should choose. Maria Helliwell, being married to an alderman, was socially a cut above the others. Priestley described her as *pompous* and *very pleased with herself*, which would be an interesting challenge, but also as *bouncing*, which, increasingly sensitive about her weight, she feared was a euphemism for *fat*. Downtrodden Annie Parker had one highly effective scene, in which she turned the tables on her bullying husband, but was otherwise dull. Clara Soppitt was a stock battleaxe who, while offering plenty of scope for humour, offered none for pathos. Moreover, her husband slapped her, and Laura still cringed at the memory of being spanked overzealously by Richard Lyons in *The Little Hut*.

'I'm so sorry,' she said, as she walked into the hall and found several of her potential rivals clustered around Derek. 'Have you all been waiting for me?'

'Not waiting, *aching*!' Derek said, his air kisses smelling of cheese.

'Where do you want me?'

'No no, my dear, the question is surely "Where do you want us?"' he replied, with what she could only describe as an affectionate glint.

Noreen hung up her coat and headed into the kitchen. The remnants of Brian's hurried breakfast were strewn across the table, but there was as yet no sign of Laura. At their first meeting, she'd explained that, like many thespians, she was not a morning person. Unfamiliar with the word, Noreen had presumed that she was confiding her sexuality, which, coupled with her plunging neckline and assertion that she'd always been tactile, filled her with alarm. A flick through her old school dictionary on her return home reassured her. That evening after laughing at her confusion, she and Barry had speculated on the type of people they'd be, if they had the luxury of choice.

'I'm a teatime person,' Barry said, banging his cutlery on the kitchen table.

'Don't you mean dinnertime?' Noreen asked, mimicking Laura's cut-glass vowels.

Accent apart, she longed to substitute *dinner* for *tea*. If Barry had ambitions beyond life as a municipal gardener, he'd never shared them with her. She, on the other hand, having left school at sixteen with three O' levels and worked as a waitress before marrying, was determined that her children should do better. As soon as Heather was old enough for nursery, she took up cleaning; to save for their education. Barry charged that she was getting above herself and that private schools would make their children ashamed of them. He hadn't been altogether wrong. She still shuddered at the thought of Craig's horror on winning a prize for industry, which he saw as a slight on his background, and Heather's repeated excuses for not inviting her classmates home. Yet, while she never failed to credit their intelligence (and industry), she was convinced that neither of them would have accomplished half as much without her support.

With their careers well established, they'd both urged her to give up work. It amused her that whenever they described it as 'demeaning', they focussed on scrubbing toilets, a task which, with a sprinkle of Vim or a splash of Harpic, accounted for at most five minutes of any day. For all their expressions of concern, she suspected that Craig was embarrassed when overseeing Brian's planning applications, and Heather, a harassed health visitor, begrudged anything that prevented her providing regular childcare. But while she loved her granddaughters and was happy to help out when she could, she had no wish to become an unpaid nanny.

Hard as it was for her children to grasp, she enjoyed cleaning. She liked keeping rooms – especially elegant rooms – spick and span. What did it matter that they weren't her own? Even so, she understood the children's objections. Although Barry lamented that, since privatisation, his job had been little more than park maintenance, it required skill. That was more than could be said for cleaning, which required little more than a shelf of products and a modicum of common sense. No wonder so many of her employers had treated her as if she were retarded.

Laura alone was free of such condescension, no doubt because, as she'd told Noreen time and again, she'd grown up with servants. In Lower Marston and several of the surrounding villages, she was known as Dame Laura, which she mistakenly ascribed to her acting skills. But for all her airs and graces, she had a good heart.

Noreen cleaned at the Hall three days a week and, despite its size, she could easily have managed in two. Some days she spent longer chatting to Laura over coffee and lunch than she did wielding a mop or duster. She knew that, regardless of her full address book, Laura was lonely.

What's more, Laura knew that she knew, which made for an uneasy intimacy. After fourteen years of watching the Hardings' children grow up and their marriage wither, Noreen was more than a domestic but less than a friend.

The yapping and scraping of two highly-strung pugs heralded Laura's arrival. They circled the room and leapt up at Noreen, who patted them as she led them through the scullery and into the garden.

She returned to greet Laura, who was casually dressed in a floral print tracksuit, with a large gold pendant and two-toned pink sneakers. She poured her a cup of coffee and offered to make some toast, but Laura replied that she was far too on edge to eat a thing. Five minutes later, she relented and asked her to fetch a box of macaroons, which she'd hidden 'from myself' at the bottom of the larder.

'You can throw away the bag. I didn't need it, but the assistant asked and I didn't want to stifle her creativity.'

After handing the macaroons to Noreen, who took one, which she insisted was her limit, Laura slipped one each in mock secrecy to her 'greedy pugs', who had rushed back indoors at the first rustle of food. Then she devoured three in swift succession and explained the source of her anxiety.

'It's the play. I can't seem to get on top of my lines.'

'You always say that. And it ends up a marvel.'

'Really? You're such a comfort, Noreen. *When We Are Married*. Do you know it?'

'I've seen the book lying around in the lounge.'

'Drawing room.'

'Sure. But except for the ones at the Stationhouse, I haven't been to a play since school.' She'd faithfully attended each of Laura's performances, several of them twice and *Mrs Warren's Profession* three times, to help fill the seats. Despite the frisson of seeing Dame Laura play a prostitute, 'the Philistines of East Cheshire,' in the words of its leading actress, 'had failed to appreciate George Bernard Shaw's mordant comedy.'

'It's about three couples who find out that the minister who married them wasn't qualified. He was a Methodist of course, not an Anglican – or Catholic,' she added, with a nod to Noreen, who never set foot inside a church from one funeral to the next. 'It gives you pause. A second chance halfway through life. Would you feel differently about Barry if you found out you weren't legally married to him?'

'I don't feel all that married to him now. He scarcely utters a word to me – or anybody else for that matter. He never had much to say for himself, but ever since the Council did away with his floral clock, he's clammed up completely.'

'Vandalism! Still, what can you expect from those vulgarians? I can't imagine not being married to Brian. Of course, we've had our ups and downs – who hasn't? – but we fit together like a pair of comfy old slippers.' Noreen bit her tongue. 'It would be a big help to me if you went through my lines.'

'I was just about to start on the dining room.'

'Oh, that can wait! No dinner parties till the play's over, and Brian's out most evenings. Rotary . . . the Chamber of Commerce . . . you name it.'

'He's a busy man,' Noreen muttered. She smiled thinly as Laura passed her the script, bracing herself for an hour-long explanation of characters she didn't know and expressions she never used.

'Let's go from the top of page fifteen. Oh, by the way, it's set in Yorkshire, but don't worry about accents. As I always say, you can pay too much attention to externals, it's the spirit that counts. Besides, I'm convinced that Maria Helliwell, my part, would have taken elocution lessons. So I'm Maria and you're everyone else. All you need remember is that Helliwell is her husband and Clara Parker and Annie Soppitt are her friends. I don't expect you to distinguish them.'

'Just as well.'

'Oh, and there's Mrs Northrop, the char. Nosy. Noisy. Determined to do things her own way. No great stretch for you there.'

'Thank you,' Noreen said, too amused to take offence.

'Oh dear me no!' Laura replied, with a studied laugh. 'That came out wrong. What I mean is that she's broad Yorkshire, but Derek has agreed that Sheila Considine can play her with an Irish brogue. She's from the Emerald Isle too.'

'I was brought up in Lyme Green.'

'But this is set before the First World War, when the Irish swarmed over here after all that business with potatoes. Now don't hesitate to pull me up on the teensiest mistake.'

Laura tried to hide her irritation. Although neither the oldest nor the longest-standing member of the company (Robin Tillotson had been a Marston Mummer when she was still in pigtails), she was widely acknowledged as its doyenne. Considering it her duty to boost morale, she wandered through the hall, chatting not only to her fellow

actors but to Marcia Rowan, the props mistress, and Julia . . .
something, the prompter, as if the absence of the director and
three of his cast from the last full rehearsal before the tech
run, presented a welcome opportunity to socialise.

The three absent actors were Lloyd and Sheila Considine
and Drew Blakeley. The Considines were doubtless in the
throes of a domestic crisis. While Lloyd was admirably old
school and had once left a burst pipe rather than hold up a
run-through of *And Then There Were None*, Sheila was a
lightweight, apt to have been distracted by anything from
a blown fuse to a cold caller. Derek and Drew's delay was
more puzzling, unless, of course, the inevitable rift between
the director and his latest 'discovery' had occurred earlier
in the production than usual. Having commiserated with
him over the fickleness of youth more often than she cared
to remember, Laura longed for Derek to settle down with
a suitably middle-aged teacher or solicitor. Then again,
with so few stage-struck juveniles in Lower Marston, his
infatuations did serve a purpose.

Just as Laura was about to propose some warm-up
exercises, Derek flung open the door and swept in, closely
followed by Drew. The usually dapper director looked
harassed, dishevelled and a touch sweaty. Even Drew,
whose woodenness dismayed the more seasoned players,
exuded alarm.

'You may as well all pack up and go home,' Derek said.
'Months of work in ruins.'

'Why, what on earth's happened?' asked Lynne Grafton,
who was playing Clara.

'It's the Considines. No, it's too sordid. I can't!'

'She was caught in a van—' Drew interposed.

'Do you mind?' Derek said. 'Well, if I must . . . Robin, you'd best sit down for this.' Robin, who refused to make any concessions to age, remained standing. 'As everyone but Lloyd knows, Sheila's been carrying on for months with Fred Mason, the artisan butcher in Knutsford.'

Taken aback by the calmness with which the news was greeted, Laura was torn between pride at not listening to gossip and fury at being kept in the dark. 'Is this the shop at the centre of the foie gras hoo-ha?' she asked.

'Exactly. The so-called *High Class Butcher and Providore*: whatever that means.'

'I think it means—'

'I know what it means!' Derek cut Drew off with a snarl. 'If you're serious about a career on the stage, I suggest you look up *hyperbole* . . . It turns out that last night, Sheila and Mason were smooching in his van.'

'Good God!' Lynne said. 'What are they? Teenagers?'

Several faces turned towards the nineteen-year-old Drew, who looked at the floor.

'He was in the front seat, on top of her,' Derek continued.

'Oh, that sort of smooching,' said Richard Lyons, Laura's stage husband.

'Naked,' Drew added.

'Semi-naked,' Derek said, with an air of rectitude that silenced Drew more effectively than any rebuke. 'It appears he went into spasm and seized up. With all eighteen stone of him pressing down on her, Sheila wasn't able to wriggle free. In desperation, she honked the horn, but there was no one within earshot except for a gang of kids who, far from coming to their aid, filmed everything – and I mean *everything*. Eventually, the police arrived and called an ambulance to take Mason to St Thomas's.'

'Then what?' Richard asked.

'The police drove Sheila home where, according to Lloyd, whom I've had on the phone half the afternoon, she was frisky. That's the word he used: frisky.'

Looking around, Laura saw that she wasn't alone in her distaste. 'So what happened?' she asked. 'Did Sheila make a clean breast of it?'

Drew stifled a snigger.

'Not on your life. Lloyd would never have known if one of his daughters hadn't rung up this morning. His grandson – he's nine – had seen the clip online. It was apparently "trending".' Derek drew quote marks in the air.

'Over twenty-four thousand views on Instagram when I last looked,' Drew added, taking out his phone. 'I bet by now—'

'Thank you, Drew. We all know how "connected"—' more air quotes – 'you are. Lloyd was devastated. He's thrown her out.'

'Don't tell me she's moved in with the butcher!' said the fretful Nancy Teale, perfectly cast as Annie.

'Who knows? Her phone's switched off. But Lloyd was adamant that he wouldn't take her back. "Dead to me," were his precise words. As for the play, he said it was him or her. So obviously, since Ormonroyd is the bigger role—'

'And Lloyd the better actor,' Nancy said.

'Quite. I assured him that we'd be sticking with him. He said he'd be here for the tech on Sunday. But what good's that if I can't get hold of a Mrs Northrop?'

'Is there no way you can persuade him to put the good

of the production first?' Lynne asked. 'It's not as if they share any scenes.'

'He was adamant.'

Laura looked at Lynne, who was happy not only to appear on the same stage as her former husband, Will, but to play his termagant wife, thus confirming her belief that the best gauge of a couple's relationship was the civility of their split.

'I've spent hours ringing every possible replacement. I even tried the Hodcott Stagers.' Laura shuddered, as Derek named their local rivals. 'Hester Bishop jubilantly informed me that their entire membership was tied up in *Half a Sixpence*. "Surely," she said, "you can find a suitable frump in Lower Marston?"'

'Bitch!' Lynne interjected.

'My thought exactly.'

'Maybe she's right,' Laura said. 'I've had one of my brainwaves. Noreen Dougherty, who helps me at the Hall.' She chose her words carefully, out of consideration not just for Noreen but for younger members of the cast who might not be able to afford a cleaner. 'She's been hearing my lines, so she knows the play. And she's Irish, so she'll have no trouble with the accent.'

'Ring her . . . ring her at once!' Derek said.

'I think I'd have a better chance if I went to see her. She's less likely to refuse me face to face.'

'We all are,' Robin said.

'Someone else will have to read my part.'

'Leave it to me,' Tessa Shipstowe said, overeagerly.

Laura left the hall and drove through the village to the millworkers' cottages. In all the years Noreen had worked for her, she'd visited her at home on only a handful of occasions, each time feeling that she was breaking an unwritten rule. This evening was no different, as a startled Noreen led her into her 'lounge'. Barry, a ferrety man who looked too gaunt for manual labour, sat in his vest, watching a game show. He mumbled a greeting but made no move to switch off the TV, so Noreen suggested that they talk in the kitchen.

Dispensing with the niceties, Laura outlined her proposal. She rebutted Noreen's objections one by one, assuring her that she would barely be called upon to act. 'Just be yourself . . . that is the self you'd be if you were living in the them-and-us world of Edwardian England. Mrs Northrop drinks and answers back. She's insubordinate and vengeful. You told me about the woman in Gawsworth who accused you of stealing. You simply have to tap into your sense memory, as Stanislavski . . . never mind! And you'll even have the chance to break a dish legitimately.' She feigned a laugh, recalling Noreen's sensitivity to her recent spate of accidents. 'Of course I'll pay your usual hourly rate during rehearsals and performances. It's the least I can do,' she said, forestalling any protests. 'No one else need know. You work hard, and it's only right that you should be recompensed when we eat into your free time.'

'But it's only four days till the first performance. You gave me a ticket. How will I learn my lines . . . know where to stand . . . and everything else?'

'Derek will take care of it. And I'll help. You'll be amazed at how you'll rise to the challenge. Let's make a deal. Come to the rehearsal with me now and, if you find you can't manage, that'll be the end of it. No one can say we didn't try.'

'Well, I'm sure that your . . . Derek will take one look at me and give up.'

'Nonsense! You'll be terrific. What's the Hollywood line? "Now go out there and be so swell that you'll make me hate you!"'

The last time Noreen had acted was as the Star of Bethlehem in the Our Lady of Sorrows nativity play. Her mother had made her a cardboard-and-silver-foil headdress. Father Damian had handed her a lit sparkler as she stepped into the chancel and, even though it fizzled out before the three wise men appeared, her Aunty Jill described her performance as dazzling. Her mother had set her heart on her playing the Blessed Virgin, but Noreen had been grateful not to have any lines.

Forgetting her lines was only one of her worries as she arrived at the Stationhouse. The millworkers' cottages were separated from the rest of the village by more than just the river. Her neighbours had neither the time nor the inclination to take part in the Players' shows, which they regarded as a middle-class indulgence. Although she'd met most of the company at Laura's parties, it was on a *May I take your coat? / Can I get you something to drink?* basis – which Craig mocked as knowing her place. She had no doubt they would go out of their way to make her feel welcome, which in itself filled her with dread.

With all eyes turned to her as she entered the hall, she felt as though she were already onstage. Laura introduced her to the director, Derek, whom she'd served several times although she didn't expect him to remember her. To her horror, he dropped to his knees and brushed her hand with his clammy lips.

'Laura always said you were a treasure and now we know why. You've saved our bacon.' The young man beside him laughed. 'Did I say something amusing?'

'Bacon . . . the butcher . . . I thought . . .'

'Don't! It's not your strong point.' He turned back to Noreen. 'Without you, all our hard – I think I may truthfully say, inspired – work would have gone to waste. We're eternally in your debt, Nora—'

'Noreen,' Laura said.

'Noreen, of course.'

'I haven't done anything yet. It may not . . . you may not think I'm right.'

'You're too modest. I can tell at once you'll be perfect. I have an instinct. Don't I have an instinct?' There was a general murmur of assent. 'Now let me introduce everyone.'

Although embarrassed for the two young women whom he identified solely as the prompter and props mistress, Noreen was glad to have been spared more of the names which she was almost as afraid of forgetting as her lines. Derek then sent the others away, declaring, with ominous emphasis, that he would work intensively with her. In a reversal of roles, Laura stayed behind to read with her, as did the young man – Hugh? – whose presence was not explained.

Derek described Mrs Northrop as a middle-aged woman who looked older than her years, worn down by relentless childbearing, grinding poverty, overwork and a feckless husband. Noreen couldn't help picturing her mother, until he added that, for all that, she kept cheerful.

She read her scenes, which she found easier than expected, although it helped that her audience numbered only three, two of whom were roundly appreciative, while the third confined himself to correcting her diction. When they reached the end, he jumped up and kissed her again, this time on the cheek. As if it were a favour, he gave her the morning off to become 'word-perfect', before calling her with the rest of the cast for an emergency rehearsal at two.

'One morning to learn the complete part! I'll never do it,' she said to Laura, who was running her home.

'Nonsense! It's like the fight or flight mechanism. Your brain goes into overdrive.'

'I think I'd rather flee,' she replied feebly, knowing that Laura would be hot on her trail.

She set her alarm for six and was elated to find that, by lunchtime, she had most of the first two acts by heart. That elation vanished when they began to rehearse and she discovered that lines, which had been crystal clear at home, turned fuzzy as she struggled to remember where to stand, where to look and what to do with her hands. She reached breaking point at the end of the first act when, already confused by the author's direction that she *may have had a drink or two* (surely he should know?), Derek suggested that it would be funnier if, before flinging the dish to the ground, she placed it on the whatnot. Assuming that his *whatnot* was the same as her *whatchamacallit*, she put it on the bureau, triggering a loud groan. Drew came to her rescue, dashing out of the wings, where he'd been chatting to the prompter, and placing it on the small stand.

For all her anxiety and mistakes and apologies for the
mistakes, she found herself enjoying the rehearsal. Her
fellow actors were full of compliments, none more so than
Lloyd, who was playing the drunken photographer and,
according to Laura, taking method acting too far.

'My dear wife has done us all a favour. Oh yes, her
ignominy turns out to be a blessing. You have more talent
in your little finger – no, your fingernail – than she has
in her whole sluttish body. But you must nurture it. And
you want to know how? I said: do you want to know?'
Unnerved, Noreen nodded. 'Give up meat!'

The next morning, Laura, as proprietorial of her
'protégée' as she had long been of her 'treasure', drove her
to the Stationhouse for the tech run, warning that they
would spend the entire day repeating cues for the benefit
of the stage management and lighting team. For Noreen,
however, the novelty outweighed the tedium. Surveying
the finished set, she was amazed at how closely it adhered
to the plan at the back of her play-script: not only the two
settees, a term she thrilled to see in print as if in defiance
of Laura's edict, but also ornaments like the leaf-shaped
dish, which wouldn't be seen even by people in the front
row.

'It's wonderful,' she said, as Derek caught her admiring
it. 'You have all the props exactly like in the book.'

'The devil is in the detail. It's my job to create the
perfect setting in which my actors – my human props – can
shine.'

Her greatest excitement was trying on her costume:
a long black woollen dress, black linen cap, ragged grey
shawl and hobnail boots. The dress, which had been made

for Mrs Considine, was too large about the bust and hips, but she was assured by Laura, resplendent in peacock blue silk, that at that period working women wore hand-me-downs. Noreen thought of her own wardrobe, full of Laura's cast-offs, and smiled.

The tech run ended at 10 p.m., which Laura claimed was a record, since she'd known several last into the early hours. The dress rehearsal the next evening was flat, with even Lloyd's Ormonroyd, for Noreen the highlight of the production, lacking zest. No one else was worried, however, since it was widely accepted that a bad dress rehearsal would be followed by a good first night.

That evening, Laura gave each member of the cast a porcelain bridal couple, adding a silver horseshoe, inscribed *Just Married*, for Noreen, who was 'such a star.' She assured her that it was only natural that she had the 'wobblies', since even veteran actors experienced stage fright.

'Whatever you do, the audience will be on your side. Derek has impressed on the *East Cheshire Chronicle* that you only stepped in on Friday. He's bound to make allowances. Break a leg!'

'You too!'

Noreen told herself that she'd be fine as long as she spotted no one she knew. Fortunately, the stage lights made it impossible to make out anything other than a gratifyingly full house. To her amazement, she was greeted with a loud laugh on her first line and even a splutter of applause as she exited, shouting 'To 'ell with 'em!', which she attributed as much to a subversive spirit in certain sections of the audience as to her delivery. Her next entrance brought her face-to-face with Maria Helliwell. Laura, usually flawless, faltered and, instead of asking for a tray with glasses, asked for a glass with trays. In the ensuing pause, Noreen impulsively mimed tippling. As the audience guffawed, Laura (or rather, Mrs Helliwell) glowered, and Noreen feared that she'd committed a serious faux pas. She escaped into the wings, where she was spun round and kissed by Derek.

'Quick thinking, darling! Once again, you saved the day.'

With twenty minutes until her next appearance, she had time to recover from the shock. The rest of the play passed in a kind of dream . . . not a blur, since she was aware of every moment, although she felt unable to control it. When the house lights came up at the curtain call, she was so taken aback by Barry's enthusiastic clapping that she failed to notice Derek's arrival onstage, until he handed her a large bunch of roses. The cast joined the audience in applauding her, while Laura whispered in her ear that 'the bouquet was my idea.'

It felt strange to be walking into the Hall for Laura's traditional first night party, rather than waiting in the porch to admit the guests. Almost as strange was to be accompanied by Barry. Touched by his congratulations, she'd pressed him to come, only to watch uneasily as he snatched a glass of champagne and stationed himself at the bottom of the stairs. Drinking steadily, he rebuffed several attempts at conversation. Each time she made to intervene, she was accosted by a well-wisher. She'd barely shaken off Laura's yoga teacher when she was grabbed by Lloyd.

'Where have you been keeping yourself all these years?'

he asked, in the over-familiar tone she assigned to his new-found freedom.

'I've told you already. I've lived in the village ever since I got married.'

'Impossible! There's no bushel large enough to hide such a blazing light.' His glazed smile showed that he too had been guzzling the champagne. 'My wife's left me, you know. Yes, of course you do. For a butcher . . . a butcher! Why, I ask you? Is there a war coming? Will meat be rationed? A butcher!' He stumbled, not only over his words.

'Sit down, Lloyd,' she said, pointing to the settle. 'You'll feel better.'

'I'll feel better if you sit down beside me.'

'I have to speak to my husband.'

Trusting that she'd made herself clear, she headed towards Barry, who was inspecting Brian's recently acquired coat of arms, only for Laura to waylay her.

'Devil on horseback?' she asked, holding out a tray.

'Shall I take that from you?'

'Absolutely not! You're the guest of honour.'

'That means so much. I was worried I might have put you off your stride. I tried to make it look as if that slip was intentional.'

'Don't give it another thought! Your improvisation was inspired. Of course, without it, nobody would have noticed. I was about to correct myself – in character – when you jumped in. But you're a neophyte.' Noreen flinched. 'Actually, yes, it's kind of you to offer. Here!' She handed her the tray.

Slipping into the accustomed role, Noreen headed to the dining room and passed round the canapés. But when

Richard Lyons and Lynne Grafton made the same joke
about taking care not to fling down the tray, she knew that
it was time to leave. Returning to the hall to fetch Barry,
she froze at the sight of Tessa Shipstowe, playing the floozy
offstage as well as on, brazenly propositioning him.

'Have you any ambitions to tread the boards?' she asked,
as if suggesting a private rehearsal.

'No.'

'Or do you and Noreen like to keep your hobbies
separate?'

'Don't have any.'

'So what line of work are you in?'

'Gardener.' He took a drink. 'Mickham Park.'

'A horny-handed son of the soil,' she said, tracing a
figure of eight on his sleeve. 'Or should that just be *horny*?'

'Actors!' he said, recoiling. 'Prancing about in other
people's clothes!' His raised voice echoed through the hall.
'Pretending you're someone else because you're sick of your
own selves . . . They destroyed my clock.'

'The Players?' Tessa asked, bewildered.

'Time to go home,' Noreen said, clasping Barry's arm.

'What clock?' Tessa asked.

'I thought you said that he didn't speak,' Lloyd said,
intercepting Noreen as she guided Barry away.

'There must be more than one bushel.'

Laura liked to lie in during performance week. Despite a
lifelong aversion to pubs, she felt obliged to mingle with
the cast in the Hollybush after the show. The previous
night she'd found herself alone with Noreen and Lloyd,
who were deep in debate about global warming (a subject

in which Noreen had never before expressed the least interest). The rare sensation of being not only superfluous but unwelcome deepened when she stood up to go and neither of them detained her. After an earlier than expected bedtime, she was sufficiently awake to join Brian for breakfast.

'To what do I owe the honour?' he asked, looking up from the *Financial Times*.

'Aren't I allowed to enjoy my husband's company before he disappears for the day? Besides, it's Friday,' she said, picking up the *East Cheshire Chronicle*.

'Of course. The review we claim never to read.'

'Not funny.'

She turned to the *What's On* page, piqued as ever by the heading (surely there were enough discriminating readers to merit an *Arts and Books*?). She struggled to keep the paper from flapping as she read the caption *A Star is Born*, above a photograph of Noreen. She skimmed the first two paragraphs, which summarised – indeed, gave away – the plot. After praising the Graftons, Lloyd's and Tessa's comic flair, and even Robin's cameo as the Vicar, the reviewer remarked on 'disappointingly lacklustre performances from Richard Lyons and Laura Harding in the key roles of Alderman and Mrs Helliwell. Given the setting, Ms Harding's performance might be likened to a soggy Yorkshire pudding.'

'Libel!' Laura shrieked, hurling aside the paper.

'What's that?'

'He calls me a Yorkshire pudding.'

'That's most ungallant.' Brian laid down his paper. 'You may have put on the odd pound but—'

'Not me, Brian, my performance! When I think of how often we've invited that man to dinner.'

'He's certainly drunk enough of my best brandy.'

'Is there no loyalty left!' Laura picked up the paper. 'Wait a minute, it's not Trevis at all. Harriet Ormerod . . . who's she? What happened to Mark?'

'Maybe he's ill?'

'That's no excuse. Has he never heard of "the show must go on?"'

'Getting worked up won't do you any good.'

'A pudding, Brian! So they send this . . . what? Sixteen-year-old intern? She's probably never seen a play in her life. There are such people.'

'So I'm told.'

'You must ring the editor at once and demand a front-page apology. At once! You have the clout. Who else takes out a double spread in the wretched rag every week?'

'Show me the review. It can't be all bad.'

'Not just a pudding but soggy! She calls me soggy! It's an outrage. Insult a professional actor, if you like. They get paid. But we do it for love. To bring a little light into people's lives. I have to go on stage again tonight and tomorrow. How will I face the rest of the cast?'

'With your usual aplomb. You always tell everyone you never read reviews.'

'But they know it's not true!' She returned to the paper. 'And if you think it could get no worse . . . Have you seen what they say about Noreen?'

'I haven't seen anything. You're scrunching it up like a rejected planning application.'

'"A last-minute substitute, with only a day to learn the

part." Nonsense! She had . . . what? Saturday, Sunday, Monday and Tuesday, whenever we weren't rehearsing. Noel Coward wrote the whole of *Private Lives* in less. "Playing the truculent Irish charwoman to the manner born" – well, no surprise there! – "she didn't merely steal the show, she committed grand larceny." See, she calls her a thief! I've had my suspicions.'

'Now you're being ridiculous.'

'I've nurtured a viper in my bosom.'

'Be fair! Noreen didn't write the review.'

'No, it was probably one of her friends.' Brian looked at her sceptically. 'Or Craig's or Heather's. You were there on opening night. You saw the way she pounced on my tiny fluff. That vulgar gesture.'

'I thought it showed presence of mind.'

'But it threw me for the rest of the performance. Harriet Bitchface is right. Not soggy, no! But perhaps a little dull. I was so knocked off balance, I never recovered.'

'Well, you have two performances left to show her and everyone else what you can do. At the village shop they call you Dame Laura.'

'Not after this.'

'I really must be off. Remember it's Friday. Noreen will be here any minute.'

'No, it's more than flesh and blood can stand! Ring and tell her I'm not well.'

'Rubbish. You'll be gracious and congratulate her. After all, you're nothing if not an actress.'

Laura had not felt so challenged by a role since she'd hosted dinner for the Hortons, days after discovering Brian's affair with Marianne. But bathed, dressed and wearing a breastplate of beads, she stepped into the kitchen to greet Noreen, who was singing – tunelessly – as she washed up the breakfast dishes.

'Morning,' Noreen said, with a smile which Laura struggled to mirror. The irony was that, under normal circumstances, she would have attributed her high spirits to *Doctor Theatre*.

'You're sounding very jolly this morning,' she said. 'Did you and Lloyd stay on at the pub long after I left?'

'We had a couple more drinks. I'm afraid we lost track of the time.'

'You're becoming very thick with him.'

'He's lonely without Sheila. He hates going home to an empty house.'

'You don't need to explain yourself to me. I'm not judging you . . . just offering a word of warning. This is Lower Marston, not Macclesfield. Tongue-wagging is the local sport.'

'I'm a married woman.'

'So was Sheila Considine. Please don't misunderstand. I'm not suggesting there could ever be anything between you and Lloyd. After all, he's a deputy headmaster. But people talk. And it reflects on me. I'm the one who introduced you to the Players.'

'Is there anything special you wish me to do this morning?' Noreen asked quietly.

'Yes, would you deep clean the oven? We had duck on Sunday. I'll get out of your way. The Mr Muscle wreaks havoc with my vocal chords . . . Anton, Henrik, heel! Anton, Henrik!'

The dogs broke away from Noreen, who was

shamelessley seeking to win their allegiance, just as she had with everyone else. She ushered them into the car and drove to Knutsford, where she spent the morning shopping but found nothing she liked enough even to return.

Arriving at the Stationhouse that evening, she was more dismayed than ever by the communal dressing rooms. At least Noreen's spot was at the opposite end of the women's room to hers. As she walked to her chair, her eye was drawn to the *East Cheshire Chronicle* next to Tessa Shipstowe's tote bag, open at the fateful page. Looking away, she greeted her fellow actors with a breezy 'Hello.' She'd scarcely had time to take off her coat when Tessa approached, brandishing the paper.

'I know I speak for us all when I say that it's grossly unjust.'

'What dear? Has someone died?'

'The review,' Tessa said.

'Oh, I never read them! They always get it wrong even when they lavish you with praise. Remember what they say about critics: eunuchs in the harem.'

'This one was written by a woman.'

'Lesbians in the locker room, then . . . whatever. Now I really must change. It's almost the half.'

'It's monstrous,' Lynne said. 'After all you've done for the village. I intend to write to the editor.'

'That's most kind, but there's really no need. Though I have to say it's the first time I've been compared to a foodstuff.'

'I thought you hadn't read it,' Tessa said drily.

'Brian read out the salient bits before he left for work. Somebody said that a bad review might spoil your breakfast but it shouldn't spoil your lunch. It didn't even do that, as I buttered a second croissant.'

'Comfort eating?' Tessa asked.

Laura didn't deign to reply.

'Noreen was singled out for praise,' Lynne said.

'It must have been the sympathy vote,' Noreen interjected.

'Nonsense,' Laura replied. 'You have an innate talent. I saw it right away. I trust you'll all give me credit for that at least. Now I really must get on or I'll let the side down even further.' She took a large peacock feather fan from her bag and laid it on the table.

'What's that?' Tessa asked.

'From last year's masquerade ball at Tatton Park. I thought it might help me to scale the dizzying heights all around me.'

The performance was an ordeal. With her actor's instinct, she could tell that everyone in the audience had read the review and was waiting for her to trip up. Having nothing to lose, she held nothing back, forcing the others to rise to her level rather than lowering herself to theirs. She introduced several new moves during the first act but promised to stick to the blocking, after Derek, aka Mr Hidebound, gave her a furious dressing down during the interval. The one thing she refused to drop was striking Mrs Northrop with the fan, which raised a huge laugh, especially when two of the feathers flew off.

On the last night, she suffered a blinding migraine and spent most of the performance in agony. Although the entire cast urged her to go home and rest, she felt honour-bound to stay for the party. Sipping a glass of mineral water on a set which, for once, she couldn't wait to see struck, she watched indifferently as Brian flirted with Amanda Belben, who'd played her niece, and smugly as Derek glowered at Drew, who slipped away with Julia . . . thingamy. Spotting Lloyd on his own, she beckoned him to the sofa, steeling herself for an uncomfortable conversation.

'This must have been a painful production for you,' she said.

'Actually, it's turned out surprisingly well.'

'You and Sheila were such stalwarts of the Players.'

'We did our best.'

'There's no hierarchy here, thank goodness, but as a senior member of the society, I feel it incumbent on me to speak out. You command a great deal of respect in Lower Marston.'

'Really? The first I've heard of it.'

'Brian and I often pick up your pamphlet on . . . what was it? *The Lost Railway Lines of East Cheshire.*'

'*Branch lines.*'

'No one knows or, indeed, values Noreen's qualities more than I do. Loyal . . . devoted . . . hard-working.'

'Woof woof!'

'Are you drunk?'

'You make her sound like a sheepdog.'

'Just look at what she's done for her children!' Laura said, determinedly. 'Of course I did everything I could to help. I took them on outings with my two – they're pretty much of an age – whenever it seemed appropriate. But when all's said and done, she's a cleaner.'

'What are you getting at?' he asked, narrowing his eyes.

'The first time she came to me, she'd never seen a

bidet.' Her voice cracked. 'She called it the little toilet.'

'So?'

'She's a woman who circles her 'i's and loops her 't's. Not your sort at all.'

'I've had a few drinks with her. I haven't proposed marriage! And I'd thank you to keep your nose out of my affairs.'

Lloyd stood up and walked away, leaving Laura feeling doubly aggrieved. Seizing his chance, Brian moved toward her.

'Ready to go?' he asked.

'Desperately, but duty calls. What do you suppose they're talking about over there?' She gestured at a group with Noreen at the centre. 'Don't stare!'

'Probably how the gun failed to go off twenty years ago in *Murder at the Vicarage* and Miss Marple had to kill Colonel Plum with a quill pen.'

'Very droll, but I caught them glancing at me. Let's find out.' As she led a reluctant Brian towards them, she was startled by a burst of laughter. 'Is it a private joke or can anyone join in?'

'Noreen was describing life in a convent,' Robin said.

'A convent school,' Will corrected him.

'And the bizarre behaviour of the nuns,' Lynne added.

'Do tell!' Laura said.

'It really wasn't that funny,' Noreen said.

'It got a bigger laugh than anything I did onstage this evening.'

'That's not true, darling,' Brian said. 'You're tired. We should say our goodnights.'

'I want to hear Noreen's story,' Laura said, sounding petulant even to herself.

'We were discussing mortal sin.'

'At a cast party?'

'No, at school. The nuns told us that the only time suicide was pardonable was when our virginity was threatened. They said that the surest way was to jump out of a window. I got six strokes of the cane for asking what we should do if we were on the ground floor.' Brian gave a strangled laugh. 'See, I said it wasn't that funny.'

'Not at all,' Laura replied. 'I've always loved that story.'

'Have I told you it before?' Noreen asked, puzzled.

'It's your party piece. But then you're quite the professional.'

'Don't be a cow, Laura,' Derek said. 'We understand you're upset about the review, but there's no need to take it out on Noreen.'

'What do you mean? I've done everything I can for her. If I weren't paying her, she'd never have agreed to take part.' Laura was gratified by the instant chill, as everyone gazed at Noreen.

'I didn't ask you to.'

'Think nothing of it. It's my privilege . . . my pleasure to help. Just like that dress you're wearing. It looked garish on me, but it suits you perfectly.'

'Come on darling,' Brian said, gripping her arm. 'Time to go home. Goodnight, all. And congratulations again!'

Much to her surprise, Noreen enjoyed playing Mrs Northrop, partly she suspected, because everything had happened too fast for nerves to set in. Even the unpleasantness at the party didn't blight the experience. The next day, Laura sent her a large bouquet of lilies and a profuse apology, attributing her outburst to artistic temperament. For a few hours, Noreen considered handing in her notice, but knowing how hurt Laura had been by the review, she decided to make allowances. If nothing else, the episode had taught her how much acting took place in everyday life.

She was touched when, three weeks after the production, the Players elected her a member, but she insisted that her future involvement would be limited to helping backstage and front of house. So she was surprised to receive a letter from Derek, inviting her to audition for the autumn production of Noel Coward's *Blithe Spirit*. She dimly recalled seeing it on television as a girl but could remember nothing about it, other than her mother's assertion that seances were blasphemous.

While scathing about 'yet another boulevard comedy,' Laura was excited at the prospect of returning to the stage, as well as repairing relations with her fellow actors who, she told Noreen with an air of bewilderment, had been treating her coolly.

'Such a pity that there's no part in it for you!'

'I've told you, Mrs Northrop was a one-off.'

'You should build on your success. There's a maid of course, but she's far too young. Coward doesn't specify her age, but Madam Arcati calls her a child. And there's no escaping the fact that society was dreadfully rigid in those days. You couldn't hope to get away with playing Ruth or Elvira, or even the dreary Mrs Bradman.'

That afternoon, Noreen broke a majolica vase. Still

seething when she returned home, she rang Craig and asked him to order her a copy of the script, since Barry refused to let her use her credit card online. The moment she read it, she saw that Laura was wrong. There was one part she could play: Madam Arcati, the eccentric psychic, who might have been modelled on her Aunty Jill.

Jill, who'd claimed to 'have the gift,' had been their next-door-neighbour in Lyme Green. Her bedsit, complete with crystal ball, tarot cards and Ouija board, was a treasure trove for Noreen and her sisters. She wore tasselled earrings, a jewelled turban, a clutter of chains and, most thrillingly, a patch over her left eye. She told the girls it had been gouged out by an angry spirit, but their disapproving mother insisted it had been split open by her drunken husband. Although born and bred in Oldham, she'd taken the professional name of Signora Silvana, adopting a heavy Italian accent for her clients.

Hearing Aunty Jill's voice more clearly with each reading, Noreen resolved to try out for the part. She presumed that Laura, despite being twenty years too old, would want to play the glamorous Elvira, and was dismayed to discover that she too had set her sights on Madam Arcati. Having concealed her own interest, she was relieved to see no sign of her rival when she arrived at the Stationhouse to audition.

Derek was seated with Juan, the Spanish exchange student who had replaced Drew as his assistant, and Lynne Grafton, the Players' secretary. Noreen read a speech she'd prepared, in which Madam Arcati summoned her six-year-old 'control', followed by a scene with Juan, whose halting delivery failed to dent her confidence.

To her astonishment, Derek stood up and hugged her. 'Brilliant,' he said. 'Truly brilliant.'

'Whatever gave you the idea of making her Italian?' Lynne asked.

'Her name, Arcati. I assumed . . .'

'Brilliant,' Derek repeated. 'So much for those – who shall be nameless – who said that you were a one-trick pony.'

'I know Laura's keen to play the part. I wouldn't want to tread on her toes.'

'You've crushed them, darling.'

'Besides, she doesn't deserve it,' Lynne said. 'Her disgraceful upstaging at the end of the run. Faffing about with that ruddy fan. Utterly unprofessional.'

Although that struck Noreen as a strange criticism to level at an amateur, she knew how seriously they took their performances and was determined to follow their example when, three days later, Derek rang to offer her the plum role.

He asked Laura to play Mrs Bradman. 'I was in two minds whether to accept,' she said, after congratulating Noreen with every semblance of sincerity. 'I'm afraid that audiences unfamiliar with the play will feel cheated when they find out how little I have to do. You'd hope for loyalty – not from you, dear . . . after all, you're a mere neophyte.' Noreen smiled. 'If it hadn't been for Brian and me – well, to be honest, me – the Players would still be performing on rickety rostra with no wings and moth-eaten curtains, in the village hall. But Brian convinced me to be the bigger person. As the saying goes, there are no small parts, only small actors.'

She proved her point in rehearsal, questioning her motivation for every move and even during the long stretches when she was idle, provoking exasperated glances from Lloyd and Sheila, back together after what she termed her 'moment of madness'. Noreen, more circumspect, thanked her for her advice, some of which was helpful, and for her compliments, not all of which were double-edged.

Noreen took the production week off work. Although she knew her lines by heart and they only rehearsed in the evenings, for once in her life she wanted to emulate Laura. The fantasy unravelled when Laura coaxed her up to the Hall to root out an Art Deco cocktail shaker, which she'd promised Marcia as a prop. So, on Thursday morning, she found herself dragging a stepladder up the backstairs and into the box room. Laura insisted on holding the ladder – which was quite steady – while she clambered up and shone a torch into the top of a dusty wardrobe.

'It must be right at the back. Though this may be the wrong wardrobe,' Laura said, after Noreen pulled out several dishes, vases and a large carriage clock. As she grabbed what turned out to be an old Thermos flask, she felt the ladder shake and heard what sounded like a faraway scream. The next thing she knew, she was sprawled on the floor, a searing pain shooting down her right leg. Laura was lying beside the toppled ladder, with Henrik licking her face. When Laura failed to respond to her call, she tried to stand, but the pain was too intense. She feared that they'd be trapped there until Brian returned from work.

Just then, Laura stirred. 'What happened? I feel . . . I blacked out. I'm fine, I'm sure . . . Oh my God! Are you all right?'

'I fell. You must have pulled the ladder down with you.'

'No, I can't have done! That's impossible. How? I'll never forgive myself. Not now, Henrik!' She pushed the pug away. 'Can you stand?'

'It's my leg. It feels broken.'

'No, it can't be. It must be a sprain. Hang on! I'll pick myself up. I'll be fine as long as I go gently. Where's my phone? I'll call an ambulance. Don't move!'

The ambulance arrived within fifteen minutes, taking them both to Macclesfield General. Noreen's leg was X-rayed and the broken bone set, and Laura was given an ECG, which revealed nothing irregular. As they sat together in A&E, Laura kept repeating that she'd never forgive herself and, although Noreen assured her that she wasn't to blame, she couldn't shake off the suspicion that she was. After all, *Blithe Spirit* turned on Elvira's tampering with the brakes on Charles' car. Might a similar thought have occurred to Laura – unconsciously, of course?

She wasn't alone in her suspicion, as she discovered when Derek called round, clutching a bottle of whiskey.

'Irish, naturally. I thought you'd prefer it to flowers.'

'I'm so sorry to have done this to you. It's not fair: to lose another actress days before opening.'

'You've done nothing. We all know who did it.'

'It was an accident. She blacked out.'

'Read your Freud, darling! There are no such things as accidents. Manifestations of deep-rooted impulses. It's what the play's all about.'

'No, I can't believe she'd do that – or even think of it. What if I'd hit my head?'

'Have you never heard the phrase "kill for a part?"'

'Surely that's just talk?'

'Laura rang me as soon as she got home, in floods of tears. That's always been her forte. Offered to take over the role, even play it Italian. Suggested that Nancy could step in as Mrs Bradman.'

'That sounds like the best solution.'

'Who for? Mother has had an inspiration! You remember my friend Vincent – no, of course you don't. You've never met him. He was in the business in his salad days. Matter of fact, he was in *Salad Days*. It's twenty years since he quit the boards. But he dabbles in antiques (some might say, horses for courses). Last week at his shop, he showed me a vintage bath chair. So elegant, I'd half a mind to buy it myself. Anyway, I've skimmed through the play and there's no earthly reason why Madam Arcati shouldn't be an invalid. Of course we'd have to tweak the odd line: no more bicycling through the lanes of Kent or darting across the living room. Instead, you'll steer yourself about ineptly, while the others scramble to move the furniture out of your way. Then for the trance, rather than falling on the floor, you can jerk the chair to and fro.'

'It might just work,' Noreen said, slowly.

'Work! It'll be a sensation. You know who will be spitting feathers. Who'd have thought that breaking a leg would turn out to be a genuine stroke of luck?'

The White Lie

I T WAS MY idea to serve snacks in the new building. One hundred and fifty years after his great-great-grandfather, Joshua Beddard, first auctioned off a handful of unredeemed pledges in his Market Street pawnshop, my husband Toby moved the firm's headquarters to the former Corn Exchange. Gutted and remodelled, the building featured state-of-the-art sales and viewing rooms, spacious offices and a large reception area with provision for a café. He outsourced the catering to a local company, the Staffordshire Larder, which brought in twenty-one-year-old Daisy Jackson as manager. So it's fair to say that, if it hadn't been for me, Guy and Daisy would never have met.

At the time, Guy was living with the elegant, erudite Viola Curtis. Although they were well matched (he was the fourth generation Beddard & Son and she its silver and *objets de vertu* specialist), I held out little hope for their long-term prospects, especially since he'd kept on his old flat as a 'bolt-hole'. Toby accused me of jinxing their relationship, but if my feelings had counted for anything, Guy would have married Claudia Ravenscroft, his Cambridge girlfriend, or Sophie, the Swiss furniture restorer, whose surname escapes me. I loved my son dearly, but I wasn't blind to his faults. Yet his looks, charm, intelligence and background made him irresistible to women. Several of my own friends had avowed that 'If only I were twenty years younger . . .', flattering themselves by a good decade.

For years, Toby had made excuses for Guy's philandering or, as he put it more charitably, 'his roving eye', but with his son and heir's thirty-fifth birthday approaching, he was starting to have dynastic concerns. My own concerns were more visceral. I'd always longed for a large family and, with Guy an only child, I ached for grandchildren to fill the void. Even so, when I heard that he was seeing Daisy (from a tearful Viola, who'd heard it herself from the office manager), I tried to dissuade him.

'You're such a snob, Mother,' he said, with an almost adolescent mixture of resentment at my meddling and satisfaction at claiming the moral high ground.

'Is it snobbish to want what's best for my son? I'm simply being realistic. Passion doesn't last forever.' Had I been braver, the word would have been *lust*. 'What lasts is shared experience, friends and values.'

'I'm done with all that. Brittle, competitive women whose brothers I knew at Rugby or Cambridge, or cousins I met skiing. Daisy's quite different. She's so sweet and unworldly, so funny. She makes me see the world in a whole new way.'

'I hate to say it, darling, but that's exactly how I felt when you were born.'

They announced their engagement three months later. Daisy's mother Lee, who called me 'duck,' and father Trevor, who prefaced every second remark with 'yunno', were content to leave all the wedding arrangements to us. The ceremony was held at the village church, followed by a reception at the Hall, on one of those perfect summer days that now seem the province of period dramas. After their honeymoon in Bora Bora, where they stayed in a replica native hut, the newly-weds moved into our Lodge.

Otto was born in June the next year and Flora fifteen months later. Although I took care not to intrude, Daisy was eager to share her happiness, and scarcely a day passed without my walking down to the Lodge with a gift or treat, first for one child and then for both. I revelled in their nascent personalities. Otto was serious and self-contained, requiring everything to be 'just so', whether it was the position of the animals on his bed or the voices of the ones in his stories. Flora was as easy-going as her brother was fractious. A pert, vivacious child, she took and gave joy in equal measure. She was even able to comfort Otto when their father bridled at his 'little despot's' demands.

For all my efforts to be impartial, Otto and I shared a special bond.

'You're the best granny in the whole wide world,' he told me.

'What about Grandma Jackson?' I asked, feigning innocence.

'She's the next best,' he said, furrowing his brow. 'But you're the bestest best.'

I felt a pang at the thought of Lee, who saw so much less of the children and had fewer opportunities to indulge them (Toby's word for it was *spoil*, which, as I pointed out, did both them and me an injustice). On the other hand, she had two grandchildren living with her, now that her elder daughter Sheila had left her husband and returned home.

'You're prettier than Grandma. You feel softer. And you smell nicer,' he said, burying his head in the crook of my arm, as though aware of his own naughtiness. I said nothing but added a bottle of scent to my Christmas list.

My fears about the misalliance began to be realised. The first flashpoint came with the engagement of a nanny, which Daisy took as an affront to her competence. While Guy grew ever more exasperated, I sought to reassure her that it would free up time for herself (and, by extension, her husband), although the only time she cared about was that which she spent with her children. Eventually, she succumbed to both pressure and tradition, choosing the youngest applicant, June Cunningham. At twenty-four, June might have been an ally, but while never openly insubordinate, she made plain her disapproval of Daisy's parenting methods. Matters came to a head when Sheila stumbled on her Facebook posts which, though never mentioning her employer by name, bristled with complaints, notably about her continuing to breastfeed her four-year-old son.

Guy was horrified by the breach of trust and humiliated by the revelations. Visiting the Lodge soon after June's departure, I gently quizzed Daisy on the wisdom of the practice, especially since she was also breastfeeding Flora.

'I have to sit down quite a lot,' she said, misconstruing my concern. 'Other than that, it's not a problem. Otto's always found it hard to settle at night and giving him the breast calms him. I didn't want him to feel jealous of the baby. The health visitor said it was perfectly fine to feed him once a day.'

I hinted that Otto might not be the only one who was jealous of the baby. It was imperative that she took a more active interest in Guy's work. When entertaining clients, he needed his wife by his side.

'Those people frighten me,' she said. 'I can't speak to them.'

'We can arrange elocution lessons.' Her horrified expression showed me that I'd now misconstrued her. 'Or an art appreciation course.'

She must have heeded my warning, since she began to attend our pre-sales parties. As I fielded compliments on my daughter-in-law's beauty, charm and even, on one occasion, wit, I congratulated myself that the danger had been averted. Then the Fairhursts, who'd appointed Guy to value their cellar, invited them both to the Grange for the weekend. It would be the first time that Daisy had been apart from either of the children for longer than a few hours but, after I promised – repeatedly – to call her if there were the slightest problem, she entrusted them to me. I tried not to betray my irritation at the regular calls and texts, which began on the drive down and continued throughout Saturday. To my lasting regret, I handed the phone to Otto while I was preparing Flora for bed. Preoccupied with her, I was startled when he passed it back to me, calmly saying 'Mummy's screaming.' It turned out that he'd told her that Flora had had an accident. By the time I'd explained to Guy that she'd merely peed on a sofa, Daisy's panic had disturbed the entire house.

'I'm afraid, old boy, your wife's deranged,' Sir Rodney declared bluntly, as Guy announced their early departure. From the way he reported the remark to me on their return, repeating it over the following months, I took it to be the moment that he gave up on Daisy and sought solace elsewhere.

◊

While his father would have been the natural choice to remind Guy of his obligations, Toby's chequered past meant that any reproof risked courting derision. So I took it upon myself to admonish him. Trusting that a public setting would lower the temperature, I invited him to lunch at the Orangery.

He arrived fifteen minutes late and immediately ordered a whisky. He warned me that he could only spare three-quarters of an hour, so I wasted no time in voicing my concerns. I assured him that I wasn't judging him and I was certain that the relationship was purely professional, but I'd heard rumours that he'd been seeing a lot – too much – of the new Chinese ceramics specialist, Huang Xue.

'Rumours? Really? Do you mean Father's pillow talk?'

'It's not just your father,' I replied, irked by his tone. 'Alicia Langley saw you walking together in Victoria Park. "How fashionable of Guy," she said, "to bring in someone from China!"' Her actual words had been *an Oriental*. 'Then she added that the two of you were holding hands.'

He downed the whisky in one gulp and ordered another. To my surprise, he seemed keen to talk. 'You were right, Mother. I shouldn't have married her.' Never had I longed so much to be wrong. 'She doesn't read the papers or even watch the news. Her world is so limited . . . no, so low. She cares about nothing above knee-height. The other evening, I'd barely walked through the door when she shrieked at me to come up to the bathroom. I thought one of the kids was ill. It turned out that Otto had shat this gigantic turd and she wanted me to see it.'

'Everything those children do is remarkable to her,' I said. 'She wants to share it with you.'

'No, she wants to show it to me. There's a difference. I've started to feel like a stranger in my own home. I truly believe that if Xue and I were having an affair – which we're absolutely not, by the way – she wouldn't care.'

'I wouldn't put it to the test.'

Suspicious of Guy's avowal, I suggested to Toby that we invite Huang Xue to dinner, together with two other young specialists, Alexandra Brooks from Clocks and Watches and Philip Fanshawe from Decorative Art. On all three cards, I wrote *and partner* in my best copperplate. Accepting, Xue wrote, with matching elegance, that she would be coming alone.

Suspicious of my motives, Guy insisted that it wouldn't be fair to subject Daisy to an evening of Beddard's gossip. I promised to veto any work talk, and when Daisy in turn begged to be excused, I not only pulled rank but, to ensure that she looked her best, booked her a hair appointment with Jackie. I was convinced that, given the traditional Chinese respect for family, as soon as she saw Guy with Daisy, let alone listened to her chatter about the children, Xue would break off any dalliance. But my scheme was thwarted when Flora came down with croup.

Forced to rearrange my seating, I put Xue next to Toby and Guy next to me, but their furtive glances alarmed me as much as an intimate exchange. By candlelight, I studied Xue's dainty, heart-shaped face, with its flawless skin, full lips and hard eyes. I had little opportunity to speak to her until we moved to the drawing room for coffee, when she mentioned that, after growing up in Beijing, she'd been educated at Rugby and Cambridge.

'Just like Guy,' I said fatuously.

She'd done a masters at Harvard, and her father had wanted her to stay on in America, but she'd chosen to return here, working in a London gallery before joining Beddard's. She was lavish in praise of Guy's efforts to expand into the Asian market. Later, when Toby and I were talking (on our separate pillows), he revealed that her father, Huang Chen, was a property tycoon and, according to Forbes, one of China's newest billionaires. 'She might have been head of some vast enterprise, but she wants to do her own thing, on her own terms. There's not much she doesn't know about porcelain. She'll have a real impact on the company.'

My main concern was what impact she might have on the family.

A fortnight later, I found out. I was enjoying a mid-morning canter when I spotted Daisy, smartly dressed, getting into her car. Given her recent isolation, I was pleased to see her out and about, and it was only the following week that I learnt she'd been on her way to consult a solicitor. It turned out that one of her former colleagues at the Staffordshire Larder was privy to all the Beddard's gossip, including the two overnight trips Guy had taken with Xue. When Daisy confronted him, he made no attempt to deny the liaison, which he blamed on her neglect. Showing more resolve than at any time since her marriage, she filed for divorce.

Guy was less exercised by Daisy's serving him papers than by her naming Xue. 'It's so vindictive . . . so primitive, which is exactly what I would have expected of her. In this day and age, there's no need to assign guilt. I'd have admitted to unreasonable behaviour – not that any reasonable person would consider it unreasonable given everything she's put me through – but I'd have been willing to do so for the sake of keeping the peace. This way she's compromised Xue.'

He moved up from the Lodge to the Hall, to remain close to the children. I started taking breakfast in bed rather than risk confronting the impeccably coiffed, impeccably dressed, impeccably mannered and dismayingly distant Xue first thing in the morning. For the daughter of a billionaire businessman, a provincial English auctioneer fourteen years her senior might not have seemed much of a catch, especially given her chilling assertion that 'I set aside the next few years to build my career. I didn't intend to fall in love until I was thirty,' but, in a rare moment of candour, she confided that passion for Guy had consumed her like 'a forest fire.' He was just as smitten, and they talked animatedly of the future both for themselves and the company, including plans to open a branch in Hong Kong or even mainland China, with her father's support.

Flora didn't appear unduly perturbed by Guy's departure. At three and a half, she found adults at once unexceptional and utterly mystifying. Otto, however, struggled to make sense of the changes to his world.

'Granny, what's divorced?' he asked, as we strolled around the lake.

'Why do you want to know?' I replied, my stomach twisting.

'This lady came to my school. She asked me to do a drawing of Mummy and Daddy, and then she asked me lots of questions about them. Lyndon Blake . . . he's seven; he told me it was because they were getting a divorced.'

I felt a surge of resentment towards both his parents, first for what they were doing to Otto, and then for leaving me to explain it.

'Sometimes a mummy and a daddy think it's best if they don't live in the same house any more.'

He thought for a moment, scuffing his shoe on a stone. 'Why?'

'There can be lots of reasons . . . grown-up reasons.'

'Is it because of us?'

'Who?'

'Me and Flora.'

'No, of course not. Not in the least. Why do you ask?'

'You always say we have the best mummy and the best daddy in the world. So's they can't have done any bad things. So's it must be us.'

'That's not true. You mustn't think that. They love you very much. We all do.'

'Then why? Why? Why?'

I clasped him to me, hoping to allay his fears as I once had those about the creatures lurking in the wainscot, but he wriggled out of my grasp. 'If they don't want to live in the same house, where will we live, me and Flora?'

'That's what the lady who came to see you will have been trying to decide. I expect it'll be some of the time with Mummy and some with Daddy.'

'Where will my toys live if we have two houses?'

'We can buy new toys. We can buy all the toys you want.'

'I want best of all to live with you.'

The family court officer who'd interviewed Otto submitted

her report prior to the final hearing. Guy had applied for joint residency, but the judge ruled that it would be less disruptive for the children to live with Daisy, spending alternate weekends and half the holidays with him. While he protested the judge's use of the word *sleepover*, which trivialised his role, Guy was relieved to be awarded joint responsibility for the children's education and welfare, along with lower alimony payments than he'd feared. This was partly because Daisy was living rent-free at the Lodge and partly because, by some subterfuge, he'd contrived to transfer the majority of his assets to the company.

Although she'd won as much as she could reasonably expect, Daisy saw herself as the loser, and her bitterness festered. She was terrified that Xue would try to turn the children against her. One evening, I caught Otto in the hall loo, wiping his face before going home. When I asked why, he explained that Daisy had made them promise never to kiss Xue. The previous weekend, she'd shaken him after finding a lipstick mark on his cheek, which she'd known wasn't mine. I suggested that, in future, he should come to me for a final inspection, like a soldier on parade (he declined to smile), and that, if I found any telltale traces, I'd rub them off. Meanwhile, I told both him and Flora that, if Daisy asked whether they'd kissed Xue, they should deny it.

'But that's a lie,' Otto said.

'It's a white lie.'

'What's that?'

'A good lie. One you tell to stop somebody feeling hurt.'

Daisy and Guy lost no opportunity to snipe at each other and, inevitably, the children were caught in the crossfire.

Daisy neglected to inform Guy about a meeting at Otto's school, which, as a father with joint parental responsibility, he had the right to attend. Guy refused to swap his weekend so that the children could spend Mother's Day with Daisy. I was angry with them both, but mostly with Guy, who was older and more powerful, not to mention in a new relationship. The simplicity and trustfulness, which had once drawn him to Daisy, had left her particularly vulnerable to the breakup. Although it was Guy who'd betrayed her, he acted as though she'd betrayed him, by failing to fulfil his expectations of a wife.

Daisy refused to let Guy set foot inside the Lodge and, since he resented having to 'wait on the doorstep of my own house', I was the regular escort-cum-go-between on the weekends that the children spent with him. Otto was increasingly loath to leave his mother, who told them that she stayed in bed with the curtains closed while they were away, 'so I can pretend it's night and we're all upstairs sleeping.' Her dishevelment when I took them home confirmed it.

One Sunday afternoon, Otto ran down to the Lodge twice to check on her, much to his father's fury. 'Anyone would think that she was the six-year-old!' he said. 'I forbid you to go there, do you understand? I forbid you even to think about your mother when you're here.'

'You can't stop me thinking what's in my head. We don't live in China.'

I ought to have spotted the danger sign, but I was too busy admiring his precociousness.

'That's a very ignorant and rude thing to say. Apologise to Xue!'

'Shan't! She's a Chink.'

Guy slapped him across the face. Otto howled.

'Come on old chap,' Toby said, rousing himself for once. 'Shall we take Dido and Circe for a walk?'

'Wait a moment,' Guy said, conscious of his father's disapproval. 'I'm sorry I hit you, Otto, but that's a bad – a very bad – word. I want to know who taught it to you. Was it your mother?'

'No,' Otto whimpered.

'I expect it was something he picked up at school,' I interjected.

'Don't ever let me hear you say it again!'

Toby took Otto outside; I took Flora into the kitchen. Guy moved to Xue, who was sitting on the sofa, flipping through a magazine, as oblivious to the disturbance as if she were in an airport departure lounge.

Midway through rolling pastry, Flora asked me to bend down and, although we were quite alone, cupped a floury hand around her mouth and whispered that it was Mummy who'd called Xue 'a Chink', when she was talking to Aunty Sheila, who'd called her 'a dirty hole.'

'A dirty—'

I stopped short and made her promise not to repeat either phrase. Later, walking back to the Lodge, I told them to say nothing to Daisy about Guy's smacking Otto.

'Is it another white lie?' Otto asked, kicking at the gravel.

'I suppose so.'

'So's we don't hurt Mummy?'

'That's right.'

'What about us? Who tells lies so they don't hurt us?'

I longed to break my own rule and blurt out that almost every word adults say to children was a lie of some sort, but I bit my tongue. Instead, I clasped them each by the hand and skipped down the drive, leaving them breathless and giggling as I delivered them to Daisy, who had neither washed nor dressed.

Xue took Guy to Cap Ferrat to meet her parents. The visit was a success and, on their return, they announced their engagement. The wedding was set for the following March and, although after thirty or more years of the one-child policy, Xue's immediate family was small, Huang Chen was flying dozens of friends and associates over from China for the ceremony. At Xue's mother's behest, Wednesday the 23rd of March was chosen as the most auspicious date. At first, Daisy refused to allow the children to attend, plunging me once again into the role of mediator; a role in which, as I reminded Toby, even a court-appointed expert had failed. I put it to her that, while she was legally entitled to withhold them midweek, it was spiteful, not to say reckless, since it would provoke Guy to retaliate.

'Of course, you take your son's side,' Daisy said.

'The only side I'm taking is the children's,' I replied. 'Flora is too young – or too placid – to act up, at least so far. But look at what you're doing to Otto! You told me that he's been disruptive at school. What about at home? The other day, I caught him pinching Flora. Up to now he's been her protector . . . I'm no psychologist, but it's patently obvious he's taking out his own feelings of vulnerability on the one person who's even more vulnerable.'

'Enough, please! I won't let anyone tell me what's best

for my children. You say you're no psychologist. Very true! If you were, you might see what all this is doing to me.'

'Everyone can see what it's doing to you. Or rather what you're doing to yourself. You're not yet thirty. You've your whole life ahead of you. You need to get out and about. Study . . . find a job . . . whatever. Meet new people. Maybe a new man.'

'Look at me! I'm a mess. Who'd want this?'

'Exactly. I mean . . . as you are now. Which is why you must make an effort. For your own sake and for the children's. At present, Otto feels sorry for you. Very soon he'll feel embarrassed. I think he may be starting to already.'

'No, that's not true!'

'Only you can make sure of that.'

In the end, Daisy relented, agreeing to let the children attend both the registry office ceremony and the reception at Weston Hall, which Huang Chen had reserved for three days' exclusive use by himself and his guests. Everything went smoothly until the morning of the wedding when, with Jackie busy doing my hair and Toby out with the dogs, Guy went to collect the children himself. I was bent over the basin when he rang, raging that Daisy was refusing to open the door. He'd tried – and failed – to break in through a window and was threatening to call the police. I begged him to wait until I arrived. Grabbing my spare keys, I dashed downstairs, with Jackie behind me towelling the back of my head. She drove me to the Lodge, where Guy stood amid shards of glass, nursing a bleeding hand.

'Just drum some sense into her!' he yelled, as I asked him to show me the wound.

I rapped on the door and called for Daisy to let me

in. Hearing nothing but a child's muffled mewling, I reminded her that I had a key and would enter come what may.

'You've got a key!' Guy yelled. 'To the new lock?'

'For emergencies,' I replied, Daisy having given it me on condition that I swore not to share it with him.

As I opened the door, Guy dashed past and into the kitchen, where Daisy was cowering beneath the table, clutching the children. He ducked down and grabbed Flora's arm; she squealed, and the Judgement of Solomon flashed through my mind. Daisy released her hold on both children, Otto scuttling to me and Flora to her father.

'That's it. Everything's all right now,' I said, hollowly. 'Go outside, darlings, where Granny's hairdresser is waiting by her car.'

'Outside!' Guy shouted, as neither seemed ready or able to move.

'We've got a wedding to go to,' I said, forcing a smile. 'I'll make sure that Mummy's all right.'

The children shuffled out while Guy glared at Daisy, his face a rictus of contempt. 'You'll regret this,' he said, thumping the table. 'I swear that I won't forget it. Are you coming, Mother?'

'You take the children. I'll be up directly. I just need a moment with Daisy.'

'Oh really? Perhaps you'd like to sit out the wedding with her? It's time for you to choose where your loyalties lie.'

Guy left, although his rancour lingered. I dragged Daisy, as pliant as a rag doll, from under the table and into a chair.

'Don't say anything, please,' she said. 'I'm sorry. So sorry.

I know that I shouldn't . . . Please don't say anything. I'm sorry.'

My bewilderment made it easy to comply. With barely ninety minutes to reassure the children, finish my hair, dress Flora and myself, and head to Tipping Street, I had no time to talk. Nevertheless, I was loath to abandon her. 'I presume that your parents are at work, but what about Sheila? Shall I ring and see if she can come round?'

'No, she'll know that something's wrong.'

'Something is wrong.'

'I'll call her, I promise. Go! You go! The children need you.'

We arrived at the registry office with not a minute to spare. The ceremony was brief and business-like. Xue looked exquisite in a feather-trimmed ivory midi-dress but, to my mind, the highlights were Flora, the sole bridesmaid, looking as if she'd stepped straight out of a Millais painting, and Xue's maternal grandmother, Zhao Mei, in a red-and-gold brocaded *cheongsam*, which stood in sharp contrast to the latest Western fashions favoured by her daughter and her friends.

The wedding breakfast consisted of a traditional ten-course Chinese banquet, blending Asian and European cuisine, overseen by a Michelin-starred chef whom Huang Chen had flown in from Hong Kong. Shortly after cutting the cake (a three-tiered chocolate pagoda, crowned by a golden phoenix and dragon), Guy and Xue left for the airport on the first leg of their trip to the Amazon. Toby and I followed half an hour later, using the overexcited children as an excuse. We delivered them to the Lodge, where, to my relief, Daisy was up and dressed and sharing a bottle of wine with her sister. While the children vied to give her their impressions of the wedding, Toby and I exchanged a few awkward pleasantries with Sheila, before returning home for a TV supper and an early night.

The next morning I was startled awake by the phone. I presumed it was Guy ringing to confirm their safe arrival in Lima, but it was Otto stuttering that he couldn't get Daisy to open her eyes. Pausing only to call an ambulance, we rushed down to the Lodge, where we found Flora howling on the stairs and Otto kneeling on his mother's bed, shaking her.

I felt for a pulse. 'Listen, she's breathing!' I said, lifting him up and pressing his ear to her chest.

'No, I don't believe you. I can't hear,' he screamed.

I went with Daisy in the ambulance to hospital and Toby took the distraught children to the Hall. While the doctors examined Daisy and pumped her stomach, I broke the news to the Jacksons. By the time they arrived, she was groggily conscious. Lee and Trevor sat on either side of her bed, stroking her cheeks and arms and peppering her with questions which she was too drowsy, sore or ashamed to answer. A doctor explained that they wanted to keep her in under observation, and her parents seemed grateful for anything that took her off their hands. Two days later, she was sectioned.

When I told the children that their mother had to stay in hospital, they accused me of telling the biggest white lie of all.

'I know she's dead,' Otto said.

Anxious to reassure them, I took them to visit her, but

she refused to speak or even to look at them, covering her face with a pillow.

I rang Guy in Iquitos and asked him to come home for the children's sake, but he said that it wouldn't be fair to Xue.

'She did it on purpose, Mother, to ruin our honeymoon. Well, I refuse to play her game.'

'But the children—'

'I know that they're quite safe with you. I promise I'll take charge of everything as soon as we get back.'

True to his word, the day after his return, he applied to the court to have the Child Arrangements Order varied. He claimed that Daisy was mentally unstable, an unfit parent and a permanent danger to the children. Although she refused to see me, Lee kept me abreast of her slow recovery, and I worried that news of Guy's application would set her back. I had no doubt that he was hell-bent on revenge, and I begged him to wait at least until she was well enough to leave the clinic. 'If – God forbid – she should do something foolish again, the children will never forgive you.'

'Children are resilient, Mother. They adapt. Look at me! Don't assume that all fathers are as disengaged as mine. Most care for their children as much as mothers.'

'But what about Xue? It won't be fair on her. She admitted to me that she lacks the maternal instinct. As a girl, she didn't even play with dolls.'

'So? We'll hire a nanny.'

Otto and Flora moved into the Jacobean farmhouse outside Stone that Huang Chen had bought his daughter as a

wedding gift. With half the rooms under renovation and
stairs and floors ripped out, I regarded it as a death trap
and offered to put them up at the Hall, but Guy believed
that it would bolster his case to have them living with him.
He coaxed Nanny Clifford out of retirement. I feared that
Otto and Flora, accustomed to their mother's indulgence,
would bridle at her strictures, but either she'd mellowed
in the years since she looked after Guy or else they'd learnt
to adapt, for they reached a curious accord.

On her discharge from the clinic, Daisy went to stay
with her parents. She rebuffed my requests to visit, but
the children saw her twice a week and said that she was
'OK' or 'good' – I couldn't tell whether their terseness was
designed to protect Daisy or themselves. She instructed her
solicitor to oppose Guy's application. Although the medical
and psychiatric reports were equivocal, her most compelling argument was that Guy had never been involved in the
day-to-day care of the children, either before or after the
divorce. Furthermore, when he heard of her admission to
hospital, he'd remained on his *pleasure cruise*, rather than
coming home to attend to them.

Since I was the one who'd, unwittingly, told her
mother of my phone conversation with Guy in Peru, I
fully expected to be the target of his fury, but I hadn't
anticipated his ultimatum.

'You must make a witness statement, Mother, explaining that Lee got it wrong: that you tried to reach me, but
we were already on the boat and out of phone contact for
the next ten days.'

'I'd have to lie under oath.'

'A white lie, Mother. Didn't you used to tell me that

they're allowed? Now's your chance to prove it. I swear on the children's lives, if you refuse, you'll never see them again.'

Terrified that he was in earnest, I filed my statement and was summoned to court, where Daisy's solicitor questioned me about the phone call. I explained that, after several failed attempts to get through to Guy, I'd given up, convinced that there was no signal in the rain forest. At least in the closed court, with only the two parties and their lawyers present, I didn't have to face Lee. I studiously avoided Daisy's gaze until I gave my testimony, when it bore into me with a mixture of disillusion and disgust. The judge ruled in Guy's favour on all three counts, granting him full custody, sole parental responsibility, and a Specific Issue Order, authorising him to take the children overseas.

'Why do you need that?' I asked, as he savoured his victory. 'Is it so you can go on holiday abroad?'

'I didn't want to say anything until we'd sealed the deal, but we're opening a branch of Beddard's in Hong Kong, through one of Chen's subsidiaries. It's the most fantastic opportunity: to be at the heart of the world's largest market. Xue and I will run it together.'

I listened in mounting despair. He hadn't wanted to tell me earlier in case I refused to make my statement . . . in case self-interest swayed me, where my duty to Daisy and an oath to speak the truth had failed.

'But what about the children? Their education?'

'There are excellent international schools out there. Harrow has a branch: co-ed from the age of two.'

'Flora's only four.'

'Exactly. Places are hugely oversubscribed, but with Chen's influence, we won't have any trouble getting them in, even as boarders.'

'You swore you'd never send a child of yours away to school.'

'Why must you put a dampener on everything?'

'What about Daisy? Will she ever see them again?'

'Of course. I'm not an ogre. She'll have them for half the holidays . . . at least in the summer.'

'And us? When will we see them?'

'You'll come out to Hong Kong. Father will have business there. For the rest, it'll be up to Daisy when they're with her.'

My perjury – my perfidy – had been justly punished. There wasn't the slightest hope of Daisy allowing me to see the children, when she held me responsible for their removal. They'd been the centre of my life ever since my first glimpse of Otto in hospital. Would I now be reduced to following them on Instagram and scheduling a weekly chat on Zoom?

Both heartened and hurt by their excitement, I asked if there were anything they'd be sad to leave behind.

'But it's not really leaving,' Otto replied. 'Daddy says we'll be coming back on a plane. With beds.'

'What about Mummy?'

'She won't care,' Otto said. 'Nanny says no mummy who loves her children tries to kill herself.'

'Nanny told you that?' I asked, although it sounded in character. 'But it's not true. Your mummy loves you very much.'

Otto put his hands to his ears and began to sing, with

Flora swiftly mimicking him. To say more would have distressed them.

'What about you, young lady?' I asked, making a game of prising her hands from her ears. 'Are you looking forward to a new adventure?'

'Where?' she asked, frowning.

'In Hong Kong, stupid,' Otto said.

'You're stupid,' she retorted. 'We're going to see Disneyland. Grandpa Chen is giving us a magic card so as we can go there just as many times as we ever like.'

'Grandpa Chen?' I asked weakly.

'Yes,' she said. 'He's Xue's daddy. He's the most importantest person in the whole world.'

'No, stupid,' Otto said. 'He's the richest.'

'Aren't you the lucky ones?' I said, with an aching smile. 'Grandpa Chen. Who'd have thought it? Grandpa Chen.'

The Mellow Madam

'Have you any comment on the story in today's *Sunday People*?'

'What?' Half-awake, Jackie fumbled on the night table for her hearing aid.

'Does your family know about your secret life? What about Beatrice?'

She clutched the edge of her mattress as the room wheeled around her. 'Who are you? What do you want?'

'Clayton Davis, night editor at the *Daily Mail*. Just a comment for now, love. And then a story. I can have Lindy Read, our top *Femail* features writer, with you in a couple of hours.'

'How did you get this number?'

'How do you think, love? You're not exactly ex-directory.' Her attempt to put him on the back foot had backfired. 'I guarantee she'll put your side of the story with sensitivity and discretion.'

'There is no story!' Her mouth was dry and her eyes strayed to the Teasmade, not set to boil for another forty minutes, even as she tried to assimilate the news that threatened to tear her world apart.

'We'll make it worth your while. Way above your usual hourly rate. Do we pay you or go through Mellow Madams?'

'There is no story. There never will be a story.' She

struggled to moderate her voice. 'I'll thank you not to contact me again.'

She cut him off mid-protest. Shivering and wheezing, stupefied and appalled, she longed to sink back into the oblivion from which she had been wrenched ten minutes before. The phone rang. Instinctively, she reached to answer, only to draw back her hand. She needed time to think. She'd always known that this day might come. When she first registered with the agency, she'd feared that every new client would turn out to be a family friend or business associate. Over the years, not only had that fear proved to be unfounded, but she'd realised that, whatever happened, the client's wish for discretion would be as strong as hers. Nevertheless, she'd taken great pains to preserve her anonymity. But a few weeks earlier, she had let down her guard. Lewis, one of her regulars, spotted an article about Beatrice that she'd cut out of *OK!* magazine. Trusting him (for no better reason she now saw than that his tastes were vanilla), she admitted that Beatrice was her granddaughter. Her complacency had been her undoing. He must have sold the story to the press, although she was at a loss to know why. He was a maritime lawyer, whose own hourly rate wouldn't have needed supplementing. Was he an outraged fan of *On the Heath*? Or, as her intimate study of the male psyche would suggest, did he want to punish her for having a life beyond his desires?

The phone rang again but she ignored it. Was it still the *Mail* or another paper with a similar request or – she waited for the choking sensation to pass – Naomi, Frank or Sam? Her children, following their father's lead, had found fault with her when she was a dutiful housewife. Their horror at the *People's* story was too dreadful to contemplate. Her first task was to get hold of a copy. Yet if the tabloids had her number, mightn't they also have her address? What if reporters were already camped outside and – what was the word Beatrice had used . . . something like *door-knocking* – waiting to pounce? She needed to get up and look out of the window. But not yet . . . not quite yet. If only she had a friend or neighbour she could send for the paper. But the only people who wouldn't be scandalised were the men who paid for her services. She must go herself, but even if there were no one else there, how would she face Mr Sharma? What if he'd flicked through the paper in a quiet moment or, worse, her picture were on the front page? Was Beatrice famous enough for that?

The thought of Beatrice tore at her heart. While the rest of the family had opposed her auditioning for *On the Heath*, she'd encouraged her, earning a sharp rebuke from Frank and Shona, who treated every subsequent setback as her fault. 'You're twenty-three years old. Of course, you must follow your dreams,' she'd told her grateful granddaughter. Would she now be the one to shatter them?

She swung her legs out of bed, to be struck by a wave of nausea. A glance at the Teasmade showed that there was still half an hour before it bubbled into action, and she had no idea how to reprogramme it. Besides, what she needed was a nip of brandy. She stood up, steadied herself and headed into the sitting room, pausing at the door as the telephone rang once again, afraid to hear the message on the machine.

◊

'Do you have anything to say about the story in this morning's *People*?'

Beatrice struggled to suppress her irritation at being
woken on the one morning during filming when she and
Reuben could enjoy a leisurely lie-in (if she were on her
socials, she would add a row of hearts and a fireworks
emoji). She gazed at Reuben, tucked under the duvet, as
deaf to the phone call as to the earthquake that had rocked
their hotel room in Magaluf. She traced her left foot along
his calf, savouring the warm, slightly damp skin, until the
hack's voice boomed down the phone.

'The story, Bea? Anything to say?'

How many more stories could there be? In the three
years since *On the Heath* first aired, her previously blameless
(some might say *boring*) life had been sifted for every scrap
of dirt. So-called school friends had twisted her short-lived
eating disorder into full-blown bulimia and the Christmas
card she sent Rabbi Berenson into a calculated affront.
Even her brother Nathan had sold a photograph of her
bursting out of a cake to sing 'My Heart Belongs to Daddy'
at her father's fiftieth, which the *Mirror* had printed with
all the female guests blacked out, making it look as if she
were performing in a sleazy nightclub.

'What story?' she asked, more loudly than necessary in
the hope of rousing Reuben.

'About your grandmother?'

'Which one?'

'Jackie Altman, of course.'

'Is she hurt?' she screamed, turning to see Reuben stir.

'Come on, sweetheart, don't play games with me!'

'Who is this?'

'Darren Littlewood, the *Sun*. We met at the Season Five media call.'

'Has something happened to my gran?'

'How about the fact that she's a high-class hooker?'

'You must be out of your mind!'

'It's the God's honest truth.'

'Is this a joke?' For a moment she wondered whether Marcia or one of her associates had set her up, although there'd have been little point without a camera to film her reactions . . . She gulped, peering at the ceiling to see if one might have been planted there, sighing at her paranoia.

'That depends on your point of view, doesn't it? Let me guess yours . . . Beatrice Altman sobbed helplessly on boyfriend Reuben Taylor's shoulder after learning that her grandmother was a hoary hooker (not bad, actually!). "How could she do this to me?" asked broken-hearted Bea . . . etc, etc. We can work out the rest. But the clock's ticking. You need to get your story out there before the proverbial hits the fan.'

'There must be some mistake. Another Jackie Altman. She's seventy-eight.'

'Really? Is that so? It's all over the effing paper!'

'Please! I can't talk. I need . . .'

She ended the call and shook Reuben awake. He stared at her with the puppy-dog eyes which, on an ordinary morning, enchanted her.

'Babes, what is it?'

'There's a story in today's *People*.'

'Good or bad?' he mumbled.

'Bad . . . very bad . . . the worst if it's true.'

She typed *Beatrice Altman On the Heath* into Google

– the search so familiar that the first two letters brought up all five words – and tentatively added *Grandmother*, only to fling down the phone as a headline appeared on the screen. *Beatrice Altman's Gran sells sex at £450 an hour.*

'Shit! Shit! Shit!'

'Babes, what does it say?'

'You read it. I can't bring myself to.'

He reached across for the glasses that he never wore in public. She called them his guilty secret. If only all guilty secrets were as harmless.

'"Beatrice Altman's Gran sells sex at £450 an hour." Wow! Do you think it's your gran?'

'Who else's?' For all that she loved him, sometimes the jokes about his one GSCE (actually, he had five) felt justified. 'Read it out to me.'

'The headline?'

'The whole article.'

'"Beatrice Altman, star of Channel Four reality show, *On the Heath*" – they call you the star, Babes.'

'Read it, please.'

'"Is in for a shock. Flame-haired Bea, who recently branded fellow cast member, Julia Wheeldon, a slag for flirting with hunky boyf, Reuben Taylor –" Honest, Babes, it meant—'

'I know. Just read.'

'"Hunky boyf, Reuben Taylor,"' he repeated, with an air of satisfaction. '"Will have to eat her words when she finds out that her seventy-eight-year-old grandmother, Jackie, may well be Britain's oldest vice girl. Jackie, who works under the name Empress Theodora for the specialist London escort agency, Mellow Madams –" Wow!

– "describes herself as elegant, gorgeous and tactile, with a deliciously naughty side. Up-for-anything Jackie offers services ranging from canoeing—"'

'Canoeing?'

'Sorry, "canoodling over a candlelit dinner to satisfying any man's wildest fantasies. When contacted by our investigator, posing as a company director from Leeds, she said she was a natural 34DD, with boobies you can suck on—"'

'That's enough! Stop!'

'Is this the gran who came to your mum and dad's for the Seder?'

'Oh Christ, what's it going to do to them?'

'But she's like a hundred.'

'Seventy-eight, Reuben. Can't you read?'

His upper lip quivered and she reached out to stroke his arm. There were times when she wished he weren't quite so in touch with his feminine side.

'No probs, Babes. We'll get through it together. Unless . . . holy fuck, what will Marcia say?'

The niggling worry at the back of Beatrice's mind thrust itself forward. Her producer's reaction was even more critical than her parents'. Her phone rang and Reuben looked at it in alarm.

'How weird is that!' he said, as he passed it to Beatrice, the caller identified simply as *God*.

Jackie waited for the caretaker to return with the paper. Although he didn't work on Sundays, Roger always offered to pick up any essentials when he took Charlie, his Yorkshire terrier, for a morning walk on Parliament Hill. Appreciating the need for companionship, she had refused to sign a letter of complaint about Charlie's barking. The managing agents dismissed the complaint and authorised Roger to take the dog on his rounds. With too much time on their hands, her fellow residents were never slow to air their grievances. Since the majority were single women of a certain age, Jackie felt like suggesting a lucrative and surprisingly pleasant way for them to occupy themselves. She chuckled – from nerves, not glee – as she pictured Jennifer Bridges and Sadie Cohen in a baby-doll night-dress or latex corselette. Then she poured another glass of brandy and wondered whether either of them read the *Sunday People*. It wouldn't be long before word got out. She doubted whether the managing agents would be as sympathetic to her case as they had been to Roger's.

Jackie had lived in South End Court for thirteen years. While happy to greet her neighbours in the entrance hall and lift and attend the summer party in the communal garden (without participating in the competitive baking that preceded the event), she'd kept to herself even before there was any call to do so. She worried about the noise of her more strenuous sessions but, fortunately, both of her immediate neighbours were deaf; their televisions drowning out the frequent yelps and occasional shrieks of pleasure. Besides, she insisted that any gentleman requesting CP wore a gag. As her clientele grew, so did the concern that her neighbours would be suspicious of the steady stream of male visitors. So she let it be known that, having kept the books for her husband's chemist shops for forty years, she was earning pin money doing the same for friends. Agreeing to take on the accounts for the Residents Association had been a small price to pay.

She'd moved here from Enfield after leaving the children's father, which was how she now chose to think of Stanley. She'd provoked predictable outrage, with Naomi demanding that she seek counselling. 'What kind of wife walks out on her husband after forty-four years?' she'd asked, which was particularly hurtful coming from someone who'd had the freedom to marry another woman. Her 'How's Father going to cope?' was as close as anyone came to acknowledging his domestic and, as it transpired, fiscal ineptitude, even if, behind the question, lay the terror that the burden would fall on her. The two boys had been as dismayed by the sale of their family home as by the break-up of their parents' marriage, as though a mother's prime duty were to serve as custodian of her children's pasts.

The house had been a wedding gift from her parents who, having lost relatives in Poland, were eager to stay close to their only child. It was for the same reason that, though neither she nor Stanley believed in God, they kept kosher and attended shul on the high holidays. The early years of marriage had been so full that she rarely stopped to ask herself if she were happy. Like other young wives in Winchmore Hill, she waved her husband off to work after a cooked breakfast and welcomed him home to a hot meal. With no frame of reference other than coy remarks at the hairdresser's, she had what she took to be a regular sex life. Confused as to why Stanley always thanked her for what was supposed to be mutual pleasure, she suspected he clung to the Victorian view that men enjoyed while women endured. It was only later that she realised the full extent of his self-loathing. After Sam was born, their lovemaking

(less a euphemism than a contradiction in terms) petered
out: an occasional sputter signalled by his clamping her
breasts and heaving himself on top of her, almost as if to
ensure that all his parts remained in working order – the
way that the dishwasher repairman advised her to run the
machine once a month to ensure that the rubber didn't rot.

Their three children had little in common beyond
their parentage. At fifty-six, Naomi was as imperious as
she had been at four, when she stripped the sheets off her
bed and demanded that her mother remake them with the
same hospital corners she herself had made for her doll.
A respected solicitor, she was married to Fiona, a charity
fundraiser, whom Jackie had warmly welcomed into the
family, denying Naomi her chance to rebel, which, she
suspected, frustrated her almost as much as rejection.

Frank was the most conventional of the three. Leaving
school at sixteen (a decision fully endorsed by his teachers),
he'd joined her father's wine business, where, to everyone's
surprise, he'd proved a success, seeking out vineyards in the
former Soviet Republics and educating British palates to
appreciate Ukrainian Merlot and Georgian Chardonnay.
She had no doubt that his regular trips to Kiev (with the
attendant hospitality) had shored up his marriage to Shona,
a woman with a kind heart but a limited vision. They had
two children: Nathan, a web designer, who'd shocked his
parents and panicked her at a recent family gathering by
revealing that his latest client was an escort agency; and
Beatrice, a bespoke cake maker with her own label, *Bea's
Bakes*, which had grown exponentially since her role in
On the Heath.

Her grandchildren were Jackie's pride and joy, although

Frank had sought to keep her at arm's length, even before the divorce. She still shuddered at being taken to task for convincing twelve-year-old Beatrice that Jews weren't hypocritical for celebrating Christmas since, while not the Messiah, Jesus had been a wise teacher. How was she to know that Beatrice would take this as a licence to send a card to Rabbi Berenson, who was preparing her for her bat mitzvah?

Her youngest child, Sam, was her favourite. The manager of a bathroom fittings shop in Finchley, he'd lately celebrated his fiftieth birthday with a black-tie dinner he could ill afford. Given her meagre divorce settlement, she wondered where he thought she found the thousands of pounds she'd given him over the years 'just to tide me over'. The truth was that Sam thought of nobody but himself and, painful as it was for her to admit, his chutzpah was part of his charm. After a protracted adolescence (he'd dyed his chest hair and gone on Club 18–30 holidays until he was forty-four), he'd married Maggie, a primary school teacher, prompting Naomi to declare, not without reason, that she should be well-equipped to handle him.

Like their sister, Frank and Sam had been horrified when Jackie left Stanley. In fact, she'd picked the moment fully aware of the indignation it would cause. As a qualified bookkeeper, she'd managed Stanley's accounts through-out their marriage. For years, she'd warned him that his finances were overstretched. But when he opened a third shop in Green Lanes, a stone's throw from Superdrug, they reached breaking point. His belief that customers valued personal service above discounted lines and loyalty cards might have been touching had it not been so patently misplaced. She packed her bags on the day that he filed for bankruptcy. By courting widespread condemnation, she had sealed her breach not only with Stanley but with her entire past.

She sold the house, dividing the proceeds with Stanley, who moved in with his sister Leah in Bournemouth. Within months, he developed Alzheimer's, lashing out at Leah with a violence that those who didn't know him blamed on the disease. The children arranged for him to go into a care home, where, according to the staff, Jackie was his most frequent visitor. Since he no longer recognised her, the visits were uneventful, and they sat together more companionably than they had in years.

Her new life turned out to be more humdrum than she'd expected. She volunteered one day a week at the Marie Curie shop, where an offhand reference to her book-keeping skills led to her being tucked away in the office, and one afternoon at the Hampstead Talking Newspaper, where she recorded articles of local interest for the blind. That might have been all there was, had a fellow volunteer, a sprightly octogenarian, not told her that, in order to keep her mind active, she was taking a course in Chinese philosophy at the City Lit.

Despite the sense of intellectual inferiority that Stanley had instilled in her, Jackie resolved to follow suit and enrolled for an evening class on Greek and Roman Mythology in Art, which promised two academic disciplines for the price of one. Fascinated, she complemented the classes with weekly visits to museums and galleries. Then one evening, flicking through the television listings, she came across a programme about Bacchus Ladies, which she assumed was another term for the Bacchantes, who had featured prominently on Greek pots and Roman reliefs in a recent lesson. To her astonishment, they turned out to be elderly South Korean prostitutes, the name derived from the energy drink they'd once sold in the parks of Seoul.

Four years after she'd left ('abandoned') their father, her relations with her children had thawed, yet she saw little of Naomi and Sam, and more of Frank only because he and Shona called on her to babysit (a word that infuriated the teenage Nathan and Beatrice). She'd understood that Asian children took greater care of their parents and was surprised to learn that in Korea, traditional family structures had broken down: first, during the economic boom of the 1960s, when the young had sought job opportunities away from home; then following the crash thirty years later, when those same youngsters, now with children of their own, were scrambling to survive. During the slump, old women without savings were the hardest hit of all, and the Bacchus Ladies, who sold bottled drinks for a pittance, found that they could earn far more by selling sex. Their clientele had rapidly expanded from pensioners in the parks to middle-aged professionals and even college students.

'Don't call me Granny,' one of the women, whom the caption labelled as *Aged seventy-four*, cautioned a student, with what might best be described as a seductive snarl. 'My pussy is still young.'

That night, Jackie touched herself for the first time in years.

The programme played over and over in her mind. Scanning the *Standard*, she found that it was being repeated at 2 a.m., three days later. She watched it again and, apart from noting how much better tended the parks were in Seoul than in London, she was most struck by the women's resilience. Cultural differences made their emotions hard to read, but while some were clearly trapped – like the woman working to buy pills for her high blood pressure, which was worsened by the work – others claimed to welcome not just the money, but the physical contact.

Jackie had kept herself trim. While not so vain as to rule out gallantry, she was regularly taken to be ten years younger and, when she looked at many of her contemporaries, she could understand why. An idea struck her: so preposterous, so provocative, so perverse. And to think she'd been contemplating buying a cat!

For months, it was less an idea than a fantasy. She didn't doubt that there were parks in London – perhaps Hampstead Heath itself – where women sold sex, but she had no intention of heading there. And she suspected that anyone copying a number for *French Polishing* from a card in Mr Sharma's window would be in need of an actual furniture restorer. Prostitution, like almost every business, had ventured online, and she had never so much as used a computer. Her first step was to sign up at Swiss Cottage library for an eight-week course in digital skills for the over-sixties, most of whom wanted to keep up with their children and grandchildren. After finding that she would have to send friend requests to Naomi and Frank on Facebook (which wasn't worth the risk) and that Sam disclosed his private life to all and sundry, she timidly typed *Mature Prostitute* into Google, only to discover that the preferred term was *escort* (the Bacchus Ladies had been less bashful) and that *mature* in this context meant *over thirty*.

She was about to give up when, in a moment of inspiration, she replaced *mature* with *granny*. At the top of the results list was *Mellow Madams*.

The banner across the home page read 'For those who believe that women, like wine, grow finer with age,' which made her think incongruously of Frank. Eight *Sensual Seniors* were on offer, five of whom were what Sam had once described as 'undressed to kill,' while the other three seemed better suited to a whist drive. Only one showed her face, a boldness that Jackie would not wish to emulate, but all of them gave their ages, which ranged from a vague *50s* to an explicit *73*. Most intriguing was the page headed *Register with Us*, which invited 'Ladies who are old in years but young in heart . . . who are comfortable in their skin, healthy, warm-hearted and good-looking' to get in touch. 'No experience necessary,' was both a prerequisite and a reassurance to one who had only ever slept with Stanley.

She called the number provided. It was answered by a woman with an affected accent, which she dropped as soon as Jackie explained her interest. They arranged to meet at the terrace café in Harvey Nichols, when Daphne – as she identified herself – came up from Dorking on her weekly trip to town. After spending longer choosing an outfit than at any time since her divorce hearing, Jackie made her way to the store, not knowing whether to be flattered or offended when Daphne, who was fifteen minutes late, instantly singled her out from several other lone women. Wasting no time on small talk, Daphne detailed the ins and outs of the business (literally, when it came to home and hotel visits), the financial arrangements and the services she might offer, some of which struck Jackie as both insanitary and distasteful, but she was determined to show willing.

'So I'll put you down as open-minded,' Daphne said.

'Definitely.'

That had been nine years ago, and she had never looked back.

While not strictly necessary given that the underground parking enabled her to leave home unobserved, Beatrice's dark glasses helped her to look the part. She sped out of the garage so fast that Reuben was unable to count the waiting paparazzi more accurately than 'six . . . um or . . . I guess, eight'. Her instinct was to slow down so that they could get a shot, but her emotions were too raw . . . too real.

She dropped Reuben at their castmate Barry's house on the way to her parents. Despite his protestations that he was here for her, she knew that his presence would make matters worse. Her father's objections to her living with a wellness coach had been compounded by comments from Leyla and Rachel, her closest girlfriends on the show, that she and Reuben were 'not on the same page' and that she was investing far more in the relationship than he was. It didn't help that his automatic response to any situation, good or bad, was 'Wow!' Although the editors bore some blame, regularly cutting away from him after that first utterance, it reinforced Leyla's assertion that he was 'thicker than his own triceps.' Beatrice had begged him, tactfully, to stop saying it, but it had struck such a chord with the fans that he had launched a line of T-shirts, emblazoned with *Wow!* beneath an image of his torso. It was now an integral part of *Brand Reuben*.

As she drew up outside Holly Lodge, she was dismayed to see Naomi's bright red Mazda (a 'dildo substitute' in Nathan's caustic phrase) parked in the driveway. Nothing was more calculated to inflame tensions than the presence of her censorious aunt. She touched the mezuzah on the doorpost more purposefully than usual and rang the bell. Her mother answered it, enveloping Beatrice in a tearful hug, which moved her, until she recalled her criticism of the overwrought emotions in *On the Heath*.

'How are you, Bubbale? Not that I need to ask. Your grandmother! It's unthinkable. What was she thinking? She's seventy-eight. Your father's beside himself. I've never seen him like this. He doesn't show it, of course . . . but inside. Seventy-eight!'

'Do you intend to leave me out here on the doorstep?'

'Why? Are you being followed?' Shona pushed her aside and surveyed the avenue. Reassured, she pulled Beatrice into the hall and slammed the door. 'We've had to take the phone off the hook. Non-stop calls. And the abuse. Your father won't tell me what they say, but I can imagine. So many vicious people out there. And your grandmother . . . your father's mother, so I keep schtum. He's beside himself.'

'Is that you, Cupcake?' Beatrice winced at the childhood nickname, which had grated even more on her since she set up *Bea's Bakes*.

'I'm coming in, Daddy.'

Beatrice followed her mother into the lounge, to find her father by the fireplace, her aunt Naomi in an armchair with Fiona perched beside her, and Nathan on the window seat, his back to the room, as if to underline his distance from the family. Beatrice kissed her father and aunts

(Fiona's concern meriting the courtesy) and was hi-fived by Nathan, who didn't look up from his phone.

'Can't you switch that thing off?' Frank asked him irritably.

'Don't you want to know what the Twittersphere is saying?'

'No!' Frank and Naomi replied in concert.

'I didn't realise you'd be here,' Beatrice said to Naomi.

'What? Stay away and miss all the fun?' Nathan interjected, still studying the phone.

'Sam has gone to collect Mother.'

'She's coming too?' asked Beatrice, unsure whether she could face her. The prim and proper grandmother with the brimful swear box, which had once consumed Nathan's entire month's pocket money on a single visit, was a prostitute. It beggared belief. This must be how it had felt when people first learnt that the earth revolved around the sun or that humans were descended from apes.

'Your uncle Sam has gone to fetch her,' Naomi reiterated.

'Along with Maggie,' Shona added.

'Dad thought that if he went alone, someone might mistake him for a client.'

'Nathan, please,' Shona said, sniffling. 'Must you make it even more sordid than it is?'

'Alright, Shona,' Naomi said. 'No need to go overboard. She's not your mother.'

'Thank God!'

Beatrice wrapped her arms around her mother, which appeared to irritate Naomi even more. 'Of course, this is all your fault.'

'Mine, why?'

'Hang on now, Naomi,' Frank cut in.

'I warned you – we all did – about going on that programme; selling your soul for fifteen minutes of fame.'

'It's been running for three years,' Beatrice replied, more feebly than she'd intended.

'Without "*On the Heath's* Beatrice Altman," there wouldn't have been a story. Mother could have carried on her disgusting activities and no one would have been any the wiser.'

'That's all right then, is it? What the eye doesn't see . . .' Frank asked, rising to Beatrice's defence, although she knew that, at heart, he agreed with his sister.

'Don't you dare twist my words! Of course it's not. But we wouldn't have had to suffer this opprobrium, which will stick to us for the rest of our lives. And all for what? A trashy TV programme full of entitled, self-centred kids, whose sentiments are as fake as their tans.'

'Rather like Gran then,' Nathan said. 'She must have to fake it . . . three or four times a day, if you believe the article.'

'Oh for God's sake, Nathan!' Beatrice said, neither knowing nor caring whether he was on her side. 'I need a shot of caffeine. Anyone else?'

Fiona's 'a cup of green tea would be lovely,' felt more like a kindness than a genuine request, enabling Beatrice to escape to the kitchen and gather her thoughts.

She had been persuaded to audition for *On the Heath* by her then boyfriend, Julius, who, two years earlier, had been rejected for *Love Island*. With his rigorous gym routine and 11,800 Instagram followers, he'd been confident of success, only to be eliminated after the first interview, when the casting director took seriously his quip that he'd rather have the £50,000 prize money than the girl of his dreams. Seeing on TikTok that the makers of a new reality TV show, set in Hampstead, were looking for couples to take part, he convinced Beatrice that it wouldn't just be fun but also valuable publicity for his line of ethically-sourced coffee beans. She was encouraged by Marcia's remark that they looked great together, although the producer later confessed that she'd sensed from the start that 'Julius was over you' and expected their breakup to be a highpoint of the first series. No one, however, could have predicted the brutal way that he accomplished it: removing his shirt to reveal that the Bea on his biceps had been altered to Beauty.

The breakup was dissected by the rest of the cast, in the tabloids and across social media. While, under normal circumstances, she would have taken time off to recover, if only by staying with her great aunt Leah in Bournemouth, she was obliged not just to remain in Hampstead but to run into Julius at the restaurants, clubs and parties that were the lifeblood of the show. Despite feeling numb and null, she was suitably emotional during scenes with her friends, dissolving in tears at the repeated claim that Julius had disrespected her. When, shortly afterwards, he introduced his new girlfriend, Melanie, to the group, she delivered the required barbs, trading insults with someone she would have preferred to avoid.

That was the nature of the show. When it was picked up for a second series, she came to accept and even enjoy the discrepancy between her on-screen and off-screen selves. Pip, an Oxford dropout and linchpin of series three, maintained that the mediated reality format exposed the illusion of personal autonomy. Beatrice, more mundanely, found it both restful and challenging to be told how to react by the cast liaison team, who claimed to know, from her expressions and body language, how she was feeling before she did herself. Although Marcia was quick to dismiss any suggestion of scripting, she acknowledged that, with the growing number of reality shows, viewers were wise to their contrivance. In more innocent days, fans had even tried to book rooms in a soap opera motel.

The irony was that Julius quit at the end of the third series. The string of interviews he gave, citing the toll it had taken on his mental health, turned out to be better publicity than his eighteen months on the show. Not only did he win an exclusive contract with Selfridges for his coffee, but he became the brand ambassador for a range of organic hair gels made from Nicaraguan tree bark. Beatrice, however, had found her niche. She'd recently signed on for a sixth series and a summer special in Lisbon. Both were now under threat, and she tried not to second-guess tomorrow's 8 a.m. meeting with Marcia. *On the Heath* prided itself on its tight production schedule. Unlike its competitors, it wasn't filmed in advance but shot, edited and broadcast within the week. How could any reality show, however mediated, ignore such a big – or rather, gross – matter as her grandmother's disgrace?

Lingering at the breakfast bar, she sipped her coffee while Fiona's green tea grew cold. With a sense of dread, she switched on her phone to find three passionate texts from Reuben, making her wonder again whether her former English master's approving 'Not a word wasted' would extend to a man who appeared to have dispensed with words altogether. Several supportive messages from her cast mates dashed any hope that the damage might be contained. A glance at her Twitter feed revealed a flood of anti-Semitic abuse. She didn't examine it closely enough to be sure, but certain trolls seemed to be under the impression that she herself was the prostitute. She couldn't suppress a mordant laugh at the knowledge that her grandmother earned as much per hour as she did per episode.

A minute later, the doorbell rang.

Jackie knew that it was a mistake to answer the Entry-phone. Of all her children, Sam was the one she thought might be understanding but, even on the intercom screen, he refused to meet her gaze. Once she'd buzzed him up, he stood in the hall, informing her curtly that he'd come to take her to Frank's. His tone brooked no refusal, and she asked, with pointed sarcasm, whether she might have a moment to get ready. He nodded his assent, declining to sit down as though afraid it would sully him.

Lipstick in hand, she stood at the bathroom mirror, before deciding that, to her small-minded children, a lack of makeup would indicate contrition. She dabbed a little scent behind her ears, draped an autumnal-shaded scarf around her neck, checked that she had her purse (security) and phone (freedom) in her handbag, and returned to the hall. They took the lift downstairs, Sam uncharacteristically squeezing himself into a corner, and stepped outside, where the absence of lurking newsmen gave her hope. As they reached the car, her new place in the family pecking order was confirmed when Maggie failed to greet her, let alone relinquish the front seat.

Sam switched on the radio, thwarting any attempt at conversation. They arrived at the house and a grim-faced Shona ushered Jackie into the lounge, where she was met by looks of unconcealed contempt from Naomi, Frank and Fiona, and horrified fascination from Nathan.

'Does no one have a kiss for me?' she asked, with forced jollity.

Nathan scrambled to his feet.

'Sit down, Nathan!' Frank said. 'Sit down, Mother.' He gestured to a ladder-back chair by the wall.

'I don't bestow my kisses that cheaply,' Naomi said.

'Nor does Gran. Four hundred and fifty quid an hour!'

'If you've nothing sensible to say, you can go upstairs,' Frank said to Nathan, who shrugged.

'Where's Beatrice?' Jackie asked. 'I saw her car outside.'

'Leave her out of it!' Shona said.

'Have you lost your mind?' Naomi asked. 'That wasn't a question!' she added, as Jackie opened her mouth to reply. 'I've been meaning to talk to you about lasting power of attorney. But it's gone way past that now. You should be certified.'

'I had Rabbi Berenson on the phone an hour ago,' Frank said, determined as ever not to be left out. 'You've brought shame on the entire community. He's offered to pay you a visit.'

'Probably wants a freebie,' Nathan muttered.

'Not another word!' Frank said.

'What do you with all the money?' Sam asked, triggering glares from both his siblings. 'I'm just saying that it's dangerous for an old woman to keep so much cash in her flat. There are lots of shady characters around.'

'They're the ones who've been paying her!' Fiona said.

'I know that money has been tight, Mother,' Frank said, softening his tone.

'It isn't about the money.'

'But surely you had enough to get by? If you needed more, we'd have given it to you.'

'Would you? Really?'

Beatrice walked into the room, forestalling Frank's reply. Ignoring Jackie, who half-rose from her chair, she moved to stand beside Nathan at the window.

'How could you do this to us, Gran?' she asked, gazing out at the garden. Her pain was real but her posture looked staged, and Jackie suspected that she'd adopted it from the programme. 'You've ruined my life.'

'That's not true! You're a strong, independent woman.'

'Wherever I go . . . whatever I do, I'll be Beatrice Altman, granddaughter of the pensioner prostitute.'

'People have short memories.'

'Not that short! Even when the scandal fades, it will be "Beatrice Altman, isn't she the one . . . ? Oh yes." Titter, titter.'

Shona crossed the room and gave her daughter the hug that Jackie longed to give her herself.

'See what you've done!' Frank said. 'How could you? You're sick. Naomi's right. You need to see a doctor . . . a psychiatrist.'

'I haven't harmed anyone. Nobody would have known.'

'Not harmed anyone?' Frank asked. 'Look at us!'

'Blood pressure, Frank!' Shona said.

'When did it start, Mum?' Sam said. 'How long? Was it already going on in Enfield?'

'*Belle de Jour*,' Maggie said.

'What?'

'The film . . . never mind.'

'Is this why you split up with Father?' Naomi asked. 'Oh my God! Did he know?'

'No. It was after I left. It's been nine years. The happiest nine years of my life.'

'Thanks a lot!'

'Don't be silly, darling. Of course I was happy when you and your brothers were children. But I've been so alone. So lonely. Unfulfilled.'

'Take up pottery,' Frank said. 'Go on a cruise. Join a bridge club.'

'I tried. That is, working at the Marie Curie and the talking newspaper.' She winced at the prospect that next week she might be asked to record her own story. 'Then there was the art class at the City Lit.'

'And a spot of prostitution was the next thing on the To Do list?' Frank asked.

'Have you ever thought about my life? No, why should you? I'm your mother. That's all that matters.'

'And a wife,' Naomi added bitterly. 'At least you were until you walked out on him.'

'I don't intend to speak ill of your father.'

'You'd better not try.'

'But he wasn't a kind man, that is husband.'

'I never imagined I'd say it,' Sam said, 'but I'm glad he's gone doolally. Alzheimer's has some advantages.'

'When did you last go to see him?' Jackie asked, harshly.

'What does that have to do with it?'

'Nothing, you're right. And why should I expect any of you to think about my life when I barely gave it a thought myself. Besides, it wasn't much different from those of my friends. True, they had husbands who booked hotels for family holidays, and not self-catering units, since what was the point of paying other people to do something *we* could do ourselves?'

'I loved those holidays.'

'I'm glad. You had your friends and games and the swimming pool. Your father had his birdwatching. And I had the shopping and the cooking and the laundry.'

'Come on! That didn't take all day,' Naomi said.

'Not *all* day, no.'

'So what would you have rather done?'

'Bungee jumping.'

'What?'

'She really has lost it,' Sam said.

'Bear with me.'

Beatrice turned away from the window and, for the first time, looked her in the eye. Seizing the moment, Jackie asked 'Do you remember when you couldn't make up your mind whether to sign up for the series, and I said that you were only young once and to go with your heart, not your head?'

'Yes, of course.'

'I wasn't even young at the time. I was sixty-one.'

'Lost it!' Sam repeated.

'Your grandfather asked me what I'd like for our ruby wedding, so I told him that all I wanted was to go bungee jumping. We'd seen the crane with the people on it when we crossed Chelsea Bridge. He looked at me as if I was mad.'

'Do you blame him?' Naomi asked.

'Yes, I do actually.'

'Couldn't you have gone on your own?' and 'Did you want him to do it with you?' Fiona and Maggie asked simultaneously.

'Yes, and no. But I wanted him to be there with me, cheering me on. Instead, he bought me a ruby ring.'

'Which will have cost him far more,' Sam said.

'I don't doubt. But that's just it. He believed in spending money on things . . . possessions, not experiences.'

'Definitely not 450 quid for an hour with a hooker,' Nathan said. 'Ow!' He rubbed his arm where Beatrice poked him.

'Quite, but then your grandfather never showed much interest in that side of life.'

'Must we?' Naomi asked.

'Yes, I think we must. Next time you speak to Rabbi Berenson about the shame I've brought on the community, Frank, perhaps you could ask him about the obligation in the Torah or the Talmud (I forget which) on a husband to satisfy his wife. It differs, depending on whether you're a camel – or is it a donkey? – driver, or a gentleman of leisure. For the last twenty years of our marriage, your father didn't even observe the lightest obligation, which, if memory serves, is on a sailor who spends half the year at sea.'

'You've certainly made up for it since,' Naomi said.

'Thank you, I've tried,' Jackie replied, with a show of nonchalance. 'I've kept in shape. Good genes . . . You've inherited them,' she added, making Naomi squirm. 'And I've had fun. The odd unpleasantness, it's true. But nothing I couldn't handle. And the men are such a mixed bunch. Some old of course, but several as young as . . .' She gave Nathan a telling look.

'Do you have no morals at all?' Naomi asked. 'While you're having fun, as you put it, what about the wives? I presume that most of the men are married.'

'That's their concern. I know the conventional wisdom is that it's women like me—'

'Prostitutes!' Naomi interjected.

'Prostitutes, thank you – who keep marriages together by providing a safety valve. But I don't intend to justify myself like that. The men are free agents. They can choose for themselves.'

'You disgust me.'

'Do I, darling? I'm sorry. You'd do well to remember that, even in this day and age, there are people who are disgusted by you and Fiona. They may not shout about it the way that they did, but believe me, they still are.'

'Are you comparing—'

'Merely stating.'

'Enough!' Frank said. 'This is getting us nowhere. What we need from you, Mother, is a cast-iron guarantee that you will give up this obscenity at once. Then we can discuss getting you medical help – counselling or whatever – and some sort of carer.'

'And financial advice,' Sam interposed. 'I'm simply saying,' he added, in response to his brother's glower. 'The agency is sure to have rooked her. And what about tax? Has she paid any? Will they deduct it from her estate?'

'Have you quite finished?' Jackie asked. 'Then, let me tell you that I've no intention of giving it up.'

'Just listen to her!' Naomi shrieked, as Fiona kneaded her shoulders.

'But you've been found out,' Maggie said.

'No, I've been stitched up. There's a difference.'

'What about the neighbours?' Beatrice asked, breaking her silence.

'You're right. They might be an issue.'

'Not too happy about the notoriety either?' Frank asked.

'That's their problem. Mine is a clause in the lease preventing me running a business from home.'

'There's a simple solution,' Frank said.

'Yes, I shall move.'

'Did you hear that?' Frank asked.

'I wash my hands of her,' Naomi said. 'She's no longer my mother.'

'You mustn't say that!' Beatrice said.

'You're the one she's hurt most of all,' Naomi replied.

'Excuse me!' Nathan interjected.

'You're not my mother, Jackie,' Shona said, 'but I think I can speak for everyone when I say that, unless you give us your solemn word to mend your ways, you'll no longer be welcome in this family.'

'Thank you for putting it so succinctly, Shona. I take it then that you won't be inviting me to stay for lunch.'

'How can anyone think of eating?'

'Then if there's no more to say, I'll order an Uber. I've no wish to inconvenience Sam again. I use them all the time. One of the perks of the job. Not just such interesting clients, but such charming drivers.'

◊

'*On the Heath's* Beatrice Altman isn't the only member of her family making headlines,' writes Lindy Read. 'Last weekend, celebrity cake maker, Beatrice, woke to find her seventy-eight-year-old grandmother, Jackie, unmasked as a £450-an-hour hooker.

'I meet Jackie in her cosy mansion block flat close to London's infamous Hampstead Heath. It's hard to reconcile the demurely dressed lady with the "escort", who boasted about her "f***ability" on the phone to an undercover reporter. But when I compliment her on her jade green cashmere skirt, she volunteers that, beneath it, she's wearing "a white lace suspender belt because it makes me feel sexy."

'"I may be a MILF but I'm no MIF," she says, serving tea on rose-patterned china. MIF, she explains, stands for *Milk In First*; MILF is best left to the imagination. She offers me a biscuit – Garibaldi, Fig Roll or Bourbon – adding that her clients prefer the traditional brands. One, who pays her to dress as a school matron and administer mild corporal punishment ("My wrists wouldn't be up to anything heavier"), likes to chat afterwards, nibbling on a Wagon Wheel.

'Chat features prominently in Jackie's description of her services, and she claims that many men want nothing more than a cuddle, followed by a "happy ending." She's reluctant to discuss more specialised practices, insisting that being open-minded doesn't mean that she has no boundaries.

'Revealing a wide expanse of crinkly bosom above her

low-cut blouse, she declares that she has regular clients aged between twenty-five and eighty. When I ask what, in her view, drives young men to pay for sex with a woman old enough to be their grandmother, she replies that they feel they have less to prove and assume that, unlike girls their own age, she'll be grateful for their attention. "That can be reassuring to someone who's insecure." Then after a moment's hesitation, she adds "And I think they think it's naughty. They've grown up watching all kinds of sex online. They want something a little bit different."

'She has been dubbed "the country's oldest practitioner of the world's oldest profession," a label she wears with pride. "Do you think I could claim an entry in the *Guinness Book of Records*?" she asks, with a dry chuckle. "That would be something, wouldn't it?" But she has no wish to become a poster girl for pensioner sex. "It is – or it should be – a private matter. Some people are still in the market for rumpy pumpy in their nineties. Others would rather have a nice cup of tea," she says, offering me a refill.

'Although no longer equal to seeing two or three clients a day, as she did when she started out nine years ago, she's not yet ready to hang up the suspender belt. "I have regular health checks. All being well, I'm good for another ten years."

'Jackie's cheerfulness falters only when I raise the subject of her family, who have disowned her since they found out about her double life. While understanding why they were shocked, she insists that she has been equally shocked by their lack of compassion. "I've never interfered in my children's personal affairs and I don't expect them to interfere in mine."

'She's particularly stung by Beatrice, claiming that she was the only member of the family to support her when she signed up for *On the Heath*. "She accuses me of damaging her career, when the truth is that she's the one who's damaged mine. If it weren't for her, the *People* would never have targeted me. Now I've been asked to leave my home. I'm being hounded by the taxman. I've received the most obscene poison pen letters and even been spat at by a woman with a pushchair in M&S."

'She hopes that, in time, Beatrice will relent. Meanwhile, whatever one thinks of her morals, it's impossible not to feel a sneaking admiration for a woman who refuses to eat humble pie. "The people I feel sorry for are the editors and reporters who set me up," she says. "They may have disgraced me, but they've demeaned themselves."'

Beatrice sat in the manager's office, waiting for her cue. On the monitor, she watched as a scattering of extras sipped the ginger ale, weak tea and sparkling grape juice that passed for cocktails at three in the afternoon. At a table alongside the dance floor, five of her castmates, their faces lit by shafts of colour from a rotating disco ball, were gossiping about Jackie.

'It's no secret that I'm not Bea's number one fan,' said Cressida, Reuben's ex-girlfriend. 'But it's hardly her fault. That'd be like blaming Hitler's granddaughter for the Holocaust.'

'Did Hitler have a granddaughter?' Barry asked.

'Who knows? That's not the point.'

'She'd have changed her name by now anyway,' Tyler said.

'And she's one hot granny,' Barry said.

'Would you?' Tyler asked.

'Defo!' Barry replied, leaning across the table to bump fists.

Cressida rolled her eyes.

'I don't care what anyone says,' Leyla interjected. 'I think she's brave. Why shouldn't an older woman lead an active sex life?'

'Grab it while you can!' Rachel said. 'My granny doesn't know what year it is. She just sits in a chair all day long, like a phone that's out of juice.'

Beatrice's cue light flashed. She walked into the club, where her friends greeted her with a show of surprise.

'How are you?' Cressida asked.

'Fine,' she replied, knowing that the team wanted her to save her tears till later.

'No, how are you really?'

Tyler went to fetch her a mojito, her favourite cocktail, if only because the green colouring was less unpalatable than the others. Leyla stroked her hair and asked if she'd spoken to Jackie.

'No. What would I say? I don't know what to think, let alone *do* any more. My whole world's been ripped apart. It's like – I don't know – getting on a plane to the Maldives and being hijacked to Somalia.'

The image was so bleak that her tears flowed naturally and, when Tyler came back with the drink, he was swept into a group hug.

After a week's absence, Beatrice was relieved to return to the show. In the immediate aftermath of the revelations,

Marcia had announced, her voice thick with regret, that she was suspending her temporarily, until they saw how the story played out. It had taken an unforeseen turn when, far from expressing remorse and retreating into obscurity, Jackie gave an interview to the *Daily Mail*, defending her right to live as she chose and sharing her hurt at her family's hostility. The response, even from the paper's Middle England readership, had been overwhelmingly positive. The following day, she appeared on BBC One's *Morning Live* and ITV's *Loose Women* (the title prompting a glut of bad jokes), where her candour charmed presenters and viewers alike.

Convinced that this marked a shift in British social attitudes, Marcia welcomed Beatrice back to the show and proposed inviting Jackie on as a guest. Though profoundly uneasy, Beatrice wasn't surprised. It was typical of a producer who, claiming that her primary concern was the programme's impact on impressionable viewers, banned smoking while sanctioning serial affairs, character assassination and treachery. She insisted that the decision on Jackie's participation rested with Beatrice alone and urged her to discuss it with Miles Cooper, the show's resident psychologist. He, in turn, advised that the best way forward was for Beatrice to 'take control of the narrative', which was all very well but, as they both knew, the narrative would still be Marcia's.

Reuben was equally keen for Jackie to take part. 'The damage has been done, Babes. And it's a killer storyline for us. Besides, I'd like to get to know Granny Jackie. That's one feisty lady.'

Beatrice's misgivings were aroused. Despite his recent

assertion to Barry and Tyler that their relationship was 'rock solid,' he had form. How could she forget Leyla's waspish warning: 'Once a fuckboy, always a fuckboy'?

'Have you ever visited a prostitute?' she asked him, hesitantly.

'What sort of question is that?'

'A simple one.'

'No, never. Well, not a prostitute kind of prostitute.'

'Is there any other kind?'

'Sure . . . like in New Orleans, when we went for Jamie Bridgeport's stag. Where you pay a girl two hundred dollars for a beer. But that was long before us. Now I wouldn't even look at one.'

'Except for my grandmother.'

'*Our* grandmother, Babes.'

Disarmed, she told Marcia that she had no objections to her grandmother's involvement and, at her request, rang Jackie who, elated by her new-found celebrity, leapt at the chance. Indeed, even as Beatrice assured Leyla that they hadn't spoken, Jackie was discussing her first scene with Xandra, one of the story producers. This was to be with Beatrice and Reuben in the Flask Café. On finishing at the club, Beatrice made her way there. After a quick costume change, she ordered a cup of fresh mint tea and took a seat.

A harassed glance at her phone betrayed her irritation as Reuben burst in, his grin newly whitened and muscles taut beneath a skin-tight cycling kit.

'Sorry I'm late, Babes. You'll never guess who I bumped into on the High Street.'

'I'm not in the mood.'

'Don't be such a grump! Close your eyes.'

'Reuben, please!'

'Trust me, you won't regret it.'

'They're closed.'

She heard the tinkle of the door chime and looked up, as Jackie's familiar fragrance wafted across the table.

'Granny,' she said, with appropriate consternation.

'Hello, darling.'

'What are you doing here?'

'I am allowed to walk the streets . . . oh dear! That came out wrong.' She chuckled. 'Mind if I join you?'

'Well, you're here now,' Beatrice replied, unsure how much of her discomposure was genuine and how much triggered by the camera.

Reuben headed to the counter to place their order.

'You've done alright for yourself there, darling,' Jackie said, fixing her gaze on him. 'A real studmuffin.' Beatrice baulked at an expression that Jackie would never have come up with alone and, for one ghastly moment, wondered whether Marcia were plotting a duel for Reuben's affections.

'This is very hard for me,' she said swiftly. 'You've really hurt my mum and dad.'

'I'm hoping you'll help me mend fences. No one likes to think of their parents having sex, I know.'

'Especially not with a string of random men.'

'I was lonely.'

'You could have joined a dating site. There must be one for the over-sixties.'

'But I don't want a boyfriend,' Jackie said, as Reuben returned. 'At my age there isn't time. This way I get all the pleasure without having to cook dinner or wash socks.'

'We share everything, don't we, Babes?' said Reuben,

whose idea of preparing a meal was mixing a protein shake.

'You're young,' Jackie said, wistfully.

'How can you be sure you're safe? All it takes is one psychopath.'

'I like to think I'm a pretty good judge of character. At my age, the biggest risk is toppling over in my stilettos.'

'Wow!' Reuben said. 'I don't know how you girls manage. In Croatia, we did a drag fashion show for clean water – for drinking, not swimming. I was afraid I'd end up in somebody's lap.'

'I doubt they'd have complained,' Jackie said with a smile.

'Hello! Earth to Gran!' Beatrice interjected.

'I'm not asking you to approve of what I do, darling,' Jackie said. 'Just to accept it. You may find it hard to believe, but since I started this work, I've become a better person. Less judgemental – even if others are more inclined to judge me. The need for love is a great leveller. I have a guiding rule; a philosophy, if you like, though it's not one you'll find in any holy book. "Be what you are and say what you feel, because those who mind don't matter and those who matter don't mind."'

'Wow!' Reuben said.

'It's not original. I read it somewhere.'

Probably a Christmas cracker, Beatrice thought.

As the director signalled that it was time to wrap, she reached across the table and took her grandmother's hand.

'I won't pretend I'm happy with what you do. But you're my granny and I'll always love you.'

'Wow, that's really beautiful,' Reuben said, as Jackie wiped away a tear. 'I'll leave you two to catch up. I've got my CBT session.'

'Really?' Jackie said, sounding surprised. 'Are you allowed to say that?'

'What?'

'Cock and ball torture?'

'No way!' Even Reuben looked shocked. 'It's cognitive behavioural therapy.'

'I've got a lot to learn.'

'We'll teach you, Gran,' Beatrice said, lifting Jackie's hand to her lips.

'Wow!'

'Cut!'

The Web of Deceit

I owe PRIMROSE Shipman an apology. Along with half the country, I rushed to judge her after her husband's arrest. How could she have slept beside a man for forty years yet known nothing of his 250 murders? Why did she get fatter and fatter and her house filthier and filthier, with visitors' shoes sticking to the grease on the carpet, if not because she'd been grappling with the gruesome truth? I've kept myself slim and my house spotless, although I've no doubt people will claim that that too is an avoidance tactic. But as a wife – not to mention one also married to a doctor – I can say with absolute certainty that she had no reason to suspect a thing.

Even though the clocks went forward in March, I still wake up at ten past six every morning, with the doorbell ringing in my ears. That first day, it was you who answered it while I lay bleary-eyed, but at the sound of voices in the hall, I put on my dressing gown and hurried downstairs. My initial feeling on seeing the police officers was one of relief. Archie, our German Shepherd, had been missing for three days and I assumed that they had called so early in order to bring him back. Had I been thinking, I might have asked myself why this should take four officers from a purportedly overstretched force, but I wasn't . . . I wasn't thinking at all.

'Is it Archie?' I asked, hoping to see, hear, smell and

be swept off my feet by a rumbustious dog. When none
appeared, I looked at the sombre faces in front of me. 'Has
something happened to him?'

'Go back upstairs, Sheila,' you said. 'Let me deal with
this.'

'I'm not a child!' I replied, fear fraying my nerves. As I
spoke, your cheeks drained of colour.

One of the officers (I was not attuned to distinctions of
rank) explained that they had reason to believe that you'd
been 'accessing indecent material' and had a warrant to
search the house.

'That's ridiculous!' I said. 'I dust every day. I'd know if
there were anything indecent.'

'On sites frequented by paedophiles,' he added,
implacably.

'I am not a paedophile,' you said to the officer. 'I am not
a paedophile,' you repeated to the others. 'I swear to you
that I'm not a paedophile,' you said to me.

I didn't realise how violently I was shaking until one
of the officers – the only woman – led me into the kitchen
and made me a cup of tea. Overriding my protests – I'm a
doctor's wife, after all – she stirred in three teaspoonfuls
of sugar. I sipped it gratefully, until I felt compelled to
break the silence.

'My husband's a GP. He's past retirement age, but his
partners have begged him to stay on. He spends hours on
the computer every evening, reviewing the latest medical
advances. He has to sift through all sorts of material. I
suppose some of it might be classed as indecent. But if
you explain the situation to your colleagues, I'm sure that
they'll understand.'

She must have replied, although I can't remember a word she said. At some point, she brought me back to the sitting room, leaving two of the officers to search the kitchen. Why? Did they think you were hiding something – God knows what – behind the baking tins or the fish kettle?

The sitting room felt different. At first, I blamed the alien presence of the policewoman, but then I realised that it was an absence. They'd stripped the television cabinet of the DVDs, so neat in their uniform cases, unlike the jumble of books on the nearby shelves. Still more shocking was the removal of the photographs: Philip in his primary school uniform; Holly and Ivy in their water-wings, huddling together on Southwold beach. Gone too was Charlie and Georgina's wedding picture, although ours remained. But then alone on the registry office steps, we lacked the bridesmaids and flower girl who flanked our son and daughter-in-law.

The policewoman assured me that they were making a careful note of everything, which would be returned to us in due course. Indeed, when they left, they handed me an itemised receipt for all that they'd taken: your computer, both our iPads and mobile phones, the DVDs, photographs and albums, as well as some cuddly toys we kept for the grandchildren when they stayed overnight. I was poised to protest. What possible relevance could a giant panda and a pink rabbit have to their investigation? But I clammed up when I realised that they were also taking you.

Stupid I know, but having pictured them taking you straight to prison, I felt a rush of relief when the officer in charge said that you were to be interviewed at Beaumont

Street station. You told me to ring Gordon Lewis and
ask him to meet you there. As they ushered you out, you
insisted once again that this was all a misunderstanding
and we would laugh about it later. I smiled as supportively
as I could, but I doubted that I would ever laugh again.
I went into your study, which looked empty without the
computer, and found the solicitor's number. As I dialled
– the first two attempts incorrectly – I gave thanks that
we'd kept the landline. How would Charley or Carla, who
regarded us as Luddites, have coped if their mobiles had
been confiscated? Ridiculous thought! I should be ashamed
of entertaining it. The children would never have visited
illicit websites.

The one virtue of the police's dawn raid was that I
reached Gordon before he left for work. I told him what
little I knew and he promised to go straight to the station.
I remembered how he'd handled the trouble with the
controlled drugs and felt reassured. He advised me to say
nothing to anyone, including the children. As I put down
the phone and gazed vacantly out of the window, I was
grateful that we didn't live on a 'lace curtain' street, where
everyone knew everyone else's business, but in an avenue,
with a ten-foot-high rhododendron hedge screening the
house.

Somehow I made my way back to the kitchen where
I must have sat for more than an hour, since the next
thing I heard was the creak of the front door and Mrs
Coupland's obligatory 'Only me!' Looking surprised to
see me in my dressing gown, she asked if anything were
wrong. Following Gordon's advice, I told her that I'd had
a bad night and went upstairs to shower and dress. The

water must have cleared my head for, when I came down and she asked with a puzzled look if we'd been having a clean-out, I replied that we'd been burgled.

'I forgot to mention it before. I must still be in shock.'

'That's terrible! Too idle to do an honest day's work ... Did they take anything valuable?'

'The computer, iPads, phones ... you know.'

'What about the photos on the sideboard? That lovely one of the kiddies in the water.'

'The frames ... they were silver.'

'And the DVDs?' She stared at the empty cabinet. 'It makes no sense. What would they want with those?'

'Who can fathom the workings of the criminal mind?' I winced at the words. 'They must have grabbed anything within reach. The doctor came home and caught them red-handed.'

'Is he alright? Did they hurt him?'

'No, they ran off, thank God! He's at the police station now, picking them out of a line-up.'

'They caught them that fast?'

'Yes, I suppose they must have done. I don't know, I'm sorry. I need to sit down. I feel sick.'

She gave me an odd look – at least I considered it odd – but asked no more questions. The rest of the morning was a blur. At one point, Louise Winthrop called, in deep distress, to ask if I had any idea why the police had visited the surgery and impounded your computer (I told her that I didn't). She said that Sylvia had tried to stop them, insisting that it contained confidential records which they had no right to remove. She became so hysterical that Louise had to send her home, leaving the new nurse to fill in at reception. The visit took place in front of a crowded waiting room and, thinking quickly, Louise informed them that the CCG auditors had discovered minor discrepancies in the practice's prescribing budget, which had to be investigated. That sounded far more convincing than my botched robbery, which, I suppose, is why she is a GP and I'm a gardener (I know you prefer *horticulturist*, but such niceties seem redundant now).

Around three o'clock, Gordon drove you home, where, without so much as a hello to me, you made for the drinks cabinet.

'Brian has asked me to explain what's happened,' Gordon said, sounding like a doctor about to deliver a terminal diagnosis (although I hardly need describe that to you!). 'He's been released on police bail, since they don't have sufficient evidence to charge him.'

'Thank God!'

'Not yet,' Gordon said, as you poured yourself a second drink. 'They have to do a forensic search of his computer. Brian has admitted that, in recent years, he's been suffering from a porn addiction.'

Suffering: that's the word I seized on . . . it was something from which you were *suffering*.

'There must be treatments for it, just as there are for drugs and alcohol and gambling,' I said, trying to focus on the underlying condition. 'We'll get through it together,' I added, moving towards you and placing my hand on your arm. When you shrugged it off, I hid my hurt by reaching for the whisky bottle and offering it to Gordon.

'Better not, I'm driving. For now I'm afraid it's a waiting game. It can take up to a year for the police and the CPS to decide whether to press charges. My advice is to live your lives as normally as possible. Brian will have to surrender his passport and report to Beaumont Street station once a week.'

'What about the Black Sea?' I asked. 'We're booked on a cruise in June.'

I blush to recall my obtuseness.

'Oh I'm sorry!' you shouted. 'Have I ruined your holiday? Take my sister! Take your lover!'

'What lover?' I asked, nonplussed. 'I don't . . . I've never had a lover.' Except you, I mouthed.

'Brian isn't himself,' Gordon said. 'It's been a stressful day. To reiterate, try to maintain your usual routine. Except that Brian's not allowed to be alone with children, nor can any child stay here overnight.'

'What about our grandchildren?' I asked.

'Any child at all,' Gordon said, staring at his feet while you stared into your glass.

'But Philip is helping Brian lay new track for the model railway.'

'No contact of any kind with children,' you cut in. 'Didn't you hear the man? Are you trying to twist the knife?'

At seven years old, Philip failed to understand why the railway extension had to be put on hold, and the one time I stood in for you was not a success. When my level crossing proved to be anything but level, he stomped down the loft ladder, shouting that train sets were 'just for boys.' Three years younger, the twins missed their sleepovers at Granny and Grandpa's. Similarly, Charlie and Georgina missed their child-free weekends, but they accepted my explanation that arthritis (a blessing in disguise) had sapped my strength. You resigned from the practice. I wasn't privy to the details, except that there was no presentation or retirement party and, immediately afterwards, Sylvia, who'd carried a torch for you for years, handed in her notice. When I tried to reach her after the trial, I found that she'd left Beeston to live with her sister in Whitby.

Although you were now at home all day, I saw no more of you than when you were at work. You locked yourself away with your new computer and I could only pray that you weren't feeding your addiction. When I hinted at it to Gordon – not my confidant of choice – he assured me that there was no danger since, under the terms of your bail, you were forbidden to delete your search history. Meanwhile, I made my own searches of helplines and counsellors, but when I tentatively suggested that you contact them, you snapped at me. 'Can't you at least wait until I'm charged? Or do you know better than the police?'

Seven months after your arrest, I found out how little I did know. You were summoned to the station and formally charged with making, sharing and possessing indecent images of children. Although when they'd searched the house, an officer mentioned *paedophiles*, I'd blanked it from my mind, kidding – no, fooling! – myself that you'd been watching adult pornography. Once again, it was Gordon who explained the facts while you remained silent. Although *making* meant that you had downloaded the images, rather than created them, his account of what they depicted crushed any relief I might have felt.

I see you so clearly as I write this that I'm afraid of reopening a wound. Yet I need to keep track of what happened and, after forty-two years of marriage, the only way that feels real is by confiding in you. Knowing that you will never read it, I can set out the charge in full.

There were 1,288 images in all, divided into three categories: A, B and C, according to gravity. Gordon's impassive description convinced me that the sobriety of judges should be ascribed to all lawyers. There were 402 in Category A, which related to sexual activity with children involving penetration or pain, or sexual activity with animals; 587 in Category B, which related to non-penetrative sexual activity with children, and 299 in Category C, which related to less hardcore images. Even though Gordon insisted that there was no evidence of any such interest in your case, for some reason my brain latched on to *animals* and all I could think of was Archie. I'd long feared that he had been snatched by a gang that organised dog fights. Now a worse horror gripped my mind.

I offered to drive you to Beaumont Street, but you chose to go with Gordon. When you returned, however, I followed you into your study and demanded answers. For months we'd talked about nothing more intimate than meals and laundry, dripping taps and burnt-out light bulbs. For my part, I was constrained by a mixture of concern and cowardice. I didn't want to hurt you, but nor did I want to address what you'd done. Knowing about it was torment enough. But with Gordon's three categories gnawing at my brain, I could no longer hide from the truth. The charge spoke of images, but each image was a child: 402 of them depicting *penetration or pain*. How much pain? What sort of penetration? I needed to see them as clearly as if I'd been watching beside you. I needed to conjure up the bewildered eyes and agonized faces and broken bodies. Dear God! Only then could I begin to understand you.

'Isn't it enough that I've been interrogated by the police all morning?' you replied. 'Must you have your pound of flesh as well?' It was only then that I noticed how much weight you'd lost. 'Have you no mercy?' you added, and I might have relented, had Gordon's list of categories not muffled your appeal.

'Do you intend to plead guilty?'

'And do the police's job for them? Of course not! They're scapegoating me. They can't catch the real criminals, the people who make the films, so they punish those who merely watch them.'

I might have challenged the *merely* and, although I've forgotten much of what we said that evening, the word has lodged in my brain. Instead, however, I asked about the charge that most disturbed me: the images you'd shared.

'They're nothing. A technicality. A means of accessing a site so as to gain the other members' trust.'

'But why should you want to access it?' Before I asked the next – the crucial – question, I pictured you in the clinic, listening to one young girl's tight chest and palpating another's tender stomach. I saw you on home visits, wiping one young boy's flushed forehead and placing a thermometer under another's hot arm, while their mothers looked on unaware. 'Your husband is so good with the children, Mrs Stewart.' I felt sick but pressed on. 'Have you always been attracted to children?'

'I'm not a paedophile!' you shrieked. 'Why won't you believe me?' The answer lay in the 1,288 images, but I kept silent. 'You don't understand how pornography works.'

'No, I don't. I'm sorry – or, rather, glad – that I don't. So explain it to me please.'

To my surprise, you were eager to do so. I suspect now that you were refining your story, to see what would carry conviction in court. In which case, you should have tried it on someone less credulous.

'The trouble started with my panic attacks. Day after day in the surgery, faced with everyone's aches and growths and rashes and never knowing whether this would be the time I got it wrong. Is it any wonder I overdid it with the pills? And you saw the side-effects first hand.' I did indeed and remember suggesting that, if you could prescribe yourself Librium, you could prescribe yourself Viagra. But you explained that the interaction would be harmful, and although of course I took your word for it, I was sure that, had we slept together rather than side by side, it would have comforted you. 'I felt ashamed that I couldn't be a proper husband to you,' you said, 'which only made everything worse: an endless cycle of anxiety, depression and self-disgust. It was then that I started to visit the porn sites. I felt dirty, so I chose the dirt.'

'You're talking fifteen years ago!'

'I know! The internet is evil; a worldwide Pandora's box. And its greatest curse is pornography. The government should ban it . . . every government should ban it. Children in primary schools are downloading smut on their phones.' I bit my tongue. 'It felt so easy to control both the stimulus and the effect, when in truth it was controlling me. I was hooked. No different from the Johnson boy, stealing his mother's bank card and shooting up in a dingy basement. Except that I was here, in my comfortable study, while you sat reading or watching television in the next room.'

'If only you'd talked to me.'

'How? One of the reasons I love you is you know nothing of such things. And I loathe myself for forcing you to learn about them. Like any addict, I craved ever more frequent and powerful fixes for my drug to take effect. I began by watching couples you might almost describe as making love. But very quickly that wasn't enough. I wanted more participants, more extreme positions, more sordid acts. It was as if they enabled me to arouse and purge myself at the same time . . . Is this enough for you? Do you want more?'

No, I wanted less, far far less, but I felt driven to ask: 'And the children? What about them?'

'They were just another deviancy . . . another aberration. I'm aware how that sounds, but you have to believe me. If you don't, who will? Whatever else, I beg you to remember: I'm a pornography addict, not a paedophile.'

402 Category A images, 587 Category B images, 299 Category C images.

I moved into the spare room, claiming that your snoring kept me awake, although you slept as fitfully as I did. Alone in the dark, I couldn't help wondering whether, had you still found me desirable, any of this would have occurred. Or was the problem rather that our story had been too romantic? If I'd played Lady Macbeth rather than Juliet in the Shakespeare programme on Speech Day, would you still have fallen in love at first sight and told your mother that same evening that I was the girl you were going to marry?

For me, our meeting felt like something out of a dream.

You were the headmistress's son, a trainee doctor with whom it was almost a rite of passage for every sixth form girl to fall in love. And I was only in the lower fifth. You were very proper, of course, and didn't ask me out until I turned sixteen the following year. I still have the ticket stub from *Saturday Night Fever*, which we saw on our first date. Eighteen months later, I had no hesitation in accepting your proposal or marrying you the summer after A levels, to the dismay of my parents. Not only were you eight years older and as yet unqualified, but I was turning down an offer to read history at Durham. Much to my amazement, given her insistence that any girl with a half-decent brain had a duty to make use of it, your mother supported us throughout, even organising the wedding, which my parents refused to attend.

We were happy, weren't we, in those early years? One reason for setting down these thoughts is to prevent myself rewriting the past. So I say again that we were happy. The children were born while you were still training. Eking out your meagre bursary wasn't easy, but I made sure that they wanted for nothing. I would be the first to admit that they have their faults. At forty-one, our daughter is too old to rely on parental handouts, while her younger brother would do well to be less smug. But when I think of some of our friends' children (you mentioned Duncan Johnson), I'm thankful that ours have turned out as well as they have. For which you deserve much of the credit.

The children loomed large in our thinking. With the court date fixed and the local paper scavenging for a story, we could no longer put off telling them the truth. I dismissed your suggestion that it would come better from me, but agreed to give you what I would once have called moral support. They both claimed to have known that something was wrong: Carla assuming that you'd been having an affair and Charlie that one of us was seriously ill. Though, true to form, neither had thought to ask.

Charlie gave no credence to your pornography addiction. I understood his horror – of course I did – but I was horrified in turn, as I watched you crumple beneath his contempt. His worst fear was for his own children, since he refused to accept your assurance that you had treated them with absolute propriety. He swore that, if he found out you were lying, he would tear you apart with his bare hands.

'That's enough, Charlie,' I said. 'He's still your father.'

'And your husband!' he replied, turning on me. 'You live with a man for God knows how long yet know nothing about him. Did you never suspect?'

'No, never. Not once.'

Should a casual remark about a pretty girl in a playground have sounded an alarm? In which case, what to make of your sister's repeated assertion that Holly and Ivy are good enough to eat?

'What did you think he was doing holed up in his study night after night?'

'Reading up on the latest clinical research. Your father's a dedicated doctor.'

'Oh yes, I bet he has the perfect bedside manner.'

'Now you're just being crude.'

'Me!'

Carla's response was both colder and more chilling. It was as though she had finally found an explanation for all her doomed relationships. The therapist, whose bills we've been paying for years only to receive an itemised account of our own inadequacies, long ago told her that her fear of intimacy stemmed from your having shown her too little affection as a child. Now – and, admittedly, I only have this at second-hand – he has convinced her that you were scared of showing her too much. Although too young to have put it into words, she claims to have sensed it, withdrawing first from you, and later from men in general. Her excitement at having achieved this 'breakthrough' even outweighed her shock at your offence. She immediately demanded that we fund an additional weekly therapy session.

'After all, you owe me.'

Any hope that the charge might go unnoticed was dashed by the front page of the local paper. Louise told me that she spent the next few days fielding phone calls from anxious parents. Although there wasn't a shred of evidence of wrongdoing, she brought in a community paediatrician to address their concerns. The broader response was predictable, and I suspect that under different circumstances I would have shared it. It came as no surprise that you were asked to resign from the Civic Society, but I was taken aback when my name was removed from the volunteers' rota at the library. 'Just until things blow over,' Edwina White assured me, with gruff embarrassment.

As ever, my main support came at the Manor: not just from my fellow gardeners but from Lady Lupton, who asked me in for tea.

'It's a truism that you can never see inside somebody else's marriage,' she said. 'In my experience, you can rarely see inside your own.'

402 Category A images, 587 Category B images, 299 Category C images.

Were there any chance of your reading this, I'd suggest that you skip the next couple of pages. You'll be no keener to relive the events of your trial than I am, although I fear that, as we serve our respective sentences, neither of us has the choice. Were there any chance of your reading this, I'd discard that metaphor. But in the privacy of my own head, it sums up how I feel.

I thought of Primrose Shipman, as I clasped your hand on the way from the car to the court. She attended every session of her husband's fifty-eight-day trial, supporting him from the public benches, despite his scarcely sparing her a glance. I have no doubt that she'd have walked beside him had he not been held in custody, even though, by any measure, his crimes eclipsed yours.

'I'm his wife,' I declared, brushing aside Charlie's objections. 'What kind of message would it send if I stayed away?'

That said, my loyalty was sorely tried by the evidence. In the past, I'd regarded *crimes beyond comprehension* as atrocities such as the Holocaust and genocides; now I found them closer to – indeed, within my own – home. I might say the same of *crimes against humanity*, for surely it defies every human instinct – every decent . . . every natural human instinct – to violate a child? So when and how does that natural instinct become distorted and depraved? Some of the images in the prosecution's catalogue were not even of children. Babies who should have been suckling at the breast were sucking on . . . I felt sickened and sullied and, above all, utterly ashamed. Returning home after hearing the prosecution case, I was unable to speak a word to you. I even left you to cook for yourself on what now looked certain to be your last night of freedom. But when we arrived at court the next morning, I thought once again of Primrose Shipman and reached for your hand.

In your testimony, you alleged that the enormity of the images was precisely why they possessed no appeal for you. After years of violent and fetishistic adult films, they were simply another colour in the pornographic palette . . . or was it titbit for the jaded palate? I may have misheard. I felt the eyes of the court boring into me, but with my gaze fixed on the witness box, I couldn't tell whether that were from sympathy or disgust. You maintained that your problem was addiction rather than attraction, something you should have sought help for long ago, but your professional status held you back.

Although the warped argument fitted the crime, it failed to convince me or, more crucially, the jury, whose guilty verdict was unanimous. Passing sentence, the judge described you as a man of previously good character, who had forfeited his standing in the community and whose name would be erased from the Medical Register. She declared that while, in some cases, that might have been punishment enough, there were aggravating factors in the length of time you'd engaged with the material, the very young age of the children involved, and the extreme acts to which they had been subjected. She was therefore sentencing you to twenty months' imprisonment.

You showed no emotion as you were led out and I tried to follow suit, although I struggled to obey the bailiff's order to rise. Having relinquished responsibility for you, Gordon took charge of me, guiding me through the cluster of reporters to the car and driving me home, where, while I'm not equating it with yours, I began my own term.

It has been served largely in isolation. With a few exceptions, friends didn't return my calls and those who did ceased when they learnt that, far from filing for divorce, I intended to stand by you. Perhaps I do them an injustice and my commitment aroused genuine suspicions of complicity. But surely they must understand that, after forty-two years, my feelings for you couldn't vanish overnight? A man – a person – is more than his crimes, no matter how abhorrent.

I felt the need to make amends on your behalf. Since I couldn't reach out to the victims directly, I decided to sponsor an Indian orphan. I explained to the agency that we didn't want gratitude and there was no obligation on Gulika to make contact. However, the representative informed me that it was their policy to foster a bond between donor and recipient, so we would receive regular progress reports and photographs. In time, he suggested, we might even like to visit her in India . . . I trust that he didn't hear me gulp. On the other hand, I see no reason why, in years to come, when she's safely in her twenties, we shouldn't invite her to England. I've had two letters from her so far, the second of which included a drawing of her village. But, when I brought it in to show you, the officer at the gate insisted that I leave it in my locker. When I asked why, she pointed to the signature: *Gulika, aged eight.*

Even after four months, I dread the prison security

checks. I tell myself that they'd be the same at an airport, but, instead of Florence or Florida or even the Isle of Man, I'm taken to a brightly lit, sparsely furnished reception hall in HMP Nottingham. In place of the hustle and bustle, the animated faces and voices, and the premature shorts and sunglasses of a departure lounge, the visitors, almost all of them women and children, are alternately careworn and resentful. The only excitement comes from the toddlers, oblivious of their surroundings, eager to see the fathers they barely know.

My first visit was only three days after the trial, but already I sensed a change in you. I was permitted to give you a single kiss, which you accepted rather than returned, and I gazed enviously at the couple beside us, well into middle age, whose passionate embrace was curtailed by an officer. I asked about your cell, your food and your fellow prisoners, smiling fatuously as if your terse replies were all that I needed to hear. Lowering my voice, I asked if anyone had targeted you on account of the children.

'Of course not,' you hissed, glancing around. 'My age and manner inevitably arouse suspicion. But I had my story ready from the start, telling them in the holding cell that I was a doctor caught forging prescriptions.'

'You are a doctor,' I said.

'Struck off!' you replied, truculently. 'Given that so many of them are users, it made me something of a folk hero. My personal officer urged me to request a transfer to the VPU – that's the Vulnerable Prisoners Unit. But there's no way I'm going to be locked up with all the nonces. Google it!' you added, at the sight of my baffled face.

Your stubbornness worried me. I've seen enough

television dramas to know of the punishments meted out to child abusers in prison. What's more, I felt that by distancing yourself from the 'nonces', you were refusing to confront your crime. That feeling deepened when you declared that you intended to appeal. Having sat through the trial, I couldn't envisage any possible grounds, and I begged you to accept the sentence, at which you called an officer to take you back to your cell.

Time passes slowly, although it feels insensitive to say so, even to a hypothetical *you*. My principal diversion has been Fraser, the rescue dog your sister Rowena brought me as a replacement for Archie. Given his nervousness around Charlie and the CCTV installer (the only men who have visited lately), I suspect that he was abused – that is, ill-treated – as a puppy, but he grows more confident by the day, and I expect him to greet you warmly on your return. He's a Labrador/Collie mix and, despite your aversion to mongrels, I guarantee that you'll be smitten – always provided I can wean him off the bed.

The big event of the last fortnight was my sixtieth birthday. I bought a card and signed it from you in case anyone should examine the small display on the mantelpiece. Please don't think I blame you for forgetting! I realise how hard it must be to keep track of the days when each one resembles the next. I rather wish that nobody else had remembered. Under the circumstances, any celebration felt inappropriate, but Georgina was determined to mark the occasion. 'That's one thing he's not going to steal from you,' she said, grimly. So we compromised on a family lunch: just the children, grandchildren and Rowena.

As it happened, you were as much a spectre at the feast

as if a place had been laid for you like Banquo. Philip, who turns eight next week, senses that something is amiss, but he knows better than to question it. At four, the twins have yet to learn such discretion and, despite Georgina's sinister probing of whether 'Grandpa touched your wee-wees', they don't understand why you've disappeared from their lives. Rowena, who alone maintains your innocence, took it upon herself to tell them that you were in Africa, vaccinating babies, 'to keep them safe from nasty diseases.' I could see Charley fuming and, after the children had left the table, he berated her for transforming a monster into a hero.

'I did it for the girls' sake,' Rowena said.

'No, you didn't,' Georgina interposed. 'You did it for your own.'

Carla abruptly announced that her therapist is convinced you abused her and that this, rather than your aloofness, accounts for both her failed relationships and her failed life. 'Why else would I be so fucked up?' she asked, at which even Charlie had the grace to groan. Max, the therapist, is helping her to 'recover the repressed memories, clear the emotional blockage and overcome the toxic trauma.' Losing patience, I reminded her that your offence involved images and there was not a scrap of evidence that you had abused anyone, either now or in the past.

'What difference does it make whether he was there in person?' Charlie asked. 'There are children who've been damaged for life.'

'I'm not denying that for an instant,' I replied, 'but you could say the same about drugs. You may or may not still use them – please let me finish! – but I know that they're endemic in the advertising world. Every sniff or spliff or whatever it is that you and your friends take at a party comes at the end of a long supply chain. Children, lured into drug gangs, are shot dead in the street.'

'You're not comparing them to the ones in Daddy's videos, I hope!' Carla said.

'No . . . I don't know. I'm just asking you to show a little compassion.'

'Do you mean to spend the rest of your life defending him?' Charlie asked. 'It was bad enough when we were growing up. His rules. His rages. His day-long silences. Now it's unconscionable.'

'A man who could upload an image of his granddaughters in a paddling pool as wank fodder!' Georgina said.

'Please!' Rowena said.

'I'm sorry if the word offends you. They're my daughters. How do you suppose I feel?'

'He cut off their heads . . . on the photograph,' I interjected feebly.

'So that makes it all right?'

'No, of course not. It's the thing I find hardest to forgive. But our solicitor explained to me: it was a kind of passport to the porn sites.'

'The abuse sites,' Georgina replied.

'It's an illness,' I said.

'It's a crime,' Charlie said. 'What you refuse to acknowledge is that he also committed it against you. He betrayed you as badly . . . worse than if he'd taken a lover every year you were married.'

'Max says that I bought into the world's most pernicious myth: love at first sight. Daddy out-Romeoing Romeo when he saw you play Juliet.'

'Except that he was already twenty-three. Eight years older,' Charlie said. 'Did nobody think that was, to say the least, odd?'

'You had to be there to understand,' I replied, stifling the memory of my parents' objections. 'It felt right; that it was meant to be.'

'I understand all too clearly. It was sick.'

'You were with us, Rowena. Tell them what it was like.'

'Yes, tell us, Aunt. Mum was clever, wasn't she? A straight-A student. And didn't Granny say that any intelligent girl who refused to take up a place at university was a traitor to her sex?'

'That's what she told me years later,' Carla said.

'Yet she encouraged Mum to get married straight after leaving school. Why? What was it she suspected about her own son?'

'She could see that they loved each other,' Rowena replied.

'A twisted sort of love,' Charlie said.

'If so, then I plead guilty. Perhaps that's why I won't give up on him. The solicitor told me that when your father was charged, the custody nurse asked him whether he'd had any thoughts of suicide. "No," he replied, "I have a wife waiting for me at home." And he still does.'

'More fool you!' Georgina said.

'I may be the only thing standing between him and the abyss.'

'Do you really believe that?' Charlie asked. 'Or is it that having been married so long, you're afraid of being on your own?'

'No, it's more than that,' Carla said. 'Max explained

how she's trapped in this image of herself as the saintly, self-sacrificing wife . . . standing by her man against the rest of the world.'

'I'm sorry if you think that. And please convey my apologies to Max. Now it's time for me to make a move.' I grabbed my bag. 'Thank you for lunch, Georgina. And thank you all for the presents. Perhaps you'll take them to the car for me, Charlie. Will two glasses of champagne push me over the limit? We'll see. It's a minor offence. But then none of us is perfect.'

402 Category A images, 587 Category B images, 299 Category C images.

When I received no Visiting Order last week, I contacted the prison. Your personal officer called back within the hour to inform me that you'd been involved in what he described as 'a spot of bother' and moved to G Wing, which I know to be the Vulnerable Prisoners Unit. He assured me that you were well but needed time to adjust to your new surroundings before sending me another VO.

I was uneasy, and when I visited you this afternoon, your faded black eye and the web of spider veins on your face confirmed my misgivings. I wondered whether any of the officers would object if I reached across and stroked your cheek, but there was no chance to find out since you pushed my hand away.

'Do you want to tell me what happened?'

'No. But I don't suppose I've much choice. It's quite simple. Jed Dickinson – one of the Wollaton Road Dickinsons – turned up here a fortnight ago with a six-year sentence for GBH and blew my cover. The irony is that I saved his life when he choked on a carrot as a baby. Or was that his brother? Anyway, the word was out and Disgusted of HMP Nottingham bashed me with a billiard cue.'

'Does it hurt?'

'No bones broken. Which is one blessing, since the doctor here is a quack. But he patched me up and they sent me to the VPU, reminding me that, if I'd only gone there at the start, all this would have been avoided. So here I am. Denied leave to appeal. Devoid of illusions. In among the beasts and nonces, where I belong.'

'Still, you'll be safe.'

'Yes. Sharing a cell with an ex-copper, who told me that, "on the out", he'd have had no qualms about "croaking" me. It's not until you hit rock bottom that you realise there's a primal urge – a basic human instinct – to feel superior to the next man. It may not be as strong as that for survival, but it comes close.'

I'd expect you to be bitter, but as I transcribe the conversation a few hours later, I'm shocked by your cynicism.

'With remission, you only have six months left to serve. Maybe the new wing will be a more congenial place to reflect on everything that's happened,' I said, weighing my words. 'To prepare you for when you come out.'

You stared at me in disbelief. 'It's a snake pit! You can't imagine some of the men . . . Every form of porn is banned, of course, even the tamest girlie mag. But by claiming to be drafting their appeals, they're allowed transcripts of their trials, which they pass between them, feeding off accounts of each other's crimes. The worst thing is that it's boys . . . most of them are here because of boys.'

'What difference does it make? Boys or girls. they're

still children.' I'm alarmed by the suggestion that yours is a more natural depravity.

'Don't be so sanctimonious! There's a headmaster here from a prep school – one where we almost sent Charlie. He admitted to forty-eight counts of indecency with under-age boys. Forty-eight!' I worried that your screech would disturb the man at the next table, but he had ears for no one but his daughter. 'He claimed that he was "bonding with them" . . . showing them affection when they were homesick. He even decried the callousness of the parents who sent them there.'

'In other words, adding perversity to perversion.'

'Don't try to be clever,' you said coldly. 'It doesn't suit you. There's another one!' You pointed at a hollow-cheeked man talking to an elderly woman, whom I took to be his mother. 'He gets six years for buggering three boys, and I get twenty months for looking at pictures. Is that justice?'

'But they were more than pictures. Surely you must see that?'

As the date of your release draws nearer, I'm increasingly perturbed that you persist in regarding them as make-believe, rather than records of actual assaults.

'The pictures – images, if you prefer – exist. There'll always be people who make them. So what's the difference if they're viewed by one man or a thousand . . . a million? I've prescribed methadone to heroin addicts. It's the same principle. Better that people watch them than groom a child online.'

'Would you have ever . . . groomed a child?' I asked slowly, revealing my greatest dread.

'No, of course not. How can you even think that? Why must you bring everything back to me?'

Because I was sitting across from you in the prison reception hall, after being body-searched, fingerprinted and sniffed by dogs. Because you were wearing a lurid orange tabard, answering to a number rather than a name. Because in six months I'd be taking you back into my home . . . maybe even into my bed, although I didn't want to think about that yet. Because Carla was busily destroying herself in an attempt to find out why she was so self-destructive. Because Charlie was refusing to let you see your grandchildren until they were eighteen and free to decide for themselves. Because with no family wishing to visit us, I envisioned our sitting alone on Christmas Day, bareheaded, eating guinea fowl. Because I was no longer sure that I loved or even cared for you, but I knew that to abandon you would be to betray everything I believed in . . . everything I believed myself to be.

'It's the internet that's to blame.'

'Pandora's box, yes I know.'

Needing breathing space, I went to fetch us both another cup of coffee, chatting for longer than usual with the woman at the counter. On my return, I found you trading smiles with a middle-aged man who, unusually, had a solitary male visitor.

'Is that your cellmate?'

'Don't be stupid! He'd cut me dead. Another chap from the unit.'

'The VP unit?'

'Where else?'

'What was his crime?'

'Three guesses! But he has his head screwed on. He explained to me that pretty soon it won't be a crime at all. Don't give me that look! Listen and you might learn something. He has a friend who's something high-up in AI technology. Cutting-edge stuff! He told him that they're now able to create computer-generated imagery, which looks totally authentic. You remember when we took the kids to see the remake of *The Lion King*? Those amazingly life-like animals?'

'That was Walt Disney.'

'But it was as real as David Attenborough! The technology's getting cheaper all the time. It's available to pornographers just like everyone else. It's a win-win situation. People will be able to watch anything they want – adults, children, whatever – without anyone actually being filmed. Which means they'll be breaking no laws. In years to come, locking people up for viewing indecent images will seem as primitive as transporting them to Australia for stealing a loaf of bread. No one else will have to go through what I have. Isn't that something to celebrate?'

402 Category A images, 587 Category B images, 299 Category C images.

The Cut

'PLEASE, MADAM, WHAT's divorce?' Ayesha asked Miss Hopkins, on her first day at school. We all laughed, which wasn't fair because she comes from Africa where people are poor.

I don't know what Mummy and Daddy's divorce cost. Giles said it was twenty pounds, but he's only five, and twenty's as far as he can count. Louise says we should be pleased if they spend lots of money, because it shows how much they love us. I wish they'd show it by buying me an Etch A Sketch or a Magna Doodle, but Mummy says that I've got too much clutter (like she hasn't!), and Daddy says that he's stony broke because Mummy's bleeding him dry.

Miss Hopkins told Ayesha that divorce is when two grown-ups don't want to live together in the same house and think that it's best if one of them – usually, the daddy – moves out.

'Why?' asked Kevin Patten.

'There can be all sorts of reasons. Usually, it's because they don't love each other any more.'

Which isn't right. Last week, when Kevin was fighting Christopher Pauling, she told us that we didn't have to like each other, but we had to love each other. Though maybe that's just when we're children.

Mummy and Daddy loved each other, until Hiliane became our au pair. She was only eighteen, which Mummy keeps on telling people even though now she's twenty. Hiliane told Giles and me that she wanted to be a nun, like in *The Sound of Music*. Mummy said she was a snake – but not like the milk snake I held at the petting zoo, but like a viper, which is poisonous. Then she told me not to worry because there are no vipers in Exeter. Except Hiliane.

Daddy and Hiliane live in Colverton, with a garden that goes down to the river, where Daddy is going to teach Giles how to fish. Daddy does business. He says he has to work twice as hard now he has two families to support. Mummy called him a bad name when I told her that. She said she was the one who supported us, because he'd hidden all his money from the judge and only gave her a pit...thing. She's a teacher at the big girls' school, which makes her sad because the girls are sloppy and don't want to learn, not like when she was their age. She used to work for a newspaper, but she can't any more because she has to make her holidays fit in with us. And she won't ever have another au pair after Hiliane.

Mummy says that Giles and me don't appreciate everything she's given up for us. She says that she never has enough time for herself, so you'd think she'd be happy on weekends when we spend them with Daddy. But she gets furious if he comes to collect us a single minute too early on Friday or brings us back a single minute too late on Sunday. He has to stay in the car and hoot because he's not allowed inside of the house, even though he's 'paying the bloody mortgage,' and he's in full view of Mrs Harper next-door, who said that he should have his thing chopped off when she thought I wasn't listening.

Giles and me share a bedroom, though Mummy says

that I'm getting to an age when I'll want some privacy. But I put all my private thoughts in this journal, and no one will ever find the key. In Colverton, we each have our own room, though Giles likes to sleep in mine. I let him so as he won't upset Hiliane, who has more moods now that she's married to Daddy than she did when she was an au pair. Giles says he hates her because she made Mummy cry, but it was really Daddy who did that. Mummy said that Hiliane was a tart, and then she put her hand over her mouth and said we must never repeat that to anyone. Giles said: 'Cross my heart and hope to die,' and so far he's kept his promise, though last weekend, he asked her if she'd rather be made of apples or jam. He looked at me and sniggered. I pretended not to know what he meant. Daddy laughed and called him a chump. Hiliane said that she'd kill for some adult conversation. I don't think she would've been a good nun.

Daddy told us that we have to be specially nice to Hiliane because she's going to have a baby. Giles, who's in Reception, doesn't know how babies are born. One thing Mummy and Daddy agree is that he's too young to have it explained to him. I know that if I had a sister who was four years older, I'd thank her for telling me so I didn't ask stupid questions like 'When are you going to the hospital to fetch it?' But I'm not allowed to say anything, just like I'm not allowed to say that Father Christmas isn't a real person, because it would upset him. I wish they thought half – even a quarter, even a tenth – as much about what things would upset me.

I hope that Hiliane's baby is a girl. Then I'll have one of each like Louise, even though the baby won't be a whole sister, just a half. I love Giles, of course, but he can be really irritating. Everyone says that the divorce isn't our fault, but if Giles hadn't had nightmares and woken us all up, then Daddy wouldn't have gone to sleep in Hiliane's room, which was furthest away. Giles doesn't have nightmares any more, but he wets the bed when we sleep in Colverton. Hiliane says he does it on purpose. I said he does it at home too, but he said, 'I never!', when he could see I was trying to make things better. Sometimes I don't know why I bother.

Giles irritates Mummy too. He can be very stubborn, which she says is 'just like your father' (she always calls him 'your father' now, never 'Daddy'). He's specially bad when we come back from Colverton. For tea on Monday, Mummy gave us fish fingers. 'Hiliane says it's wrong to eat food that comes out of a packet,' he said, which is like two times silly, because he doesn't like Hiliane and fish fingers are his favourite. Mummy smacked him and he cried. I don't know why, but then I started crying too.

'You shouldn't hit us,' I said to Mummy, getting down from my chair to give Giles a hug, which made him cry louder. 'Daddy says that if we aren't happy here, we can always have a home with him.'

'Be my guest! Go and live with your father and that tart. At last I might get some peace and quiet.'

Giles and me were so shocked that we stopped crying. After a moment, Mummy stood up and kissed us, and we started crying again, but in a good way. 'You know I'd never let anyone take you. You're my life.'

Now I'm going to lock this up so that no one can read it, specially the bit about the smack.

◊

Mummy has met a boyfriend, Max, though he's fifty years old, which is fifteen more than her. He's taller than Daddy, with a smiley face and black hairs on his wrists as well as his head. He puts his watch in his pocket and wears a bow tie like Doctor Who. When he talks, he makes 'a's sound like 'e's and 'r's sound like 'w's, because he was born in Austria, though he came here when he was twelve. He's kind and generous, which I know aren't the same but it's specially nice when they are. He bought me a Kaleid A Sketch, which is like an Etch A Sketch, only better because you can draw in shapes and colours and they move. He bought Giles an Evel Knievel Stunt Cycle, which does jumps and somersaults. I'm sure that, if Daddy had bought it him, Mummy would say it was dangerous, but because it's Max, she just smiled and said 'As long as it doesn't give him ideas.'

Max asked Mummy to marry him, and Mummy told him that she had to ask us before she said 'yes' (though I think she'd already decided). I'm happy because ever since she's had a boyfriend, Mummy doesn't shout at us so much. Giles is happy because on the nights when it's too late for Max to drive home, he feels protected if there are burglars. Hiliane is happy because Daddy won't have to pay so much money to Mummy. The only person who's not happy is Daddy, who said 'I hope that man doesn't think he can buy my children's love.'

'He's promised to buy me a micronaut,' Giles said, when none of us thought he was listening.

The best thing about the wedding is that I finally get to be a bridesmaid. Louise has been one three times, but I don't have any cousins, or maybe I do but I've never met

them, since no one in Daddy's family wants to speak to
him. The worst thing is that it's going to be in an office
instead of a church, because Mummy's Jewish. She never
told us up to now. 'You mustn't think I was hiding it,' she
said. 'But we – your father and I – didn't want you to grow
up with all that mumbo jumbo.'

'Can I still say the Lord's Prayer in Assembly?' I asked.

'Of course. You can say whatever you like. Don't get
me wrong! A lot of beautiful things have come out of
religion: poetry, art and music. But a lot of terrible things
too: hatred and prejudice and cruelty and violence. Your
father's parents cut him off when he married me. I wonder
if they'll kiss and make up now he's with Hiliane.'

'She wanted to be a nun.'

Mummy snorted, but not as long or as loud as she did
before she met Max. He's Jewish too, though he doesn't
believe in God. The person who does is Mutti, his mother,
or at least she believes in believing (which makes no sense,
but Mummy says that I'll understand when I'm older).
Mutti and Vati, Max's parents, left Austria with Max and
his sister Hannah forty years ago. I asked why they didn't
go to Israel like Becky Adler did when a racial man set
fire to her synagogue, but Mummy said that Israel didn't
exist then, so they came to England where they felt safe. I
said that Becky's family didn't feel safe here any more, but
Mummy said that that was a bit extreme.

The next Saturday after Mummy told us she was getting
married, Max drove us to Bridford to meet Mutti. Her real
name is Mrs Durkheim, but Max said that we should call
her Mutti, even though we're not related. Giles said that it
sounded like putty, and Mummy turned round in the car

and gave him one of her looks, reminding us both to be on our best behaviour.

'I reminded Mutti too,' Max said, to make us smile.

'You can't tell that to a grown-up,' Giles said.

'She's not the easiest of people. You have to take some of the things she says with a pinch of salt.'

Giles laughed and pinched me, but I didn't pinch him back because I'm more mature.

Max and Mutti live in a huge house with black-and-white stripes like a zebra. There are wooden floors, which creak even when you tiptoe, and curtains across the doors. Mutti was waiting for us in the hall, which isn't the same as what we call a hall, but a long room full of pictures and furniture and dust. She wore a black-and-white dress. 'Do you think she's trying to look like the walls?' Giles asked me. I shushed him, but the room was so long that she couldn't have heard.

'You may kiss me,' she said to me, leaning down so that I could reach her cheek, which felt like dandelion fluff and smelt of oranges and cigarettes. 'Not you!' she said to Giles. 'How do I know where you've been?'

'I've been to the Berni Inn,' he said, crossly. 'I had Chicken Maryland – a whole one, not a children's portion – and Black Forest gat . . . Black Forest cake.'

'You bought him German food?' Mutti asked Max.

'Not now, Mutti please.'

'How quickly you forget!'

'The war's been over for thirty years,' he said, breathing with loud puffs.

'Has it? Don't fool yourself!'

'That's enough!'

'And so it begins. I'm to be silenced in my own home.'

'Not at all, Mutti,' Mummy said, in a voice like she had toothache. 'We feel privileged that you want to share it with us.'

'Come now, you're an intelligent woman! "It's high time Max settled down," my friends have been telling me for years. "And you should have grandchildren." "Grandchildren, pah!" I said. "He has his girlfriends. Why complicate life? When he's old and sick, he can hire a nurse."'

'Don't you want grandchildren?' I asked.

'Bella!' Mummy said.

'You're a very forward little girl,' Mutti said. 'I came to this country in 1938. I managed to save my own children. But my sisters' children, my cousins' children, my friends' children: all dead!'

'Was there an earthquake?' I asked, looking at the three grown-ups in turn.

'This is what you teach them?' Mutti asked Mummy. 'And no, I don't want grandchildren; I want peace of mind. Now I'm tired. I need to rest. We'll get to know each other soon enough.'

She moved slowly out of the room, which was so big that it had another door at the far end from where we walked in.

'She'll come round, I promise,' Max said, kissing Mummy. 'Time for the grand tour.'

He showed us all through the house, which was built when Henry VIII was the king, though he couldn't tell me which of his six wives was the queen. Giles whispered to Mummy that the old wooden chests in the corridor scared him. 'Do you think they're where Mutti hides dead children?'

'Don't be silly,' she said, which meant *Don't show me up*.

'She doesn't like children. She said so. I bet there are skeletons and stuff inside.'

'Stop it!' Mummy said, more crossly.

'Look!' Max said, lifting an old red cloth off one of them. 'You'll see, they're empty.' Giles clung to Mummy, as Max opened the lid. 'Good God!' He pulled out two tins of pineapple. 'There must be a hundred of these in here.'

'I like pineapple,' Giles said.

'Isn't it enough that she keeps a packed suitcase under her bed? I'm one of Devon's deputy lieutenants. What more can I do to reassure her? I'd better go up and have a word. I was rather short with her before.'

Max left us in a small room that was all made of wood. A maid, who looked like Sarah in *Upstairs Downstairs*, brought tea for Mummy and orange squash and biscuits for Giles and me.

'Wouldn't you like to live here?' Mummy asked. 'So many exciting places to explore. You haven't been outside yet. There's a wood where you can build a den. And a lily pond, though you mustn't go too close.'

'Will she be here?' Giles asked.

'Who's she? The cat's mother?' Mummy asked.

'No, Max's,' I said, which made Giles fall about giggling.

'Of course. It's Mutti's house.'

'I don't like her,' Giles said. 'She's a witch.'

'Don't be ridiculous! She's just not used to children.'

'Because she kills them all.'

'I don't want to hear any more of your nonsense.'

'Like the witch in "Hansel and Gretel". She locks them in a cage and fattens them up and then puts them in the oven.' He flapped his arms up and down.

'Stop it now!' Mummy said, her face gone white. 'You're never ever to mention putting people in ovens again. Do you understand me? Never!'

After Mummy and Max got married, they went on honeymoon, and Giles and me went to stay with Daddy and Hiliane. But Hiliane had more moods than ever because she was soon about to have her baby. She said it kicked her from inside, and she blamed Daddy for not wearing a pompom. And Daddy blamed us for making noises and upsetting her, even when we were as quiet as whispers and held our breath outside her room (until we laughed).

Mummy and Max came home and we moved into the black-and-white house with Mutti and Jess the maid, who said on our first day that we were going to be best friends, which is true. There are twelve bedrooms in the house, like a hotel, but Giles still sleeps with me because of ghosts. Max promised him that there aren't any, and Mutti said all her ghosts were in Vienna. Max told her off for 'scaring the children', though it was only Giles who was scared. He asked Mummy if Mutti's ghosts could fly to England on a plane, since ghosts can become invisible. Mummy said that they weren't that sort of ghost, which scared him even more because he didn't know there were different sorts.

Mummy keeps telling us what fun it is to be here, like she did when we went to Jersey and it rained all week. I don't think she likes it as much as she expected. I listened when Max told her that it was never easy for two women to

share the same house (you'd think she'd know that already
after living with Hiliane), but that Mutti wouldn't be with
us much longer. I repeated it to Giles, which was a mistake.
The next time she told him off for running in the hall,
instead of walking like a well-brought-up boy (which is
really a way of telling off Mummy because she's the one
who brought him up), he said that she wouldn't be able to
shout at him soon because Max and Mummy were going
to send her away.

Mummy said that that was a lie and made Giles go
upstairs to his room, which wasn't fair since it was true,
even if he oughtn't to have said it.

Mutti said 'Out of the mouths of babes,' which I was
glad Giles didn't hear now that he's moving up to Year
One. Then she reminded Max that the house belonged
to her and told us a long story about one of her friends
who didn't give her nephew a single penny out of all her
money, after she found him measuring the doorways of
her house. 'When all he was doing was seeing if they'd be
wide enough for a wheelchair.' It was the first time I ever
heard Mutti laugh.

Mummy took Max and me for a walk into the wood
and said that the house should be big enough for us to stay
out of Mutti's way. Giles said he was sure that she turned
up her ear thingy on purpose when she knows we're near
so's she can shout at us. I keep hoping she'll be like Heidi's
Grandfather or Mrs Medlock in *The Secret Garden*, who
start off being mean and grouchy and end up being kind.
But maybe that only happens in books.

It's not always easy to keep out of her way. When Max
took Mummy to a lieutenant's dinner in her long green

dress, and Jess went to the cinema on her evening off, Mutti had to look after us. She tried to send us to bed half an hour before usual.

'It's still not seven o'clock,' Giles said.

'I thought you couldn't tell the time.'

'But I can count the ding-dongs on your clock,' he replied and stuck out his tongue.

'You're a very ill-mannered boy,' she said, though I could see in her eyes that she wasn't as cross as she sounded. 'Now do as you're told and get ready. Make sure you brush your teeth properly or they'll all fall out and you'll have to get false ones.'

As we walked upstairs, Giles mumbled that he was sure she had false teeth because she was really old, and that some night when she was fast asleep he was going to creep into her bedroom and pull them out, one by one, until she screamed for mercy. While I put on my pyjamas, he played with his red car. So when Mutti came to say Goodnight, he was still in his clothes. She told him to get changed at once, but he sat down on the bed and lifted his arms in the air, the way he does when he wants Mummy to take his T-shirt off for him.

'Can't you undress yourself? What are you? A baby?' Mutti asked.

'Yes, I'm an ickle-wickle baby,' Giles said, falling backwards and giggling.

'I've never heard such rubbish,' Mutti said, tugging off his T-shirt and vest in one go.

'Ow! That hurt.'

'It serves you right,' she replied. She stroked his shoulder, then jerked her hand away like it was burnt.

Giles lay down all floppy on the bed as she pulled off his trousers and pants. He jumped up again when she shrieked and pointed to his willy.

'What's that?'

'It's rude. You're not supposed to look.'

'Unbeschnitten! Du bist unbeschnitten!' she said, like she was back in Vienna.

'What?' Giles asked, his bottom lip trembling.

'What kind of Jew are you?'

'I'm a half, Mummy's half.'

'Then why have you still got that?'

'I don't understand.'

'You don't have to understand. You just have to do. Your mother . . . "She's divorced, with two children," Max told me, "but not to worry. She's one of us." Pah! You're doing what the Nazis couldn't: destroying the Jews from the inside.'

Giles started to cry.

'He hasn't done anything wrong,' I said, cuddling him.

'No? Six million of us died, and he spits in their faces.'

'I don't spit! I don't!'

'He doesn't spit, I swear.'

'Then what's that? That filthy piece of skin. I didn't know . . . they should have warned me.'

Now Mutti was crying too. She hurried out of the room, even though she has poorly legs, leaving Giles half-undressed. I wiped his tears and helped him put on his pyjama bottoms. Then I switched off the light and ran back to bed, not caring if I trod on the cracks.

The next day was Saturday so we didn't have school. Giles told Mummy what had happened, but he spoke too quick for me to make out most of it. When he finished, he put his arms around her and sobbed. 'I don't want to be filthy.'

'You're not. Absolutely not. You never could be. You never will be.'

'So will I have to have my willy cut off?'

'No, of course not. Not at all. But some boys do have the tip – just the tip – of their willies not cut but snipped off. It's healthier . . . cleaner. And it makes their families happy.'

'Mutti isn't my family. She said so.'

'But doing this might help her feel that she is. And that would be a good thing, wouldn't it?'

'I 'spose so.'

'If you like, we can talk it over with Max. He'll explain what it means much better than me. Then you can decide if it's something you want to do, now or at some time in the future. But first, I must tell you both about Mutti. I'm well aware that she's not an easy person. There again, her life hasn't been easy. When she was younger – not much older than I am now – there were people who hated Jews so much that they killed them. They killed the whole of Mutti's family.'

'Even the children?' I asked.

'Even the children.'

'But not Max and Hannah?'

'No, they escaped. Though they were the only ones. And things weren't easy for them even here. Their father was sent to prison.'

'Why? What did he do wrong?'

'Nothing. But he'd come from abroad so he was treated

as an enemy. To put food on the table, Mutti became a maid.'

'Like Jess?' I asked.

'As best she could.'

'Then you'd think she'd be nicer to her.'

'Indeed, you would,' Mummy said, giving me a hug.

'Was Max's daddy let out of prison?' I asked.

'Yes. And after the war he helped to rebuild the homes and schools and hospitals that had been bombed. And soon – remarkably soon – he made a fortune and bought this house.'

'So Mutti stopped being a maid?'

'Mutti stopped being a maid. But even then there were some people who didn't like them.'

'Did they want to kill them too?' Giles asked, his eyes opening wide.

'No, nothing as terrible as that. But they didn't want Jews to share their special places or to become too important.'

'Do people want to kill us?' I asked.

'No, of course not. Not in England.'

'Becky Adler's father said they did, when the man tried to burn down the synagogue.'

'That was a lone maniac,' Mummy said firmly. 'He was sent to hospital, not prison. There'll always be mad people who start fires.'

'Like Granny?' Giles said.

'Putting grapes in her microwave isn't the same thing.'

'Does it hurt if you have your willy cut off?' he asked.

'Not cut, darling. Snipped. And it's done in your sleep. So you don't feel a thing.'

'What if you wake up in the middle?'
'That's impossible. You're sleeping far too deeply.'
'Even if you have a nightmare?'
'Even then.'
'If I have it done, will Mutti like me?'
'She likes you now. She just doesn't always show it.'
'I want her to show it.'
'I know. And I'm sure she will.'

Giles said that Mummy had lied to him. Although he
didn't have to spend the night in the hospital, his circum-
cision (which is the name of the operation) really hurt. But
he was given ten days off school and heaps of presents. Best
of all was a go-kart from Max, which he was waiting till
he could sit down comfortably to try out. Mutti said that
it was ridiculous to make so much fuss of him. 'You might
as well congratulate the boy for breathing.' But I could tell
she was pleased.

Miss Robbins, who's in charge of Year One, wasn't so
pleased. She gave Giles a red behaviour mark for showing his willy to the other boys in the playground, which
wasn't fair because they'd asked to see it. Then she said that
it wouldn't be right for him to be Joseph in the Nativity
play and made him swap with Douglas Heaton, who was
King Herod. Mummy was angry and said 'Why doesn't
she go the whole hog and give Herod a hooked nose?'
Giles thought having a hook for a nose sounded brilliant,
but Mummy said that wasn't the point. She came to school
to make one of her fusses, but she had to say sorry when
Miss Robbins explained that Giles had been telling the
other boys that their willies were ugly and they had to

have them snipped or God wouldn't love them. There'd been complaints.

Daddy came to the play, as well as Mummy and Max, but Hiliane stayed at home with Jeremy, her new baby, who was too little to be left on his own. So as not to make anyone upset, I sat next to Louise and her mummy, who said that I had an old head on young shoulders, which made me feel like a cut-out doll. Daddy was pleased that it was our year to spend Christmas with him, though he said that having a new baby was 'bloody expensive,' so Santa might not be as generous as usual (I think Giles is starting to suspect). Mummy and Max are flying to the south of Africa, where they have Christmas lunch on the beach. Jess is going to her sister's, and Hannah is coming to stay with Mutti, so she won't be left alone.

'I'm seventy-eight years old and they think I need a babysitter!' she said. Mummy said that Mutti and Hannah have 'issues.'

Giles was sad to see the photos of Jeremy in Daddy and Hiliane's lounge, where there used to be us (I was too, but I hide things better). There was a big tree with an angel on top and loads of decorations for 'Jeremy's first Christmas,' which I thought was silly because he's only just learnt to smile. Hiliane's parents came from Paris. They spoke French the whole time, which I thought was rude, since they'd spoken English when Hiliane was our au pair. So Giles and me made up our own language, but he kept getting it wrong. Anyway, all they cared about was Jeremy.

Giles wanted to know if Jeremy had been cut (*circumcised* is too hard for him). Mutti had explained that it's supposed to happen when a boy is eight days old. The doctor – though he's called something else – puts a drop of wine on the baby's tongue and he doesn't feel a thing.

Daddy, who was still cross with Mummy for persuading him to let Max be 'mutilated' (I was shocked when I looked up the word), said 'No way I'm going to subject another son of mine to that!' Giles, who has seen Daddy without his pants, said he was only saying that because nobody had done it to him, and now he's too old. He said that we should do it to Jeremy, while his willy was too small for it to hurt. I said that it was dangerous, but he said that Daddy had sharpened his carving knife for the turkey.

'He told me it could cut through the bones.'

'What about all the blood? Hiliane will go mad if we mess up his cot.'

'He's got his nappy. There was no blood on my bandage. I asked the nurse to let me have a look.'

I thought it over in my head, and I agreed that if Daddy and Hiliane weren't going to do it then we should. Even though Jeremy was only half our brother, I didn't want him to be filthy. He would thank us when he learnt to talk. So when Daddy drove Hiliane's parents into Exeter for some last-minute shopping (when they'd have to speak English or else they'd buy the wrong things) and Hiliane was having a rest, we borrowed a bottle of wine. The cork crumbled into bits when I tried to pull it out, so we put it at the very bottom of the rack where Daddy wouldn't find it till we went home. Then I had a brainwave and took a bottle of wine vinegar out of the larder, which I was sure would work just as well.

We crept into Jeremy's room, which smelt of poo. I

lifted him out of the cot and undid his nappy, which was even smellier. He opened his eyes and looked happy to see me. Giles touched his willy (it's allowed with a baby) and tugged the skin to see where to cut it, which was going to be harder than we thought. He wondered if it would be better to use scissors, like the ones Jess has for chicken. I put a drop of the vinegar on my finger and wriggled it in Jeremy's mouth. He howled and I tried to shush him, when Hiliane rushed in.

'What are you doing?'

'It's alright,' I said. 'He doesn't like the taste of the vinegar.'

'What?' She grabbed Jeremy from me and pressed him so tight that he howled louder. She was kissing him all over the soft part of his head, when she saw the knife. 'What's that? Are you trying to murder him?'

'No,' Giles said. 'We just want to snip his willy.'

'Monsters!' she screamed, or something like it, and ran out of the room so fast I was scared she'd fall on top of Jeremy and squash him to death. We heard the click as she locked the bathroom door.

'She didn't understand,' Giles said. 'It doesn't hurt if you have it done when you're a baby, Mutti said.' I said we should go and explain, but when we knocked on the door, Hiliane turned on all the taps. We took the carving knife and the vinegar back into the kitchen and waited for Daddy to come home so we could explain to him instead. But we didn't get the chance. As soon as she heard the front door opening, Hiliane shouted for him to come upstairs. He hurried up, with her parents behind him, even though she hadn't shouted for them.

'Are we in trouble?' Giles asked.

'Of course not,' I said, though when Daddy came downstairs I could see that we were. His face was red and his body shook like when we broke his weather thermometer, which didn't work anyway, but this time he didn't shout. Instead, he looked at us like Granny does when we visit her in the home and she's forgotten who we are.

'Are you insane or plain evil?' he asked.

'Giles wanted to circumcise him while he's still a baby and it doesn't hurt,' I said.

'So that God will love him, like he does me,' Giles said.

'Your brother's a Catholic!' Daddy said. 'On both sides. I can't . . . I just can't . . . Stay here. Whatever you do, don't take a step outside that door.'

He left us. Giles said that being in the kitchen made him feel hungry, but I told him to wait since grown-ups don't like you to eat when they're cross. A few minutes later Daddy came downstairs with our suitcases and then went back for Giles' Panda, who doesn't fit inside a case.

'I know you weren't trying to hurt him. You thought – God knows why – you were doing him a favour. But you have to understand, Hiliane's his mother. She's afraid to have you here any more.'

'So where will we go?' I asked.

'I've spoken to Mrs Durkheim, and I'm taking you home.'

'You said this was our home, the same as where we live with Mummy.'

'And I wish it could be. I really do,' he replied. 'Go and sit in the car.'

Hiliane and her parents didn't say Goodbye or Merry

Christmas, which people say even to strangers. After starting the car, Daddy suddenly stopped. He jumped out, leaving the door open and the engine running. He came back with his arms full of presents from under the tree. We returned to Bridford, where he put the cases and the presents in the porch. He gave us each a quick kiss on the top of our heads and drove away.

'You foolish children,' said Mutti, who was waiting for us in the hall.

'I thought you'd be pleased,' Giles said.

'Foolish, foolish boy! Come through quickly. Now I must either call back your mother and ruin Max's holiday, or look after you myself when I was hoping for some peace.'

'I can stay a little longer,' Hannah said.

'I said that I was hoping for peace! You two are in disgrace. So please don't expect any sort of festivities. Crackers! Whatever my faults – and I'm sure my daughter will be happy to list them for you – I'm no hypocrite.'

'Really? Not even in Vienna, where we lit the tree and opened our presents on Christmas Eve? We ate pumpkin soup and carp with our gentile neighbours.'

'You were too young to remember.'

'I was eight when we left.'

'Your father wanted us to fit in. Maybe that's why we were punished.'

'Were you punished because the Jews killed Jesus?' I asked.

'No, because the Christians killed Jews. Six million of us.'

'But not you?' Giles said.

'No, not me.'

'I'm glad.'

'Cupboard love.'

Giles was scared that she was going to lock him in a cupboard, but Hannah explained it was just a saying. She tried to make Christmas as jolly as possible, though it was too late to buy decorations and our only presents were the ones we brought back from Daddy's, which had been left by Mummy and Max. She taught us to play gin rummy, but Giles struggled with the numbers on Mutti's old cards, which were in 'v's and 'x's. We watched loads more television than we would have been allowed to at Daddy's, or even if Mummy had been here. My favourites were *Basil Brush*, *Pinocchio* and *The Sound of Music*, which I'd seen two years ago in the cinema, but Giles had been too young. Mutti left the room when the children were hiding in the graveyard. I told her not to worry; everything turned out fine after they climbed over the mountain. But Hannah said I should leave her alone with her thoughts. Even though the story was happening in Salzburg, not in Vienna, she was thinking of all the people who were dead.

Daddy didn't call us on Christmas Day. Mummy called at three o'clock when she still hadn't had lunch, even though she was two hours in front of us. She said she knew about the trouble at Daddy's, but she didn't tell us off. I said we'd had roast lamb and pineapple, and Hannah made us hats out of newspaper. Mutti had tut-tutted, but she didn't make us take them off. Mummy said that 1978 was going to be the best year ever, and I said 'Promise,' and she said 'Cross my heart and hope to die,' which made my eyes prickle, so I passed the phone to Giles.

Max said Merry Christmas to me and to Giles and something longer to Hannah, but Mutti didn't speak to him, even though I could tell she wanted to. 'He'll be home within a week,' she said. 'There's no point wasting money.'

The next morning I got a shock when it was Jess who opened the curtains.

'I'm sorry,' I said.

'What do you mean?' she asked. 'What for?'

'Did Mutti make you come back from your sister's because we're a handful?'

'Two handfuls,' Giles piped up sleepily.

'Not at all,' she said, but I didn't believe her because her smile was so sad. 'You must hurry up and get washed and dressed.'

She wouldn't let me wear my red sparkly top, even though Boxing Day is a holiday, with a chain of holly and bells around it in the *Radio Times*. So I wore my brown jersey and blue trousers. Giles said he didn't care what he wore and put on his same clothes from yesterday. Jess took us downstairs, telling Giles that it wasn't a morning for jumping. We went into the hall, where Hannah was crying and Mutti had a face like Giles had broken her most precious vase (which he hadn't). Even more strange, an old lady and an old man, who only came to see Mutti at tea time, had come before breakfast. Mutti began to speak, but she got a frog in her throat, so the old man spoke instead.

'I'm afraid there's been a terrible tragedy. Yesterday evening, a terrorist gang broke into the hotel where your mother and stepfather were staying and murdered several of the guests.'

The old lady said '*Schvartzes!*' and the old man said 'Shush!'

I wondered why he was telling us the story, which we could have watched on the news, but then he said that Mummy and Max were two of the people that were murdered. Everything started to sink in for me, though not for Giles. He asked when they'd be coming home, and Hannah cried louder and pressed him to her bosom till his face went red. 'I want to see Mummy,' he said, wriggling out of Hannah's arms from underneath. 'When can I see her?'

'Not in this world, *liebchen*,' the old lady said. 'But she'll be waiting for you in the next.'

'No!' Mutti shouted at her, like she was a child. 'We'll have none of that nonsense!'

'He's five years old,' Hannah said.

'I'm six!' Giles said.

'Then you have to be very grown-up,' the old man said.

I tried to understand that I would never see Mummy's face again, but I was afraid I was forgetting it already, like a dream that disappears as soon as you start to write it down. 'I'm going upstairs,' I said without looking at anyone, and ran up to my room where I have three photo albums of my whole life, which Mummy and I made together. She didn't even mind when there were pictures of Daddy, as long as there were none of Hiliane.

I want every word in this journal to be true, so I won't write much about the next few days, which were blurry, and not just because of the tears. I tried not to cry in front of other people, even Jess, since I didn't want them to try to comfort me or tell me I was being brave. The one person I wanted to comfort me was Mummy, but if she'd been here then I wouldn't have needed comforting in the first place. I specially didn't want to cry in front of Giles. He cries when he sees anyone else crying, even if he's not feeling sad, just like he laughs at jokes he doesn't understand so as not to feel left out.

Daddy came to visit us. He didn't look angry any more, but he still didn't like to be inside the house. So when Jess had made sure we were well wrapped up, he took us for a walk by the pond. He said how sorry he was and how much he'd loved Mummy before. He wished that things had been different and, in a voice like Miss Hopkins during prayers, he said we should always remember that we come from love.

'Will we live with you now?' I asked. 'You said it's what you've always wanted.'

'I did. I do! But it's not quite that simple.'

'Because of Hiliane?' I asked.

'She's afraid of Giles. I know it sounds cruel, but she says he has a demon.'

'Like Granny?' he asked.

'That's dementia. I wish you got along with Hiliane the way you did when she first came to us, but I have to accept things as they are. She's threatening to take Jeremy to live in France. I can't face losing them. Not again.'

'So where will we go?' I asked, trying to make it sound like an ordinary question.

'If only you had close relatives. But with my parents out of the picture and your granny needing care herself, there's no one. I hoped that Mrs Durkheim might let you stay here. I'd be happy to contribute, though heaven knows she has enough money! And it's a wonderful house to grow up in.'

'It's full of things that break,' Giles said.

'Maybe it was too soon to bring it up. She's still in shock. The bodies haven't even . . . But she insists it's not practical. So I think that the best thing would be a completely fresh start.'

'Like what?' I asked, feeling hurt, frightened and sad all at once.

'A new family,' he said, scraping a dead leaf off the sole of his shoe.

'With more children?' Giles asked.

'Possibly. But most likely a couple who aren't able to have any of their own, who'll be so happy to have two such special children to love.'

'Then why aren't you?' I asked, which was a mistake because Daddy started crying. That made Giles cry too, and not just with tears but with snot.

Giles thinks that being dead is like being broken. He asked Mutti one lunchtime if they'd take Mummy and Max to be mended in hospital in Africa or bring them back here. Mutti put her hand on top of his and said that they won't ever be coming back. Hannah said 'Excuse me' and left the table.

Hannah's eyes are redder than Mutti's, but it doesn't mean that she's sadder. One time, Giles and me saw Mutti coming out of Max and Mummy's bedroom, looking like she was going to fall. Giles ran up to her and held her hand. 'Don't worry,' he said. 'I've decided that being dead is like going to sleep, but with no bad dreams. Then you wake up the next morning, but not in Heaven. You wake up here or in Africa. That's what I've decided.'

Mutti started crying, then I did, then Giles. For the first time, the tears made me feel better.

I tried to remember what it felt like to be six, but my head was so fuzzy that it was hard to remember what anything felt like before I knew that Mummy was dead. Sometimes Giles got really upset and asked me to tell him stories about her, and at other times he acted like nothing had happened, driving his go-kart up and down the terrace, until Mutti went outside and told him he had no heart.

'I do too,' he said, pressing her hand on to his chest. 'It's banging even faster now you shouted at me.'

'You foolish child!' she said, stroking his hair and then snatching her hand away. 'Do you want me to catch my death out here?'

'No, no more people dying,' Giles said, and pushed her towards the house.

We were all having lunch when Mutti said that she was shocked by Daddy.

'Not in front of the children,' Hannah said.

'Why not?' she replied. 'Isn't it better that they know the truth? All those lawyers! All those demands for custody!'

'I don't like custard,' Giles said, just as Jess brought in a plum tart.

'Then when he gets what he says he wanted, he runs away,' Mutti said.

'Go into the parlour, children,' Hannah said. 'Jess will give you your pudding there. I need to talk to Mutti.'

'Can't we stay if we're very quiet?' I said, sure that she was going to say something important.

'Like mouses,' Giles said.

'Go quickly,' Mutti said, 'before I cut off your tails.'

Giles shivered and squealed, but with a smile because at last she was playing a game with him. The curtain by the door was a perfect hiding place, and Jess let us stay there, even though she shook her head.

'You may not want to face the truth either,' Mutti said to Hannah. 'But why did he fight their mother tooth and claw? I'll give you one word: revenge.'

'You'd know all about that.'

'Very amusing! But to abandon his children . . . to leave them orphans!'

'Families aren't only the people who share your blood.'

'Maybe not for you and your friends. In my world, the meaning is precise.'

'You could keep them here. They'd be company for you.'

'I like to play patience, not rummy.'

'It's what Max would have wished.'

'That's not fair!'

'Nothing in this life is fair, least of all what's happened to those children. Max told me that, against all his expectations, he couldn't have loved them more if they were his own.'

Giles gasped, and I pressed my hand over his mouth.

'Even supposing I wanted to keep them, it would be utterly irresponsible. I'm seventy-eight. How can I look after two young children?'

'You'll get help. A nanny. Just as you did for us.'

'I have osteoporosis and a stent.'

'You'll outlive us all.'

'All I'd want is to outlive their adolescence.'

'What's adol . . . science?' Giles said, jumping out from behind the curtain before I could stop him.

'What are you doing?' Mutti asked. 'You were told to go to the parlour.'

'Listening.'

'People who listen at keyholes never hear good of themselves.'

'It wasn't a keyhole; it was a curtain.'

Hannah laughed.

'But we did hear good,' I said, owning up to listening alongside him. 'Hannah said that Max loved us like his own children and would want you to keep us here.'

'Would you want to stay with me?' Mutti asked softly.

'I do. Yes. Yes please.'

'What about you?' Mutti asked Giles.

'Me too. Though I don't want you to shout at me unless I do something really bad.'

'Are you planning to do something bad?'

'No! No, I promise. It's just sometimes, by mistake . . .'

'We understand,' Hannah said.

'It's not just up to me,' Mutti said. 'There are lots of people to consult. But if you do stay, there'll be rules. More rules even than you have at school.'

'I like rules,' Giles said.

'Since when?'

'I know the rules to all my games, or else you can't play them properly.'

'We'll be very good. And tidy,' I said. 'We'll make our own beds. And I'll make Giles's. We'll help Jess to clean the house.'

'I won't ever break anything,' Giles said.

'Is that a fact?' Mutti said.

'And I'll never put pepper in your handkerchief,' Giles said. 'I mean...' He looked at me in horror.

'That was you?' Mutti said sternly.

'Max said it was him,' I chipped in.

'I remember.'

'So it must have been. Grown-ups don't lie.'

'I'll bear that in mind.'

'And we won't have to celebrate Christmas next year,' I said, 'or have any special presents.'

'A small celebration may not be such a bad thing. As my daughter has reminded me, we had several in Vienna. Perhaps it's time for a touch of home.'

'Whose home?' Giles asked.

'Mine,' Mutti said. 'Ours.'

Sands of the Sahara

THE MORNING SKY looked grey, although it may have been the grime on Maisie's windows. It was years since they had been cleaned. That was what came of living on the fourth floor. To any suggestion that the stairs were too steep, Maisie replied that the exercise kept her in trim. Besides, she quipped, going out was always an adventure since she never knew what the weather was like on the ground. Most people, however solicitous of her welfare, had the grace to smile, but not her niece Jean.

'What about when you get outside only to you find you have to come straight back up to put on another layer?' It was always a *layer*, never a coat or a cardigan. 'We both know who'll have to look after you if you have a heart attack or a stroke.'

'Don't worry, dear,' Maisie replied. 'Whichever it is, I'll try to make it fatal.'

'Now you just want to upset me.'

Jean: such a nothing of a name! How she'd begged her sister, Irene, to choose one with more of a ring to it. Flora or Virginia or Daphne. But Jean had been Derek's mother's name, which came as no surprise to anyone who knew her, and Irene had deferred to Derek on that as on so much else. The word *doormat* sprang to mind . . . or rather, it would have, if it weren't Maisie's rule never to think ill of the dead. Jean's marriage had been no more satisfactory

than her mother's, but at least she'd had the sense to leave
Harry once their children, Scott and Sandra (names for
which there was no parental justification), had grown up.
She got a job as a floor-walker at Debenham's and moved
into Maisie's spare room. It was an arrangement that suited
them both, at any rate on paper. Maisie had to admit that
the extra cash came in handy, and Jean lived more centrally
than she'd otherwise have been able to afford on the pretext
of caring for her aunt. But, as Maisie had made clear on
more than one occasion, a pretext was all that it was. After
a lifetime's coyness, both personal and professional, about
her age, she had embraced her ninth decade with pride.
Now, rapidly approaching her tenth, she was as fit as a flea.
She climbed the four flights of stairs to the flat with only
one or, if she were alone, two short breaks on the landings.
Given how many of her contemporaries had taken their
final bows, it seemed almost indecent to remain in such
rude health.

Yesterday, she and Jean had had words. As Maisie woke
from a fitful sleep, the memory came back like heartburn.
Jean, whose boast of calling a spade a spade was best kept
for her customers, had reminded her that not only was
she eighty-nine, but she herself was sixty-four and nearing
retirement. Sandra wanted her to live with her and her
three charmless children in Aylesbury. Maisie had hinted,
tactfully, that what she really wanted was an unpaid
cook, cleaner and babysitter. Jean then made a hurtful
and unfounded accusation, which she subsequently withdrew, but the damage had been done. She was keen to
take up Sandra's offer; the problem, according to her, was
Maisie.

'I couldn't rest easy knowing that you were here on your own.'

'As you say, that's your problem. I've lived in Kilburn for more than thirty years. I'm not about to move now.'

It was true that the neighbourhood had changed radically over time (she no longer knew any of her neighbours for a start), but she liked to think that change was one of the things that kept her young. Besides, she was fond of the Dewans who ran the Super Saver Mart, even if Mrs Dewan did expose more of her midriff than was seemly for a woman her age.

'I've never seen the appeal of a sari.'

'What?'

'Don't worry. I'm not gaga.' Maisie replied, refusing to elaborate.

'You see, it's time to think seriously about Whitefields.'

'No, Jean. Absolutely, definitely not.'

'You said yourself how happy Phyllis Jameson is.'

'Of course. She never had her own dressing room. She spent her life in the chorus.'

Maisie, on the other hand, had been a star. At Drury Lane in the twenties and thirties, her name had rarely been out of lights. *Footsteps on the Stairs*; *The Perfect Gentleman*; *Sweet Dolly Daydream*: what memories they conjured up! And with them, those of her leading men: Jack, Ivor, Bobby. Leading men had been real leading men in those days, from their pomaded heads to their co-respondent shoes. Their contemporary counterparts wore dishevelment like a badge of honour. And leading ladies had been real leading ladies, with the admirers to prove it. On the first night of *Footsteps*, Badger Fawcett had drunk

champagne from her tap shoe. Not to be outdone, Teddy
Newell had filled her dressing room with lilies every day
for months. Brett Stephenson had given her a Daimler,
complete with liveried chauffeur. His contrition, when his
creditors reclaimed it, was so piteous that she forgave him
on the spot.

How did the song go?

'We're three little flirts
In our tangerine skirts,
With our eyes and our hearts open wide.
We're three little girls
In our sequins and pearls,
Wondering which one will be the first bride.'

The first bride, yes . . . that had been Clara, or was it
Diana, or even Ruby (her ladyship for a year or so), but
not Maisie. She'd had her share of proposals but, as she
always replied, in a line from *Sweet Clementine*, she was
wedded to the stage. Although her mother had fussed and
fretted, she'd been confident enough of her appeal on both
sides of the footlights to defer any thought of marriage
and retirement (the one following the other as inexorably
as the closing notice after a flop). Then the war came and
life changed for ever.

She could date that change to the day: not the 3rd of
September 1939, when Hitler rejected the British ultimatum, nor whenever it was in 1945 that the Americans
bombed Hiroshima, but the 18th of May 1944, when Ivor
Novello was sent to prison over a mix-up with petrol
coupons. It was a national scandal that the idol of millions,
a composer whose 'Keep the Home Fires Burning' had
been sung by every soldier in the First War and whose *The*

Dancing Years had entertained thousands of playgoers in the Second, had been used so shabbily. She had written to the prime minister, who left it to a secretary to reply. Had he forgotten the effusive letter he'd sent her during *Time for Tiffin*? Or was he, like the magistrates, making the point that, in wartime, nobody received special treatment?

The war over, Ivor returned in *King's Rhapsody*, but when he invited Maisie to lunch at the newly opened Le Caprice, it was to explain, with profuse regret, that there was no part in it for her. She received the news with the gallantry that had charmed the critics in *The Angel of the Crimea* and was rewarded with a smattering of applause when she entered her box on opening night. Ivor triumphed, but it was a last gasp. From then on, the West End was to be colonised by Broadway. Ruritania was annexed; realism was king. She chose to believe what her agent told her: 'You're a princess, sweetheart, not a cowgirl,' over what her mirror told her: Your ingénue days are past. She took *The Perfect Gentleman* on tour, but audiences were no longer content with elegant escapism and after a series of poor houses, she returned to London and unofficially retired. That had been almost four decades ago and it was hard to know where the intervening years had gone.

She had enjoyed her life, even if the second act had failed to fulfil the promise of the first. She had no intention of burying herself in Whitefields or, as she dubbed it, 'the chorus girls' graveyard.' She knew better, however, than to share that with Jean, who had a cruel tongue.

'What gives you the right to be so high and mighty?' she'd asked. 'Has anyone under a hundred even heard of Maisie Perceval?'

The answer was an emphatic *yes*. A few months ago, she'd received a letter from Niall Bradley-Smythe of the Actors' Relief Fund. The Fund, founded by Sir Henry Irving in 1886, was holding a charity auction to mark its centenary and asking 'a host of theatrical luminaries, past and present, for contributions.' Theatrical luminaries: words which brought tears to Maisie's eyes! Theatrical luminaries: words which she emphasised (without the redundant 'past') when relating the message to Jean, who suggested, with typical peevishness, that she should be a beneficiary of the Fund, not a donor. Having replied to Mr Bradley-Smythe (on a freshly bought pad of Basildon Bond), that she would be honoured to help, Maisie was determined to provide something special. With Jean muttering ominously about broken hips, she tottered up the ladder into the loft and rummaged through the three large metal trunks, in which she'd preserved costumes, trinkets, cards and other memorabilia.

Had Jean, a woefully inadequate torch-bearer, not been with her, she'd have gladly spent all day examining items which for years she'd confined to memory. But with Jean's frozen shoulder compounding her impatience, Maisie settled on the slave girl costume she'd worn for the Happy Harem number in *Sands of the Sahara*: a diaphanous turquoise bustier with silver tassels, matching pantaloons with a coin trim and a gauze face veil. She had long since sold the large black opal Brett had given her to sport in her navel. The show had run for more than 400 performances, and Maisie had taken over as Princess Leilah when Margot Tremayne left with what was delicately described as 'gastric trouble'. Such nonsense that opals were unlucky stones!

To Maisie's surprise, Mr Bradley-Smythe came to collect the costume in person, explaining that he lived 'just up the road in Queen's Park.' Pouring him a glass of water as he mopped his brow, Maisie assured him that the stairs took some getting used to. Looking ruefully at his stomach, he remarked that his 'hubby' had bought him a gym membership for their fourth anniversary, but he'd been too busy to use it.

Maisie flinched, which she feared he misinterpreted. Her objection was solely to a diminutive that was especially unbecoming in a man with a double-barrelled name. She had no time to elucidate, since he insisted that he had to dash, grabbing the costume, which she'd lovingly packaged in a vintage Madame Isobel box – almost worthy of its own lot. He barely noticed the tea things, which she'd set out on the sideboard, or the scrapbooks, which she'd artfully placed behind them, picturing him slowly turning the pages with a mixture of admiration and regret for the heyday of the West End. He did, however, take two photographs of her as Princess Leilah, with Billy Howes as Kingsley, the shy but dashing Oxford archaeologist who rescued her from the barbarous Sheik Hassan, to include in the catalogue.

At last, the great day dawned. Maisie was gazing out of her bedroom window, the view blighted by a recently built tower block, when Jean entered with a faint knock, fostering the illusion of privacy.

'I'm off,' she said. 'It's dismal out there. If I were you, I'd spend the morning in bed.'

'But Jean dear,' Maisie said, struggling to maintain her

smile, 'you've forgotten that I'm due at the Savoy at noon for the auction.'

'You're not still planning to go?'

Disdaining to reply, Maisie shot a pointed glance at the gilt-edged invitation on the dressing table.

'It looks like rain.'

'I'm taking a cab.'

'You must have money to burn,' Jean said, in the resentful tone she'd inherited from her mother, then adding more gently, 'You will take care not to overdo it, won't you?'

'I may not be in the first flush of youth, but I'm not on my last legs yet.'

'I meant with the outfit. Women are less dressy than they were in your day.'

'I'm all too well aware of that,' Maisie said, eyeing Jean's low-heeled shoes. 'But I have no intention of looking as if I'm queuing for a seat in the gods. Mr Bradley-Smythe told me, confidentially, that there'd be wall-to-wall stars. There'll be photographers everywhere.'

'But they may not focus on you. Remember, even Phyllis Jameson thought you were dead.'

As Jean moved to the door, Maisie stuck out her tongue at her, a gesture so vulgar that she shocked herself. She took a quick sip of tea when Jean turned round.

'People are fickle. I don't want you to be hurt, that's all,' she said, with unwarranted solicitude.

No sooner had she heard the muffled thud of the warped front door than Maisie ran a bath. She poured in two capfuls of foaming verbena oil to soothe the myriad aches and pains that she'd downplayed for her niece. After drying herself, she put in her rollers – she could live with the transition from ash blonde to grey, provided her hair retained its 'natural' wave. She then began the delicate process of putting on her face. She sat at her dressing table, which she'd kept in defiance of Jean's complaints that it took up too much space, there being a perfectly good mirror in the bathroom. Makeup was an art and, like any other, it required not only a practised hand but the right tools and a congenial setting.

Plucked, pencilled, powdered, rouged and with her lips in the bee-stung pout she had pioneered in the twenties, she examined herself with relief, if not satisfaction. She put on the white Jacquard cocktail dress which, after weeks of indecision, she'd chosen from her mothballed wardrobe, added a diamanté dragonfly brooch with matching earrings, and encircled her wrists in a rattle of bangles. She completed the ensemble with a black felt toque and a fox fur stole, discovering as she fastened the clasp that one of its glass eyes was missing. Stroking its muzzle, she made her way downstairs, ready for the cab.

The driver drew up and she waited for him to step out and open the door, which he finally did with bad grace. The cab smelt of tobacco and stale breath, and the moment they set off, he lit a cigarette. Maisie coughed loudly to no avail and she wondered whether coughing were a sign of approval in Africa, like burping in China. The traffic was heavy, but the driver rebuffed her attempts at conversation, even when she asked about the two smiling girls, whose photographs were displayed on the dashboard. She hoped to impress him with the glamour of the occasion, but he explained brusquely that he'd never set foot inside a theatre. 'I only drive there, my love,' he said, with a rasping

laugh. 'Too pricey. Some of us have to save our pennies.'
Maisie edged her stole over the brooch, trusting that he
realised it was paste.

They turned into the Savoy forecourt and, in part
because she felt embarrassed by the grubby minicab in
the line of gleaming limousines and taxis, and in part
because of his remark about pennies, she handed the
driver a ten-pound note and told him to keep the change
(something that she must on no account admit to Jean).
This time, he jumped out of his seat and held open the
door for her, which would have been more gratifying had
Faye Trevis not pulled up immediately behind them in a
chauffeur-driven Rolls.

The photographers swarmed round her, but Maisie
didn't begrudge her the attention. Faye was a trooper,
who had never stopped working, on stage and film and
even on the dreaded box. She longed to catch her eye, but
she knew better than to distract her from the cameras.
She hurried into the vestibule, where a pallid young man
in a burgundy tuxedo pointed her towards the Lancaster
Ballroom without asking her name. Confident now that
she looked the part, she strolled through the opulent foyer
for the first time since Ruby Baxter and her third (or was
it fourth?) husband had invited her to a supper party to
celebrate Princess Margaret's wedding. A table outside
the room was piled high with catalogues. She picked one
up and moved to the door, only for a young woman with
braided hair sticking up like antennae, to call out that it
cost twenty pounds.

'I'm so sorry,' Maisie said, praying that her rouge would
hide her blush. 'I presumed they were free.'

'It's for charity,' the woman replied, tartly.

'Yes, of course.' Maisie lent towards her. 'I've donated,' she whispered, reluctant to appear boastful to the couple behind her.

'It's for charity,' the woman reiterated, as implacably as a well-drilled stage doorkeeper.

'Twenty pounds, you said,' Maisie replied, fumbling first with the clasp on her bag and then with the zip on her purse. She handed over her last two ten-pound notes, clutching her bus pass for reassurance. 'Keep the change,' she said, hurrying away, as the woman looked at her with alarm. She showed her invitation at the door and entered the ballroom, savouring the perfumed plushness. Like wine, she mused, at the very moment that a gangly waiter, his face pitted with acne scars, approached her with a tray of drinks. Jean's voice echoed in her head, reminding her of the doctor's injunction. Muffling the sound, she took a glass and drank it with unaccustomed urgency. She surveyed the people milling around and shrank into her shadow. It wasn't that she felt out of place so much as out of practice. She spotted one or two faces she thought she recognised, but she hesitated to greet anyone after the humiliation of hugging an unsuspecting newsreader in Boots. If only she weren't so cowardly about her cataracts!

The waiter, who alone acknowledged her presence, asked if she wanted a top-up. Surprised to find that her glass was empty, she would have said 'no', had he not advanced towards her at the same time as a portly middle-aged couple, who might have seen – even celebrated their engagement at – one of her last performances. She smiled graciously, to put them at their ease.

'We saw you standing on your own. So I said to Harry
– this is Harry.' He doffed an imaginary hat. '"Remember
what they told us on the cruise." So here we are. I'm Sheila,
by the way.'

'Maisie,' she replied. 'Maisie Perceval,' she added, with
a hint of a rebuke.

'We've driven up from Woking.'

'Oh no, I'm long retired.' Catching her puzzled glance,
she gestured to the piano trio on the podium. 'The music's
a little loud.'

'But who can complain when it's a medley of Broadway
hits?' Sheila asked. Maisie, who had often complained that,
like their military counterparts, American musical stars
were overpaid, over-sexed and over here, smiled thinly.

'Have you got your eye on anything special?' Harry
asked her.

'I hear that there are some gems from pre-war productions,' Maisie replied tentatively. '*Sands of the Sahara.*'

'Phew, no competition there! We're really keen on some
of the *Joseph* stuff.'

'Joseph?'

'I've warned my good lady that we'd have to take out
a second mortgage for the original Dreamcoat, but there's
a programme from the Young Vic première, signed by
the entire cast, and the conductor's score from the Albery
transfer that we might just about manage. Good luck
with . . . what was it?'

'*Songs of the Sahara,*' Sheila interjected. 'He never
listens!'

Maisie watched in dismay as they walked off, accosting
a handsome young man who signed their catalogue. She

was starting to feel uncomfortably flushed. Her fox fur was heavy and, although its jaws were clamped tight, its teeth seemed to be nipping her bosom. She longed to take it off, but her hands were shaking and, besides, she didn't want to draw attention to her brooch. She should have heeded Jean's advice to dress casually. Young people today – and almost everyone was young to her – had no sense of occasion . . . or of respect, she decided, as the waiter, with a discernible smirk, asked whether she wanted another glass.

'I'll have you know,' she said, drawing herself to her full height, 'that Badger Faucett drank champagne from my shoe.'

'There are no animals here, madam,' he said, with a look of concern. 'Would you like to sit down?'

'I'm quite capable of finding my own seat,' she replied, waving him away. Feeling her legs a touch wobbly, she staggered to a chair three rows from the back. Once settled, she opened the catalogue, eager to find her costume. She skimmed through the screeds from various knights, dames and associated notables, of whom only Faye herself, a trustee of the Fund, shared her roots in musical comedy. The others were all from the straight – or, as she had known it, the legitimate – theatre. With no sign of the auction starting, she allowed her mind to wander. If she'd been born fifty years later, might she have made the leap to dramatic roles, giving her Hedda, her St Joan and even her Lady Macbeth? Might it have been Dame Maisie sending her good wishes from a rehearsal room in Stratford?

She shook the notion out of her head and turned back to the catalogue. She finally found her costume, but there was no accompanying photograph, let alone of her in Billy's embrace. To make matters worse, it was misattributed to 'Miss Maisie Perceval in *The Desert Song*.' She felt invisible – and not just to the couple who brushed past, flicking her face with their coats. *Sands of the Sahara* had run for 418 performances and she hadn't missed a single one. The King and Queen had attended a gala, at which she was presented (they'd put her in mind of a pair of skittles). How could Mr Bradley-Smythe, who'd described himself as a 'walking theatrical encyclopaedia' have failed to spot the mistake?

Thumbing through the catalogue, she noticed that the lots increased in importance as the sale progressed. Hers was the third, after a collection of vintage postcards of pier pavilions, and a flyer for a benefit performance of Billy Smart's Circus for *handicapped and underprivileged children*. After hers came set models, props and costumes; photographs, posters and programmes; autographed letters, scripts and scores and, in pride of place, Noel Coward's makeup box. Overwhelmed by lassitude, she shut first the catalogue and then her eyes.

Roused as ever by applause, she looked up to see a rotund comedian in a lurid checked suit mounting the podium. He bellowed a greeting at the audience. 'Don't worry, they haven't been starving me. The doors in this place are so narrow, I had to leave half of myself outside.' He had his own television show and his routine revolved around his girth ('I thought I'd reached rock bottom . . . rock bottom, missus. I couldn't reach my own!'). Jean was a fan but, as a former dancer, Maisie failed to find obesity amusing. He began by welcoming everyone to 'this upmarket B&B,' warning them (superfluously, in Maisie's opinion) that he was lowering the tone, but promising that he was only the first in a line of celebrity auctioneers. 'There'll be proper thesps – yes, right proper ones – for the smart stuff later. Now let's make a start, then we can get down to the real business of the day: lunch. I jest!' The pianist, who'd remained on the podium, played a dissonant chord, and a woman at the front tittered. 'Now be fair, madam. My stomach may be large but it's not loud. That rumble you just heard was Big Ben.'

For all Maisie's disdain, his banter galvanised the audience. Bids were brisk, with the pier postcards and circus flyer fetching £95 and £50 respectively. The next lot was hers. Mr Bradley-Smythe had indicated that the costumes would be modelled by current West End performers. He must have been saving them for later, since her slave girl costume was merely held aloft by a statuesque redhead in a silver sequin trouser suit, who handed it to the comedian with the flourish of a magician's assistant. He stared first at it and then at the catalogue with mock incredulity.

'I know they call them the Roaring Twenties, but this is ridiculous.' He let the material glide through his fingers. 'Did the show ever run or did the police close it down?'

The audience laughed in what Maisie trusted was commiseration for a comedian dying a death.

He started the bidding at £100 and, with no takers, dropped it to £75, £50 and then £20. 'Twenty pounds, do I hear twenty pounds for a piece of musical theatre audacity . . . I mean history? I assure you that this is the authentic costume, worn by Miss Mopsy – whoopsie – Maisie Perceval for over four hundred performances.'

Never had anonymity felt such a blessing. From now on, Maisie not only wanted no one else to remember her past, she wanted to forget it herself. 'Twenty, who'll give me twenty? All right then, ten.' A man in the centre of the room raised his hand. Maisie craned forward, but all she could see was that he had blond hair and wore a blue military-style jacket with gold epaulettes. How apt for her knight in shining armour! The one mystery was why he'd waited so long to bid. 'Do I hear fifteen? Fifteen, anyone? And we'll throw in a kiss from the lovely Tracey.' The redhead gave a practised smile. With no counter-bid, the comedian brought down his gavel and the costume was sold. He turned to the next lot: two spotlights from the old Mercury Theatre in Notting Hill.

Maisie slumped in her seat. She barely registered the subsequent lots, although the regular bursts of applause signalled that the bidding was spirited and prices high. She looked up during a lengthy ovation to see the comedian quit the podium, passing the gavel to the presenter of a television arts programme. Several people seized the opportunity to slip away, among them her St George. She felt a desperate need to speak to him; not to thank him, which would have left her further exposed, but to ascertain his interest. Murmuring apologies to her neighbours, she crept out, afraid that she'd lost him, but to her relief, he'd stopped in the foyer to light a cigarette.

'Young man,' she called, but he failed to respond. 'Young man,' she repeated, grasping his arm. As he turned, she realised that he hadn't slighted her. He was considerably older than he appeared. His hair was bleached, his eyebrows shaped, and he was wearing a thick layer of foundation. Indeed, he was the only person at the event who looked to have taken as much care with his makeup as Maisie herself. Her heart raced, and she longed to escape but, having waylaid him, she felt obliged to stay.

'I saw that you bought the slave girl costume,' she said. 'Are you a collector?'

'Yeah right! My shoebox in Woolwich is a shrine to this glorious business we call show.' Maisie was nonplussed. 'No, duckie. I'll use it for my act. I'm a drag artist.'

'A drag artist?' she repeated blankly.

'I put on a wig and falsies and wow them at the Black Cap.'

'I know what a drag artist is, young . . .' She stopped herself. 'Douglas Byng was a dear friend of mine. Although he designed all his own costumes.'

'Bully for her! We can't all be Susie Seamstress. I have a friend too, Nellie Bradley-Smythe, the brains behind this shindig. He said I'd be sure to pick up some fabulous frocks. And this one's perfect for my new number. To the tune of 'Baubles, Bangles and Beads', it's Oral, Anal and . . . sorry, too much information!' He slapped his wrist. 'A few snips to the bodice. A lorryload of glitter. A rhinestone in my belly-button and there you have it, Princess Lay-down, the desert's favourite watering-hole. Thank Jessica for Maisie Perceval, may she rest in peace. Ta ra!'

Mortified, Maisie watched as he walked away. She should have taken Jean's advice and disposed of all her treasures years ago. Far from being an expert on stage history, Mr Bradley-Smythe must have plucked her name from the dwindling list of her contemporaries who were neither dead nor dotty. He'd sounded so impressed by her career when he wrote, and yet, in the event, he hadn't spared ten minutes to leaf through her albums. He'd been

lax with the catalogue entry, hired that brash compère and
had a friend whose diminutives were even more distasteful
than his own. Jean had been right. No one remembered
Maisie Perceval. Her vanity had been duly punished.

She needed to use the powder room but dreaded
running into someone she knew. What if Faye came in to
repair her makeup? She couldn't bear to be the object of
her pity. The once alluring prospect of a reunion, followed
by lunch – perhaps even here at the Grill – now horrified
her. Focussing on her feet, like her friend Myra after her
stroke, she left the hotel and trudged to the bus stop. Her
eyes were bleary, but she managed to make out the three
digits of the 139, which would take her straight to Priory
Road. The conductor lost patience as she scrabbled around
for her pass ('Take your time, lady, I don't retire for another
three years'). Behind her, two girls giggled, but Maisie was
past caring.

The walk home from the bus stop was gruelling, but
she refused to rest for even a moment. To a mugger, her
jewels might look real. With the street door shut firmly
behind her, she clung to the wall to catch her breath before
dragging herself up the stairs. She laughed at the thought
that her rhythmic steps (left foot, pause; right foot, pause)
might be the basis of a dance routine. But, by the time
she reached the flat, she found that her cheeks were wet
with tears.

With plenty of time to change before Jean returned,
she decided to have a quick lie-down. The next thing she
knew, Jean was standing beside the bed, rattling a tea cup.

'You look worn out,' she said, as Maisie took a grateful
sip. 'I told you it would be too much for you.'

'It would have been too much for anyone. Such a glittering occasion. So many stars. The champagne flowing like . . .' She took another sip of tea.

'Stop right there! Some of us have to live in the real world. And the costume?' she asked, more gently. 'Did it fetch a good price?'

'You don't want to know,' Maisie said, feeling that that much at least was true. 'If I told you what it went for, you wouldn't believe it.'

'Don't be so sure. Some people have more money than sense. I've been telling you for years to sell those old keepsakes. Maybe now you'll listen. We could finally get colour.'

'Sandra has a colour set, doesn't she?'

'What do you think? This is 1986.'

'Well, you'll soon have a chance to enjoy it,' Maisie said, her lips parting in a genuine smile. 'I realised today how much I've missed the company of my fellow artists. Civilians never quite understand. Tomorrow, I'd like you to call Whitefields and find out if they have any vacancies. It was foolish of me to dismiss it out of hand. If you're free on Saturday, we could take a trip out there and look around. It's too long since I've seen dear Phyllis.'

Cabin Fever

WITH HINDSIGHT, IT was reckless to travel. The first case of novel coronavirus (soon to become Covid-19) was identified in China on the 31st of December 2019. Just three weeks later, Alice called and invited me to accompany you on what she innocently described as the 'holiday of a life-time': an Antarctic cruise setting sail on the 11th of March. And to be fair, none of us could have predicted how far, how fast and how fatally the virus would spread.

Alice and her siblings had booked the cruise as a fortieth wedding anniversary present for you and Alwyn. Anyone who knew you knew that it was your dearest wish to visit Antarctica. I doubt very much that Alwyn shared it, but anyone who knew him knew that it was his dearest wish to please you. So, despite the seasickness that had made even Channel crossings an ordeal, he agreed to brave one of roughest sea passages in the world.

Given the cost of the eighteen-day cruise, which included stops in the Falklands and South Georgia, along with a preliminary visit to Buenos Aires, any Early Bird Discount was welcome, so the children had booked fifteen months in advance . . . and six months before Alwyn dropped dead in the pulpit last June. They were determined that you should still go, although you admitted privately that their 'Dad would have wanted it' refrain was wearing thin. You were reluctant to venture all that way alone, but neither

Alice nor Robin, whose high-powered jobs had paid for the trip, nor Beth, who was busy looking after two young children, was free to join you. While the obvious candidate was your sister Rose, Alice feared that putting the two of you in such close quarters for an extended period would risk more turbulence in the cabin than at sea.

As your oldest friend, her godmother and 'almost one of the family,' I was, according to Alice, the ideal travelling companion. Moreover, I had been recently bereaved myself and would benefit from a change of scene. While not as untimely or shocking as Alwyn's, Mother's death had hit me hard. Apart from my three years at Cambridge, I'd lived with her my entire life. But when her gradual decline accelerated, until she woke up each morning unsure of who she was, answered the phone with the TV remote, and startled passers-by in the park by claiming she was being abducted, I had no choice but to place her in a home. Once there, she faded away in a mere four months. Despite all the letters I received praising me as a devoted daughter, I remained wracked with guilt.

Alice's talk of 'blowing away the cobwebs' struck a chord with one who spent her days surrounded by second-hand books, and her evenings in a rambling house whose every surface groaned beneath Mother's knick-knacks. So, on the 9th of March, leaving the shop in the capable hands of my assistants, Tara and Rachel, and my cat, Cheshire, in the safe hands of my neighbour, Mr Bushell, I met you at Heathrow for the flight to Buenos Aires.

I mustn't make too much of our rashness. In the weeks leading up to departure, we read and watched frequent reports of the Covid outbreak on the *Diamond Princess*, the cruise ship stranded off the port of Yokohama for twenty-seven days. One distraught passenger described it as 'like living in a giant Petri dish.' I witnessed sick passengers being carried off the ship like ancient mummies and, while I was loath to disappoint you, as well as to miss our first holiday together in forty-two years, I called Alice to cancel. She asked me to speak to Robin, who was in regular contact with the cruise company. He relayed their assurance that, with only a hundred or so passengers and a similarly sized crew, the *Ocean Spirit* was the antithesis of the *Diamond Princess* which, with nearly four thousand passengers and fifteen hundred crew, resembled a floating village. Following the latest medical advice, the company had implemented enhanced screening and sanitary measures. Far from putting ourselves in danger, we'd be heading to the most isolated – and secure – place on earth.

While insisting that he didn't want it to influence my decision, Robin explained that, without official government guidance not to travel, neither the cruise nor the insurance company would be required to refund the cost. Reluctant, I suspect, to place me under further obligation, Alice had refused to tell me how much that was. Robin had no such qualms, revealing that, even with the Early Bird Discount, it came to almost £1,000 per person per day. I was horrified. The most expensive holiday I'd ever taken, an all-inclusive two-week dialysis cruise to the Canaries with Mother, had cost us around £2,000 each. There was no way I could countenance their losing that amount.

After a whistle-stop tour of Buenos Aires, we took a flight the next morning to Ushuaia, where we were to board ship. It was on the bus to the hotel that one of our group, checking his phone, informed us that while we were in the air, the World Health Organisation had designated Covid-19 a global pandemic. Unsure how this might affect the voyage, we resolved not to join in the general speculation but to wait to hear from the cruise director. No sooner had we settled into our room than we received a call asking us to meet her in the lounge at six.

Janine, sporting the cruise line's primrose T-shirt (which did her no favours), introduced herself and immediately declared that she was here to set our minds at rest. I sensed you tense – less, I suspect, at her objective than her manner. She announced that there were nine different nationalities among the passengers, and another half-dozen among the crew, yet not one of our respective governments had advised against making the voyage. There had been only two Covid cases in the whole of Tierra del Fuego but, to ensure our protection, the crew, who'd arrived in port yesterday after fifteen days at sea, had been denied shore leave. She would stake her life (a phrase that would come back to haunt her) on our enjoying an untroubled voyage. She told one persistent questioner that if he and his wife were unhappy with the safety provisions, they were free to disembark, much as the manager of my mother's care home had told me that if I thought she was being over-medicated, I was free to remove her. Then, lightening the mood with the offer of complimentary champagne, she invited us to take our places for dinner.

One of the advantages of the *Ocean Spirit* over the two dialysis cruises I'd taken with Mother, was the open seating at meals. As it turned out, the six people who joined us at our hotel table became our closest companions throughout the voyage. Jane and Douglas Parker were a softly spoken couple in their mid-eighties, whose son Brian, a sergeant in the Royal Fusiliers, had died of injuries sustained in the Falklands. They had long planned to travel to the battle-fields but, wishing to pay a private tribute and avoid any sign of triumphalism, they'd steered clear of the official tours. They trusted that the cruise would help to ease the pain of their visits to Port Stanley and Goose Green.

Elliot and Rhoda Jefferies were a handsome couple from Cincinnati, Ohio, 'in the good old US of A,' as the ebullient Elliot put it. They took turns to tell a story that smacked of much retelling. In the summer of 2015, they'd quit their jobs and were now almost halfway through a ten-year programme of world travel. They'd spent the winter exploring Chile and, while they preferred to venture alone, planning their own itineraries and taking local transport, that was patently impossible in Antarctica. While the rest of us admired their enterprise and even Jane, the most diffident of our fellow diners, quizzed them on their memorable experiences, you, with that Puritan conscience I'd first observed in Cambridge and which had been honed by forty years as a clergy wife, appeared to take their project as a personal affront.

'Are you writing a book about the trips or are they purely for pleasure?' you asked, with thinly veiled disapproval.

'Neither,' Rhoda replied. 'We see the world, meet new people, learn about different ways of living. And we make videos for our YouTube channel which, to our amazement, attract an average of 500,000 views.'

'But what about your home? Your families? Your friends?' you added, unimpressed.

'It sounds wonderful,' I interjected quickly. For all your skills in the surgery, you were prone to blunders outside it. As a childless couple in their mid-forties, they were escaping a life in which they'd be forever peripheral. For the first time since coming away, I missed Cheshire.

The third couple to join us was by far the oddest, so much so that, at first, I took them to be strangers. 'Much better to break the ice here than wait until we're surrounded by it on the ship,' the elegant, immaculately coiffed woman said, with a throaty chuckle. 'I'm Frances – though my friends call me Frankie – and this is my grandson, Guy.' She thrust a braceleted arm towards the stringily handsome young man beside her.

'I'm Carla and this is Henrietta,' I replied.

'I don't usually expect so much drama at the start of a cruise,' Frankie remarked.

'Do you go on many?' Jane asked.

'Half a dozen a year. Like you, I live to travel,' she said to Elliot and Rhoda, who looked uneasy at the association. 'At my age, what else is there?' She smiled at her grandson, who scowled. While he was in his mid-twenties, she could have been anything from a feisty seventy-five to a well-preserved ninety. '"Been there, done that!" is what I want carved on my tombstone. That's why I've no desire to be cryogenically frozen or whatever. What else would there be, other than to do it all again? But don't worry, I'm not one of those competitive cruisers. You know the type: "We loved Shanghai." "Oh really? Next time you must try Shangri-La."' She winced as she sipped the Argentinian champagne. 'No wonder it's free.'

'So the Antarctic's the final frontier?' I asked.

'I wish! I came here five years ago. It's for Guy. He's just been surfing in Costa Rica. Now he wants to hike up a glacier.'

'Are you keen on sports?' you asked him politely.

'It depends who's asking,' he replied, taking out his phone.

'Well, I am,' you said, nonplussed.

'Don't mind Guy,' Frankie said indulgently. 'He's laconic.' Guy glowered at her. 'Look it up! What about you two? Are you veteran cruisers?'

'This is my first,' you replied. 'But Carla's been on several with her mother.'

'Two,' I interjected, hoping that no one would ask for details.

'We'd already planned this trip when my husband died in June. Carla nobly agreed to step into the breach.'

'A true friend,' Frankie said, with what I trusted was an involuntary twitch.

We'd been friends for almost forty-three years, having met at Newnham in 1977, when you were in your second year reading medicine and I was a fresher reading English. We lived on the same floor in Old Hall, but the first time we spoke was in the laundry room. I lent you two 10p pieces for the tumble dryer, and it's only now, as I write this, that I wonder if your lack of change was a ploy. Surely you must have known how many coins the machine took? The following afternoon, you knocked on my door, bringing the money, along with two Fitz-billies' eclairs, and as we sat by the fire devouring them, you leant over to wipe a spot of cream from the corner of my mouth, first with your thumb and then your tongue.

Later, you denied making the first move and while I admit that such boldness was out of character, I have my diary as proof. In any case, that first move was swiftly followed by a second, third and fourth, which were both instinctual and mutual. I was at once amazed, euphoric and confused, as you brought out feelings in me that I'd thought were found only in novels. You said that you could never have imagined falling in love with a woman, and I replied that I'd have chosen you even if I'd been as sought after as Zukeika Dobson.

'Zuleika who?' you asked, and for a moment I worried that we might not be compatible.

You insisted that we told no one of our relationship. Although sapphism wouldn't have damaged my hopes of becoming a writer (hopes buried so long ago that weeds have grown over their grave), you explained that prejudice was rife in the medical profession. I was happy to keep a secret that made the relationship feel doubly special.

My world fell apart in May 1979 when, shortly before my Part Ones and your Finals, we attended (separately, of course) our friend Monica Llewellyn's twenty-first birthday dinner. At the end of the toasts, you stood up and said that, since it might be the last time we'd all be together, you wished to announce your engagement to Alwyn Sinclair, the chaplain of Christ's. I burst into tears. I have never since let my guard down in public and, even then, I was quick to blame my outburst on the champagne. In our short, tense meeting afterwards, you maintained that you'd broken the news in company so as to make it easier for me. The only thing it made easier was my contempt for your cowardice.

Plumb, rubicund and nearing forty, Alwyn was an unlikely candidate for a whirlwind romance. Given your heavy schedule of lectures and practicals, not to mention the hours you spent with me, I failed to see how you'd had time to meet, let alone fall in love. I speculated that he was gay and the engagement a front, but you swore that it was genuine. Over the years, I came to appreciate Alwyn's qualities. He was a good man: intelligent, wise, humane. Although I never understood his passion for fly fishing and my palate was too unrefined for his vintage wines, we shared a love of the Metaphysical poets. His monograph on Henry Vaughan was prominently displayed in my shop, long after it had been remaindered elsewhere. Even so, you never convincingly explained how you'd surmounted the barrier of faith. I was the one with the vestigial Anglicanism, while you'd proclaimed yourself an unflinching atheist. But then if you'd chosen to be a wife, why not go all out and marry a vicar?

At least with me, you could be yourself – or rather, the hidden side of yourself. Was that why you treasured the week every August when Mother stayed with Aunt Judith in Torbay and you came up to Lincoln? Even after the children were born, you claimed that brief respite from the dual demands of surgery and vicarage. Mother always prepared a guest room, but after the first visit when you stole into my bedroom saying that you were too used to Alwyn's snoring to be able to sleep in silence (an excuse so ridiculous that we both burst out laughing), you slept with me. While a part of me longed to punish you for the pain you'd caused, a wiser and, thankfully, stronger part knew that, were I to push you away, I'd punish no one more

than myself. As you squeezed in beside me, I savoured the
familiar contours of your body and the chance to pleasure
you in ways which I felt sure were beyond Alwyn's ken. I
taught myself to be grateful for what I had.

Those summer idylls lasted seven years. On the eighth,
Uncle Joseph's bronchitis forced Mother to postpone her
trip to Torbay. It was too late to change your plans, so
you were trapped in the guest room. Even the weather
conspired against us, dashing any hope of intimate picnics
in the Wolds. But neither my mother nor the rain cast as
deep a shadow as your unease (I refuse to call it conscience).
I doubt you'd remember words which, in the absence of a
confidante, I committed to my diary, but you described my
mother's presence as providential. It laid bare how dishon-
ourable you'd been, not just to Alwyn and the children, but
to me. You were holding me back from true fulfilment;
preventing my building a life with someone else – 'man
or woman', you added with brutal condescension. From
then on, although we spoke regularly on the phone and
you invited me to family celebrations (I was, after all,
Alice's godmother), there was always a distance between
us.

We boarded the *Ocean Spirit* the morning after our arrival
in Ushuaia. Jacinto, our personal steward, escorted us
to our suite. 'I hope that you will be satisfied with my
services, madams,' he said, bowing stiffly. 'It is my intention that you will be leaving with a bright smile on your
faces.' My smile couldn't have been brighter as I wandered
through the sitting room, bedroom and bathroom, and
into the closet. You, on the other hand, were offended

by the opulent fixtures, from the Japanese heated loo seat to the Nespresso machine with its selection of pods.

'Such profligacy! Alwyn would have deplored it.'

'Then it's lucky you're here with me,' I replied without thinking.

We joined our fellow passengers on deck to witness our departure, then headed to the lounge for the captain's welcome. With a wave that flaunted a fresh array of bracelets, Frankie beckoned us.

'I've saved you two places.'

'That's kind,' you said curtly. 'Where's your grandson?'

'Over there at the bar, chatting to the waitress.'

'He must be relieved to find some young people on board.'

'Just as long as he doesn't forget that his job is to look after me,' Frankie replied, with surprising asperity. I wondered whether Guy and I would both discover the hidden cost of a free holiday.

The captain introduced himself and his senior team: the chief engineer, the hotel director, the doctor and, 'most importantly,' the executive chef, who, like his counterpart on the *SS Renal Failure*, received the loudest applause, before handing the microphone to the 'indefatigable' Janine.

Janine, who appeared to regard herself as a cheerleader as much as an activities director, declared that, though it was late in the season, March was her favourite month to visit Antarctica. 'Most of the other cruise ships have left, so there's no competition for landing rights. True, some of the ice has melted, so the scenery may be less dramatic. On the plus side, we'll see the most spectacular sunrises and sunsets. It's the best time to spot whales – orcas,

sperm whales and humpbacks. And while there are fewer
penguin chicks, we'll get to watch fledglings taking their
first steps into the water and, if we're lucky, the leopard
seals lying in wait for them.'

I must have looked taken aback, since Frankie leant
over and whispered 'It's all red in tooth and claw on the
White Continent.'

After lunch, we attended a talk on Amundsen's polar
expedition by Ralph Foster, one of the three guest lecturers.
We then returned to the suite, where you emailed your
children and I stood on the balcony, watching the ship
navigate the Beagle Channel. Visibility was poor and the
air damp, and I was about to head inside when a familiar
voice hailed me over the glass divider.

'What are the chances?' Frankie asked.

'What indeed?' I replied, already dreading your
reaction.

'All alone?'

'Henry's writing to her children.'

'I get the feeling she doesn't like me.'

'Not at all! She's naturally reserved and her husband's
death is still very raw.'

'I've buried three husbands,' she said, so jauntily that I
pictured her wielding a spade. 'It gets easier.'

'I don't think she's planning to remarry.'

'What about you?'

'Me? Oh I'm far too fond of my own company.'

'I need another pill, Frankie,' Guy called out, the name
flustering me until I realised that she would have vetoed
Granny.

'Poor dear,' she said, casually. 'It's a millpond right now.

Just wait till we hit the Drake Passage. It's reckoned to be the roughest sea in the world.'

'So I keep hearing. I wish someone had warned me before I signed up.'

'Wait there! I'll grab some scopolamine patches for you both. I have a stack.'

'I'm not sure Henry – Henrietta – will approve. Don't forget, she's a GP.'

'She'll forget herself soon enough, when the ship is listing in forty-foot waves.'

As I suspected, you were outraged by Frankie's doling out a prescription-only drug. But lacking your professional ethics, I gratefully accepted and stuck the patches behind my ears before going to bed.

I was lulled to sleep by a gentle swell, only to be jolted awake when two drawers slid out of my night table and the room was transformed into a fairground tilted house, with the floor and walls at impossible angles. My body appeared to have contracted so that my head and stomach occupied the same place on the bed. You were equally disoriented and after struggling to stand up, you opened the curtains with the remote. Although we were on the top deck, the waves crashed over the balcony and against the windows as though we were trapped in an aquarium.

Abandoning your scruples, you asked if I had any of Frankie's patches. I passed them between our beds, but even that slight movement was precarious, as I found myself raising my hand when I thought I was reaching across. Somehow we must have fallen asleep, because the next thing I knew it was 6 a.m. and the captain was addressing us over the Tannoy. 'Due to the extreme weather conditions,' he announced, 'all passengers are kindly requested to remain in their cabins. The restaurant staff will provide a full room service.' The prospect of food made my stomach heave. Grabbing one of the fallen drawers, I tipped out its contents just in time to vomit.

The drawer remained beside me for the next thirty-six hours, during which I seem to remember our both praying for death, although, in truth, you were little more than a shape on the periphery of my consciousness. At some point, I crawled into the bathroom and peed in the shower because I couldn't summon the strength to haul myself on to the loo. Then, in the early evening of our third day, the tempest stilled with startling abruptness. You drew back the curtains to reveal that the sky had been restored to its rightful position, the gunmetal grey now a silvery blue. My senses were so at sea (ha!) that it took me a while to register that the waves had subsided. Slowly, we regained our bearings, showered, dressed, called for Jacinto to clean the room and, finding to our surprise that we'd also regained our appetite, went down for dinner.

We milled about outside the restaurant, among passengers recounting their experiences of the storm. One large man, with stray strands of hair on an otherwise bald pate like a five-year-old's scribbles, blustered that he'd known worse on the Serpentine. He was shamed into silence when a second man told him that the woman in the cabin adjacent to his had broken her leg when she staggered to the bathroom.

'There'll be no zodiac trips for her.'

'At least she'll be able to enjoy the views from her balcony,' the large man replied.

'There are no balconies on deck three.'

The next morning we made our first landing, on Robert Island, one of the most northerly of the South Shetlands. The landscape was unremarkable, with only scattered patches of snow on its mossy slopes. The wildlife, however, was breathtaking. First, a lone fur seal lolled on a block of ice, much like Cheshire in a sunbeam. Then a vast colony of penguins waddled across the rocks, like miniature Charlie Chaplins. Both the noise, pitched between a honk and a bray, and the stench of ammonia and rotten shrimp made me shudder. Yet as I watched the parent birds regurgitate food for the half-moulted fledglings, the more intrepid of which followed the foraging adults down to the shore, I realised that, for all turmoil of the elements, coupled with the emotional turmoil of being back with you, I was glad to have come on the cruise.

Whereas you kept a precise log of the journey to email to your children and grandchildren each evening, I had only Tara and Rachel and a few friends and neighbours to whom to send cards from Port Lockroy, the southernmost post office in the world. I knew that I'd have to limit my display of snapshots to the occasional penguin, seal or whale. So I ignored the names of individual coves and bays and islands in favour of general impressions: the blush of dawn on the glaciers; the iridescent turquoise of the iceberg-strewn sea; the cobalt blue streaks across a snow-capped mountain. Even when the cold pierced my cheeks like needles and the damp seeped to my marrow, I delighted in the sublime setting, the pure air and the ethereal light. While I struggled to identify the seabirds, except for the wandering albatross (a particular thrill to a woman brought up on Coleridge), I loved to watch the various skuas, shags or whatever, as they shadowed the ship.

One name that has lodged in my mind is Deception Island, although less for the trip ashore than for its after-math. The day began badly, when you upbraided me for refusing to take part in the traditional dip in the thermal waters of Paradise Bay. Instead, I stood with Frankie on the cinder-covered beach, clouds of steam coiling round my legs, before rushing up with a towel and a flask of hot chocolate when you emerged, teeth chattering in the glacial air. We returned to the ship, where the restaurant staff were waiting with plates of goulash. But when I reached for one, you slapped my hand away.

'No, not for you!' you said. 'You don't deserve it.'

Behind us in the queue a woman tittered, although it was plain to me that you weren't joking. Abandoning your plate, you took the lift upstairs. Unsure how far your voice had carried, I was anxious to avoid the other passengers and followed you, playing for time by taking the stairs. As I entered the suite, I heard you running a shower, so I retrieved my book and curled up on the sofa, but the words swam before my eyes and the paragraph made no more sense on the fourth or fifth reading than on the first. You reappeared, wrapped in a bathrobe, a towel turban-ing your hair, and perched on the stool in front of me. I waited for you to speak but, instead, you fixed me with a disconcerting stare.

'I cricked my neck while I was swimming,' you said finally. 'Will you rub it with this wintergreen?'

'Of course,' I replied, surprised by the equanimity of

your tone. I stood behind you, dabbed my fingers in the ointment and loosened the top of your robe, at which, to my further surprise, you untied the belt and let the robe slip off your shoulders. We'd been painstakingly modest around each other, changing in the bathroom so that neither of us should be disturbed, offended (or, dare I say it, aroused?) by a glimpse of naked flesh, and here you were, stripped to the waist. I focussed my attention on the nape of your neck. I felt you responding to my touch, but I was too confused and afraid to acknowledge it, until you twisted round, clasped my hand and cupped it to your breast. Dumbfounded, I continued the same rhythmic rubbing, before I came to my senses, leant over and kissed you.

'Oh, your lips are chapped!' you said.

'So are yours,' I mumbled, loath to break away.

'It's not fair. You have me at a disadvantage. You're fully dressed.'

You pulled me into the bedroom, where I peeled off my multiple layers: fleece and woollies, waterproof trousers, two pairs of socks and leggings, down to my thermal underwear. Far from performing a seductive striptease, I felt as though I were mimicking the antics of a pantomime dame.

We slipped into your bed and, with the temperature a steady twenty-five degrees, I couldn't pretend to be shivering from the cold. I'd given you no more than a discreet peck on the cheek in thirty years, and now my hands were free to roam at will. Our bodies had changed, and we had the scars to prove it: yours from the C section; mine from the laparotomy. You were fuller around the hips and thighs and crinklier under the arms. I feared that you would find me scrawny, but the moment we embraced, it was evident that the changes were skin-deep.

We giggled a lot and spoke very little. You'd always preferred to make love in silence and after so long apart, reflexes were safer than words. We clung together as the sky outside darkened. I'd have been content to lie in your arms all night, but we couldn't cancel dinner with the Parkers, given Jane's broken leg.

'You both have some colour in your cheeks,' Frankie called out from the captain's table. 'Deception Island must have worked its magic.'

'Do you think she heard us?' you whispered, as we hurried past. 'The walls can't be all that thick.'

'Of course not. Besides, we've made more noise eating breakfast.'

After dinner, we left Jane and Douglas to enjoy the cocktail pianist, while we retreated to the suite and a bracingly sleepless night. The following day, we sailed through the Lemaire Channel. Despite your suspicions of 'the witch next door,' we stood on the balcony, listening to the crunch of the ship gouging through the pack ice, and the rumble of snow sweeping down the mountainsides. We watched a pod of humpback whales, the size and shape of primitive submarines, spouting, breaching and diving, but when Janine announced over the Tannoy that an orange orca calf had been spotted to starboard, we chose to stay put, our hands tightly clasped on the balustrade.

The next morning, we crossed the Antarctic circle and made what turned out to be our final landing, on Detaille Island. While the more adventurous passengers, including Guy and the Jefferies, trekked up what Janine warned them was a deceptively gentle incline, the rest of us visited a former British Antarctic Survey base camp, which had been abandoned in haste when its supply ship became icebound. It had remained untouched since 1959, with socks and long johns hanging in the bunk-room and copies of *Weekend*, *John Bull* and *Star Weekly* open in the operations room. Most poignant of all were the Scotch Oats, HP sauce, Horlicks and Bovril in the larder, which made me nostalgic for foodstuffs I'd never even liked. I fear that I betrayed my shallowness since, while you extolled the majesty of nature, I was imagining the stories behind the empty bottles of gin.

Unlike those sequestered scientists, we couldn't escape what was happening in the wider world. I sometimes felt like the only passenger not in regular email contact with home. News of the pandemic was grim. We were sitting at dinner with Frankie, who was wearing yet another sumptuous outfit, Elliot and Rhoda, who'd just uploaded a video of the Deception Island swim, and Jane and Douglas, who'd spent the afternoon on deck playing draughts, when Guy, who possessed a seemingly inexhaustible supply of internet access cards, reported what he'd read on Facebook. He grew almost animated as he described how, in the nine days since we'd embarked, the number of Covid cases globally had exceeded 300,000, including more than 10,000 deaths.

'This really is the safest place to be. I'd be more than happy never to leave the ship,' I said, giving you a meaningful glance.

'I wouldn't be so sure,' Frankie said, stroking Guy's cheek.

'What do you mean?' you asked sharply. I suspected that Frankie's proximity to her grandson underlined your separation from yours.

'As always, the first thing I did was make friends with my steward. There's not much gets past him. He used to be a lawyer in Manila, but he earns more money here, which he needs to support a son with Down's and a cousin with leukaemia, though that's by the by. He says there've been six cases of fever on board (four passengers and two crew) – some with coughs and chills, some with vomiting, some with diarrhoea. But the captain's instructed the doctor to downplay it.'

'Nonsense,' you replied. 'That would be totally unprofessional, as well as a violation of his oath.'

Whether from solidarity with a colleague or concern for your distant family, you were out of sorts and our lovemaking that night was perfunctory. I drifted off quickly, only for you to banish me from the bed in the early hours because you were hot and cramped. I lay awake listening to you wheeze but, when I asked if you wanted anything, you stifled a cough and feigned sleep. The next morning, your face was flushed, eyes red and nose streaming, but you dismissed my worries, pulling rank and claiming that the air conditioning irritated your chest. We went down for breakfast, but you left early, grumbling that the kedgeree tasted like wallpaper paste and the toast like cardboard. Returning to the suite, I found you stretched out on your bed in the throes of a coughing fit.

'You're wasting his time,' you said, when I insisted on calling the doctor. 'He'll simply tell me to rest and keep hydrated.' As it turned out, you were right, but I was grateful for his proficiency and, as I followed him into the corridor, I took the opportunity to voice my fears.

'Do you think it might be Covid?' I asked hesitantly. 'It seems most unlikely. I mean . . . how? But both last night and this morning in the dining room, there were all sorts of rumours doing the rounds.'

'It's impossible to know, since the additional sanitary measures the company assured me they'd put in place didn't include testing kits. All I can tell you is that there are nine similar cases on board—'

'Nine? I thought it was six.'

'It was.'

For the rest of the day I sat by your bedside, praying for a sign that the fever would break. Instead, it worsened as you complained of headaches, nausea and a sunburn-like sting on your cheeks. You were living proof that doctors make the worst patients, railing against me when I brought you drinks and flatly refusing to swallow more than a spoonful of the soup I'd ordered. You accused me of smothering you, and I wish that that had been the only reason for your shortness of breath. Although we were both baffled as to how you'd contracted the virus, we had no doubt about what it was. Your greatest fear was infecting me. So, for your peace of mind and my own protection, I scoured every surface three times after you tottered to the loo and washed my hands whenever I touched you, even singing the recommended two rounds of 'Happy Birthday'. Given that we'd shared a bedroom, to say nothing of a bed, I had little hope of remaining healthy, but the longer I did, the more use I would be to you.

The next morning, the captain addressed us over the

Tannoy, insisting that there was no cause for alarm, but
following an outbreak of fever on board, he had taken the
decision to abort the cruise. The *Ocean Spirit* was leaving Antarctic waters and would no longer call at South
Georgia or the Falklands but instead head straight back
to Ushuaia. All being well, we would arrive there in five
days' time. What he failed to mention was whether we'd
be allowed to dock. On the 15th of March, three days after
we set sail, the Argentinian president had announced
the closure of his country's borders for fifteen days.
We'd calculated that they would reopen just in time for
our return. But that return had been brought forward.
One part of me – a romantic part, which I thought had
long been silenced – wondered whether we were to be
a ghost ship destined to roam the seas forever, like the
Flying Dutchman or, more fittingly given the birdlife,
Coleridge's *Speedwell*. The rational part retorted that that
was not so much romantic as adolescent, and ordered
lunch.

Passengers were once again confined to their cabins,
and I felt for those on the lower decks with no balconies.
Even Frankie and Guy's tempers were fraying, judging
by the muffled shouts that filtered through the wall. My
heart ached for the Parkers, who had been planning their
Falklands expedition for decades, only to return home with
nothing to show for it but Jane's broken leg. My overriding
concern, however, was you. I couldn't bear to think that
we might have reconnected, only to be torn apart. I'm not
naïve. I didn't expect that at sixty-four you would abandon
your family and friends and move to Lincoln, or invite
me to live with you in Sherborne. But I did envision our

spending weekends and holidays together, maybe even following Frankie on the cruise circuit.

'Not on your life!' I hear you saying. 'Anything but that.'

Fever rampaged through the crew as well as the passengers, but according to Frankie, unless they worked in the galley or their symptoms were severe, they were required to remain on duty. She added that since they'd spent almost a month at sea with no shore leave in Ushuaia, they blamed the passengers for bringing the infection on board. Any signs of resentment were concealed behind the napkins and scarves that served as makeshift masks when, three times a day, they delivered meals to our door.

The only person to enter the cabin was the doctor. He brought you paracetamol, throat lozenges and his last antihistamine spray, although he described it to me as 'whistling in the wind', his words accentuated by the violent squall lashing the ship. He told me that there were now more than fifty cases on board, the most serious being Douglas Parker, who needed supplementary oxygen. Given that it took me all my time to chivvy you to drink, keep you fresh, and change your sheets (in the face of hurtful protests), as well as scrubbing myself with soap and the bathroom with bleach, I wondered how the injured Jane would cope. The doctor promised to report back on his next visit, but he never came. That evening, Janine announced that 'our valiant doctor is on the sick list. From now on the waitstaff will bring any medicines with your meals.' As she urged us all to continue sharing our positive energy, I experienced my bleakest moment yet.

Your skin had turned the colour of parchment, but your temperature remained stable at around 39.3. I managed to

coax you on to the balcony, parroting my mother's plati-
tudes about the benefits of sea air but, even clad in a fleece,
down jacket and parka and wrapped in blankets, you
complained of the cold. When I helped you back to bed, I
found you drenched in sweat. As I sponged and dried you,
you begged my forgiveness for putting me through this and
promised to make it up to me on our return. Then, clasping
my hand, you told me that the greatest regret of your life
was abandoning me. Although I suspect that that was the
fever talking, not the heart.

Either because of the small complement of passengers
or our isolation in the South Atlantic, or else because Covid
was now so widespread that another infected cruise ship
had little news value, your children's emails gave no indica-
tion that people at home were aware of our plight. To spare
them unnecessary worry, I agreed to keep up the corre-
spondence in your name. After consulting the guidebook, I
described imaginary visits to the penguin colony on Paulet
Island and the Shackleton memorial on Elephant Island,
although I feared that my creative powers would desert
me when it came to the Falklands. Glancing through your
recent messages to capture the desired tone, I was moved
by your flattering comments about me, not least when you
assured Beth that 'Aunt Carla is a far easier companion
than your father – and not just because she doesn't snore!'

The ever-resourceful Janine assembled a programme
of entertainment, which was streamed to our cabins.
Dennis Richards, the ornithologist and only lecturer still
standing, gave three talks on the birds of the southern
hemisphere. The pastry chef demonstrated how to make
floating islands, tarte tatin and tiramisu, and the hotel

director taught the art of napkin folding. There were two dedicated film channels, with a disconcerting preponderance of disaster movies, which I had neither the time nor the temperament to watch. My main respite was chatting to Frankie. Shielded by the Perspex balcony divider, we tracked the mounting number of casualties, like characters in an Agatha Christie novel, and compared the progress of our patients. Given that nursing came even less naturally to her than to me, it was fortunate that Guy's symptoms were mild. As he rallied, he grew increasingly fractious, raging against the confinement, the boredom, the food and, above all, his grandmother.

'As soon as I get out of this hell-hole, I'm going to sue you for everything you've got,' he shrieked one afternoon.

'Whatever happened to "blood is thicker than water"?' I asked, as she hastily shut the balcony door.

'Thank you for not suspecting anything.'

'What is there to suspect?'

It was then that she confessed the truth: Guy wasn't her grandson but a paid escort. 'I have two daughters from my first marriage, both of whom hate me, and five grandchildren, two of whom I've never met. I need young people around me. Their vitality . . . their passion is what keeps me alive. And yes, we do sleep together, in case you're wondering.' I affected nonchalance. 'Do you think me very wicked?'

'Not at all.' I wasn't sure what I felt, other than a genuine admiration for her spirit and a grudging one for her ability to keep up the facade.

'Promise you won't say anything to Henrietta. It will only confirm her low opinion of me.'

I gave her my word, and I only wish that I were breaking it now. For an instant I thought of repaying her confidence by telling her about us, but I pictured your distressed face and the moment passed. Moreover, despite my regard for Frankie, I refused to equate her secret with ours.

As we'd suspected, the Argentinian ports remained closed, forcing the captain to sail to Uruguay. Here too we were denied entry, and he anchored twelve miles off the coast of Montevideo. In his regular briefings, he assured us that the cruise company was in close contact with the Uruguayan authorities, who were eager to assist, but protests against cruise ships had erupted worldwide and they feared riots on the dockside if we were permitted to disembark. As the deadlock dragged on, they sent a pilot boat with medical supplies, protective equipment, and a team of doctors to treat the sick and test for Covid.

'Where are the people smugglers when you need them?' Frankie quipped.

Soon afterwards, Reuters reported our predicament. Less helpfully (at least for me), our mobile signals returned at around the same time and within an hour all three of your children called. No longer able to prevaricate, I did my best to prepare them before passing the phone to you. Nevertheless, they were horrified by your few stuttered words in a cacophony of coughs and croaks. Robin swung into action, calling back three hours later to say that he'd spoken to both the British Embassy and a colleague in the Uruguayan office of Citibank, who promised to put pressure on the government through his contacts in the ministry of finance.

The following morning, he rang to tell me that the

British Hospital in Montevideo had agreed to admit you and arrangements were underway for your transfer from the ship. While greatly relieved, I was puzzled by the hospital's name, until Robin explained, impatiently, that it had been founded in the nineteenth century for Uruguay's prominent British colony. During the Falklands War, wounded British servicemen had been airlifted there for treatment. In a bitter irony, one of the contingent of three passengers and two crew members who were being admitted alongside you was Douglas Parker. Unable to visit the battlefield where his son had been shot, he was now to be a patient in the hospital where he'd died.

My last glimpse of you was on a stretcher being lifted into the perilously rocky pilot boat. As a mere travel companion, I received no information from the hospital, but Alice texted me that evening with an update, which was grave. You'd suffered gastrointestinal bleeding and kidney failure and been placed in an induced coma. The next forty-eight hours would be critical. It was then that I began this account of the voyage. Addressing it to you was my way of keeping you alive.

Even now that I've received the news I most dreaded, I feel compelled to continue writing. To nobody's surprise, I tested positive for Covid, as did seventy of our fellow passengers, although not Frankie. So far I've remained asymptomatic, and my fatigue has been purely emotional.

I know that dates and times are no longer your concern, but I include them for the sake of completeness. We were kept in quarantine during the lengthy negotiations for our return. Then on the 10th of April, we learnt that a plane had been chartered to take us to Miami, where a second plane would be waiting to fly us home. I packed both our suitcases and gave our leftover currency to Frankie's fund for the family of her steward, who had also died in hospital. We disembarked, to be whisked on to buses and rushed to the airport. The authorities had cordoned off the road, ensuring that there was no traffic, but long stretches were lined by Uruguayans who, far from protesting at our presence, cheered and clapped.

'Why on earth are they doing it?' Frankie asked me across the aisle.

'Sympathy? Solidarity?' I suggested. 'Because they too have suffered and survived?'

'Because they're peasants with no other excitement in their lives,' Guy interjected from two rows behind.

In Miami, I said goodbye to Elliot and Rhoda, who'd curbed their wanderlust 'until conditions improve,' and, at Heathrow, to Jane Parker, who was too heavily sedated to say more than that she would be staying with a cousin while they awaited news of Douglas. After living cheek by jowl for so long, Frankie and I risked a kiss in the baggage hall, to be told by Guy that the only safe contact was an elbow bump.

'Not with my joints,' Frankie replied.

To my surprise, Alice was waiting for me in the arrivals hall. I was deeply moved that, despite her grief, she had thought to meet me. She explained that she had come with Robin and Beth to collect your coffin which, unbeknownst to me, had been transported in the aircraft hold. Steadying myself on my trolley, I choked back my tears. She added that her brother and sister had gone with the undertaker to customs, but she'd wanted to make certain I had everything I needed. I assured her I had.

I attended your funeral via Zoom. I chose the conservatory as the most chapel-like room in the house and watched as Alice, Robin and his wife, Beth and her husband, Rose, and a gnarled-looking woman whom I took to be your aunt (Hilary or Hilda?), sat as if estranged in a church that should have been filled with family and friends, colleagues and patients, and Alwyn's former parishioners. Alice tells me that they're planning a memorial service once the pandemic ends.

Meanwhile, you may be amused to know that I received a letter from the cruise company, offering me a free voyage ('of commensurate value') when travel restrictions are lifted. I forwarded it to Alice. Not only did your children pay for the trip, but I couldn't imagine myself or any of the passengers on the *Ocean Spirit* ever setting foot on board again.

That was to reckon without the indefatigable Frankie. We've kept in touch, and when I called to express my disgust at the company's token gesture, she told me that she'd already written to accept.

'You win some; you lose some. I don't intend to stay at home a moment longer than necessary. I've made provisional bookings for the Black Sea in August and the Caribbean in October.'

'Will you be taking Guy?'

'What do you think?' she asked, with the same throaty chuckle as on our first meeting. 'He's ancient history. But I'm sure I can persuade another grandson to join me.'

In the Event of

W HAT WORDING WILL you use on my death-site, Mother? *Much loved daughter of Edward and Susan* . . . that is your prerogative. *Sister of the late lamented Sarah* . . . that would be more contentious. *Aged twenty-two* or *twenty-two squared* . . . *Cruelly taken from us in a freak accident* . . . that depends on your credit with your fellow arbiters. *Family messages only* . . . that may solve the immediate problem but could give rise to heresy sites, and we both know where those lead.

History does not repeat itself. All life extends to infinity. Those in the top bar can expect regeneration, while the rest can look forward to painless non-existence, their experiences filed in the collective memory. Suicide is said to have been eradicated from the Controlled World, along with shame, despair and God. So what went wrong: for me, for you, for Sarah? She is the unseen factor in our family equation. Her death-site was deleted, but her death has dominated our lives. You will ask yourself through your tears – I do not speak lightly – how we could both have chosen such a savage, antisocial way to die.

Your friends will rally round you. Once the alerts are posted, your mailbox will brim with condolences. I trust that you will remember to warn the authorities and prevent another crash, like the one that followed Father's gold service bar. It will be hard for people to find the appropriate words, even with the aid of the sentiment check. As they speak of your grief, they will doubtless be thinking of my ingratitude: how you might have used your loyalty bar to obtain a place on the Lazarus list but preferred to secure your immortality by another route . . . one that has turned out to be a dead end.

I do not deny that I was born with every advantage. Our dom was on base two of the Bunker, a floor above the primes. Your top-bar status entitled us to optimum nutrition and access to all levels of Life Services. We had exclusive use of two sub-Saharans, whom I know that several of your friends considered feckless, but I shared your belief that, while they might not have been as reliable as animatrons, they had their own distinct qualities. Besides, you maintained that as an arbiter, you were obliged to take a lead in helping aliens, just as you were in recycling waste. To allay further misgivings, you explained that before being licensed to come to us, they had undergone a strict six-month quarantine and were both sterilised and sterile.

To the best of my recollection, my early childhood was untroubled. You enrolled me in playgroup at the age of three, telling me later that, unlike most children who shrank from the unfamiliar faces on the screen, I at once began to make friends. The group was, of course, restricted to the children of top-bar parents: arbiters, innovators, and tribunes. Even there, however, I was privileged. Father's job ensured that I was among the first to be allotted one of the new-generation playtrons. This unleashed a storm of jealousy in the group, with one mother threatening to withdraw her son unless I kept the toy off-screen. Father pledged my compliance, apologising for any upset we'd caused, although I suspect that he was secretly pleased to have had the chance to display his prestige. Such local difficulties aside, you were both free to devote yourselves to your work, confident that I was occupying my time constructively.

I would be the last to complain of parental neglect. The balance between my emotional and intellectual development was constantly monitored. While you were no doubt influenced by your experience with Sarah, most of my friends reported a similar routine, mocking the overprotectiveness of their top-bar parents, who had them regularly examined by a team of medical, behavioural, nutritional, social and technical assessors. You even employed image enhancers to retouch my avatar every two months, ensuring that I presented the best version of myself. For all of which I thank you.

Constancy, control and contentment were the watchwords of our world, and I had the good fortune to enjoy all three. I remember the first time I felt pain, an experience so singular that it seared itself on my brain. One of the sub-Saharans – who had, after all, been selected for their dexterity – dropped a plate on my foot. My screams brought you running from your desk. I can still picture her anguish when you excluded her on the spot, refusing to reconsider, even after the medical assessor declared that no bones had been broken and the behavioural assessor that, with skilled counselling, I would suffer no long-term trauma. Looking back, I would swear that her replacement arrived the next day, but I know that I must be mistaken since you would never have hired anyone who hadn't been fully decontaminated and reprogrammed.

An even more tenacious memory, one that resisted concerted attempts to dismiss it as a figment of my imagination or an early screen story I had muddled with time-life, was of my first meeting with Arthur; a meeting that has remained unexplained until now. I was playing in the hall, when a sub-Saharan admitted two strangers. She later swore that she had taken them for neighbours. but even though the interrogator believed her, you had her excluded. The pair were a boy, little older than myself, and a man who might have been his father. They were oddly dressed, with old-fashioned breathing equipment like fishbowls. His clothes apart, the boy looked much like any of my friends, but glimpses of the man's wrists and scalp revealed pronounced wrinkles and blotches. I know now that these were signs of age, but in our stories, even grandparents had smooth skin and luxuriant hair.

'It's uncanny,' the man said. 'You're her twin.' The boy stepped forward to touch me, at which point the sub-Saharan realised her mistake and pressed the alarm. The man grabbed the boy and ran off, pursued by the custodians. I was less frightened by the intrusion than by your subsequent panic. You claimed that the pair were surface people who had infiltrated the Controlled World either through bribery or a chink in the ventilation system. I quickly realised that I must ask no more questions or risk causing you distress. I tried instead to discuss the matter with my friends but, as though I had violated regulations, the signal cut off. After that, you made me promise not to mention the incident to anyone. I kept my word, but I never stopped thinking about it. For all the air of mystery, it thrilled more than it threatened.

Shortly afterwards, my friend Judith disclosed the secret of my identity. You have since told me that I should never feel inferior for having been cloned. In which case, why did you hide it from me for so long? According to the site – and you have always done everything by the site – parents should reveal a clone's origins by the age of five. Yet you left me to hear it from Judith, who'd heard it from her parents. We were chatting much as usual, when I said something to annoy her. She replied that what I thought wasn't important because I was going to die young. Instantly, the screen went blank. I knew about death and dying from stories, of course, but my direct experience was limited to playtrons that had short-circuited. Even though they were rapidly replaced, I was left with a profound sense of loss.

I had never imagined anything like that happening to me, so I asked you about it during the evening nutrition. The sad, shocked expressions on your and Father's faces attested to the seriousness of the matter. You refused to discuss it that night, but you both took the next day off work, accompanying me to the screen room, where you accessed a specially coded site . . . the first of the many specials to which I was about to be introduced. We listened, while a velvet-voiced woman spelt out the party line on clones. She insisted that, far from being derided as freaks of science, we should be regarded as an elite, since our replication was both genetically and socially exclusive. She urged us to be grateful to our parents, who had not only undergone an exacting assessment process and a range of invasive tests, but had made a substantial financial sacrifice.

I myself was subjected to such frequent assessment that the knowledge that you had been put through a similar process was not as compelling an argument as it might have been. Nevertheless, I sat quietly until the end of the talk when you asked if I had any questions. 'Yes! Yes, I do. Yes, I have. Who am I? If I am not me and your daughter, then what am I? Am I a unique clone or one of many? Are there other Sarahs scattered about the Bunker?' For I soon found out that you had given me not just my sister's genes, but her name; a fact that both comforted and dismayed me.

I doubt that at the time my questions were so neatly phrased, but however much I overstate my articulacy, it is impossible to overstate my desire for the truth. To be fair, you didn't equivocate but explained that you and Father were indeed my biological parents. Having lost a daughter aged twenty-two to a rare virus, you had been so heart-broken that you devoted all your energy and resources to recreating her.

My first thought was 'Why didn't you have another child?' Top-bar parents were authorised to have two children and, while happy enough with my playtrons, I longed for a time-life sister or brother. You described, as candidly as you could to a seven-year-old, how you had been unable to conceive again. Like most top-bar women, you had opted for a uterine pregnancy, but an infection after Sarah's birth had damaged your fallopian tubes.

I did not dispute your assertion that no child had ever been more loved; although over time I began to wonder whether you loved me for my sister or for myself, not least because I was increasingly confused as to who that self was. Given that you were so determined to create an exact clone that you'd not only harvested Sarah's DNA but used it to fertilise one of her own eggs, then surely, in loving me, you were simply loving her?

Once I knew the truth about Sarah, you sanctioned other people to talk about her. The unanimous view was that she had been an exceptional person: kind and loving, intelligent and beautiful; all attributes designed to encourage me, but all, except for the last, having the opposite effect. One of my friends used to complain about being compared to her older sister, but it was far more unnerving to be compared to my older self. I was afraid that I would fail to live up to her and invalidate your sacrifice. While my biology set studied the respective influence of nature and nurture on human development, I felt myself to be a prisoner of both: not only formed from the same genetic material as Sarah, but living in the same environment with parents who treated me in the same way.

My greatest fear was of dying young, not because, as Judith had insinuated, very few clones have so far lived out their natural span, let alone been eligible for a place on the Lazarus list, but because I was convinced that my replication of Sarah would extend to dying at the same age. I was particularly alarmed by the mention of a virus. I knew, of course, about screen viruses – the Moderator regularly declared them to be our number one threat – but I had never heard of their affecting people.

You sought to reassure me, insisting that Sarah's death was the direct result of her having moved to her own dom. You and Father had been opposed to it, since for one thing she could afford nowhere lower than base eight. But she had been resolute, alternately cajoling and pleading (so much for Little Miss Perfect, though I knew better than to say so!). She had joined two friends, a girl and a herm, but, as Father explained, like so many young people, they neglected to look after themselves. There had been a problem with the screen filtration system, a virus mutated and Sarah died.

Conscious of the pain it caused you, I took care not to broach the subject again. Instead, I questioned Grandmother who, initially evasive, referred to Sarah's death as a *tragedy*. The term was unfamiliar to me and when I searched the dictionary, I found that it had been blacked out. So I asked you (maybe you remember), but rather than explaining, you demanded to know where I'd heard it. To protect Grandmother, I said that it was in one of the stories I was reading. You looked sceptical. After all, it was your job to ensure that such archaisms were excised from the screen. Nevertheless, you gave me an explanation of sorts, describing *tragedy* as an old-fashioned word for *sadness*, with violent overtones, which had no place in the Controlled World.

I am sure that you suspected Grandmother, since you closely monitored our next few sessions of kinship chat. My biggest worry was that you might forbid me to attend her eightieth birthday party in the summer. I was wild with anticipation, since it would be only my third ever journey out of the dom. The first, of course, had been to watch Father collect his gold service bar at the Tribunal, and the second to make my vows at the Junior Citizenship ceremony at the Grand Rotunda. It was my good fortune that, for propaganda purposes, the Moderator had decided to hold the ceremony in public that year. It remains one of the most memorable days of my life, marred only by my failure to meet up with any of my friends, either because their image enhancement had been too rigorous for me to recognise them or because, notwithstanding the packs of custodians, their parents had refused to let them linger outdoors.

The new trip promised to be even more momentous, since we were not only travelling to another bunker, but staying for an entire week. Despite the discomfort and delays of the transit, the repeated decontamination checks, the chafing of our biosuits and the custodians' sniffing, I relished the journey. My excitement soared on reaching Grandmother's dom, which was larger than ours, although two bases higher and less efficient. It took me a while to realise that when she spoke of housework, Grandmother meant the things that she did for the house rather than the house did for her. Her only dom-help was an old-fashioned serviteur, about which you were scathing. 'Let's have one thing or the other,' you said, 'a sub-Saharan or an anima-tron. This is the worst of both worlds.'

No sooner had we entered the dom than Father started coughing. He claimed that the dust irritated his chest, but I was sure that it was Grandmother, who irritated him far more in person than she did on screen. I was embarrassed that he made his feelings so obvious, but I couldn't deny that Grandmother was a disappointment. Although her image enhancement had been crude and often out of synch, it was a shock to see her so grey and gaunt and smelling faintly of damp. I whispered to you that the best birthday present we could give her was a cell regeneration course, but you replied that, even if we could afford it, she was ineligible, being only in bar two. She had asked for a cat – a time-life cat to replace the one she had recently lost, but you told her it was perverse to want something that was expensive to feed, difficult to control, bad for the environment and prone to disease, rather than a low-energy, low-maintenance petron. When she refused even to consider one, you added that her stubbornness had blighted your life.

The most fascinating feature of Grandmother's dom was that it spanned two floors. I was forbidden to go upstairs, ostensibly on account of the poor ventilation, but more probably, as I soon discovered, because it was crammed with books. At first I was confused by seeing familiar names: *Pollyanna*, *Jane Eyre* and *Pippi Longstocking* in an unfamiliar setting. Instead of compact files to click on and scroll through, they were unwieldy objects with pages to turn by hand. Moreover, on opening them, rather than a soothing voice narrating the story, I had to struggle with the print. Every few lines, I had to put down the book to let my thoughts catch up with the words.

Even so, I knew that I had stumbled on something of value. I sneaked three of the books down to my room and, putting my playtron on full blast to distract you, seized every spare moment to read. I began with *Jane Eyre*, which I'd enjoyed on screen but found so much richer on the page. The differences were profound. Far from being pretty, Jane here described herself as plain, which had the unexpected effect of making her more likeable. Mrs Rochester wasn't working on a farm after losing her memory, but locked up like a mad dog in the attic of Thornfield Hall. When Jane returned there after the fire (which had been started intentionally), she discovered that Mr Rochester wasn't merely suffering from heatstroke but was blind.

I was startled and disturbed, confused yet elated, curious to know how Grandmother had come by such treasures. One day when, despite your disparagement of Life Services in Bunker G, you and Father were both connected in interspace, I questioned her. She was reluctant to speak out for fear of displeasing you but, when pressed, she explained that she had preserved her parents' library, from a time when books were read for the words as well as the stories. She recalled how you had loved them as a girl and, later, so had Sarah. Your name came as a surprise, but Sarah's was an inspiration; her love for books validating mine. Warning me to keep them hidden, Grandmother gave me *Jane Eyre*, *Ballet Shoes* and *Cold Comfort Farm* to take home. Her last and most precious gift was a link to three heresy sites, which published books unarbited.

My efforts to conceal the contraband were no match for the scanners. You were outraged, railing against my duplicity. Father spoke of the selfishness of hoarding paper at a time when the last remaining trees in Constitution Square were dying. You spoke of your deep hurt that your own daughter should so denigrate your life's work as to choose to read books which, in their primitive state, were inimical to personal growth and civic harmony. When I mentioned that Sarah had enjoyed the same books, you accused me of deliberate malice.

This marked the start of my rebellion. I know that I'm passing over scores of smaller incidents, but a suicide note calls for a certain succinctness. Grandmother died before I could sound her out further, but her revelations about Sarah had confirmed my suspicions that the dutiful daughter existed only in your and Father's minds. She too had defied your ban on unarbited books. What had they meant to her? With no one to ask, all I could do was explore the heresy sites for myself, finding beauty even in works that I barely understood. Taking my cue from the sites, I created alternative histories to cover my tracks. I grew ever more secretive and withdrawn. Were these feelings unique to me or universal in adolescence? There's a word that you didn't expect to see here. Why have you and your colleagues erased it from controlled speech? How can you hope to understand the feelings if you proscribe the words?

Death haunted me. I was terrified of an afterlife; not of punishment (I never became so beguiled by my reading as to believe in God), but of the prospect of your cloning me again. I posted files in a private mailbox and made you promise to pass them on to the next Sarah, to spare her similar soul-searching. You pleaded with me not to torment you. You swore that you would never survive the death of a second child, much less be able to carry a third. Ever practical, I pointed out that that was no obstacle, since you could simply opt for a laboratory birth or enlist a sub-Saharan. That was when that Father intervened, declaring that even if all else were equal, you couldn't afford it because you were still making the final payments on me. You added bitterly that, in any case, you had learnt your lesson; it would be throwing good money after bad.

You nevertheless paid for me to attend a clone support group, commending it as the highest rated in all Life Services. I logged on for my initial session with a mixture of curiosity and truculence. It was the first time I'd knowingly met any of my fellow clones. I'd often wondered whether any of my friends were like me. With more than three thousand names in my address book, it stood to reason that some must have been, but it always felt insensitive to ask.

On the evidence, my fellow clones were not the best balanced of people – but then, if they had been, they wouldn't have needed support. There were five of us. Our convenor, Jeremy (who also ran a group for uterine twins), said that he wanted to keep the sessions intimate, but Joeıluckless, our most recalcitrant member, insisted it was rather that no one else could afford the fees.

Joe's donor had been an actor from the era before animatrons, a notion that the others found bizarre, but having read the unarbited *Cold Comfort Farm*, I knew that it was once the norm. Joe's story made mine seem almost commonplace. A tribune's widow had fallen in love with his donor after secretly screening some of his films. Sparing no expense, she sent a team of gene-jackers to the Surface World to have him illicitly cloned. She raised Joe as her son until he turned eighteen, when she demanded that he become her lover. He was traumatised. Not only had he known her as his mother, but he felt a strong, albeit unexpressed, attraction to his cousin. He was at a loss to explain it, until he read on a heresy site that, contrary to his screen persona, his donor had been a herm. He informed the widow, who accused him of fraud and threatened him with exclusion.

My closest ally in the group was Jean, who had been cloned by her own daughter. She'd claimed to be so devoted to her mother that she couldn't face the future without her but, according to Jean, her actions suggested the opposite. Nothing but blind hatred and a desire for revenge could explain her rigid control over Jean's nutritional

prescriptions and her monitoring of her Life Services, not
to mention equipping her, at seventeen, with the avatar of
a twelve-year-old, which made girls her own age dismissive
of her and boys afraid to talk to her.

The remaining members were Ruby, a twenty-year-
old, who rejected image enhancement to display her badly
scarred face, and Stanley, a twenty-three-year-old, who
appeared only in silhouette. It turned out that both of their
donors had been treated by the same backstreet geneticist.
Stanley's donor had been a champion boxer before the ban
on contact sports. About twenty-five years ago – you'll find
all the details in the memory cache – there were moves
to relax the ban, and he had himself cloned in readiness
for a comeback. In the event, the ban was upheld and he
took out his frustration on Stanley, the constant reminder
of his crushed hopes. When Stanley grew old enough to
fight back, the man threw him out, leaving him to fend
for himself in the hinterlands, until he was rescued by an
anti-cloning activist, who signed him up for the group.

I had never known anyone as angry as Stanley, whose
violent outbursts against his donor prompted Jeremy to
warn that the group would be shut down if it breached
Life Services rules. He did, however, form a close bond
with Ruby, whose story neatly chimed with his own. Her
donor, an avatar model, had brought her up with exceptional severity, regulating her every impulse, even denying
her independent access to a screen until the welfare assessors intervened. When Ruby was ten, her donor began
dressing them alike, in a vain attempt to bridge the age
gap, although she waited until she turned eighteen to
reveal the full extent of her plan. This was to train Ruby

for another three years and then kill herself, entrusting Ruby, now at the peak of her beauty, with her stellar career. Horrified, Ruby had grabbed a knife and gouged her cheeks. Deprived of her destiny, the donor took an overdose, leaving Ruby consumed by guilt.

Saying nothing to the rest of us, Ruby and Stanley started to meet outside the sessions. Then, one day, with a mixture of diffidence (her) and defiance (him), they announced that they had fallen in love and intended to quit the group. Whether because he feared that he would never again achieve such a result or else that their relationship was doomed to failure, Jeremy chose to dissolve the group. He assured Joe, Jean and me that, while as clones we might feel especially vulnerable, our concerns about the loss of selfhood were common throughout the Controlled World. I later heard that he went on to run an animatron dependence group, but I've been unable to confirm it.

I scarcely need to remind you that the next two or three years were painful for us all. Like Ruby, I was deeply disturbed by my dual identity, although I directed my anger toward you rather than myself. To everyone's relief, when I turned eighteen, you and Father allowed me to move into my own dom with a girl and boy from my citizenship group. I would have preferred a herm, not least for symmetry, but with the success of the realignment programme, they were harder to find. I lost my hymen to a junior innovator and built up my immunity to the opposite sex. I made friends in time-life and joined a group of tectonic explorers, who made unauthorised climbs to the Surface World. My dom-mates urged caution, citing the twin dangers of capture by the custodians and exposure to disease. I don't know whether it was the Sarah in me or just the 'me', but I scoffed at their warnings and embarked on a strict fitness regime.

The night of my first sortie arrived. We broke into Transit Depot Three and clambered on to a freight train. As we hurtled through the labyrinth of service tunnels and into the hinterlands, I felt like an avatar in a heresy game. We stopped at a large purification complex, where our leader (no names, no scapegoats) ushered us into an unscanned ventilation shaft. I scaled the vertical ladder, my senses alternately heightened and numbed. Suddenly, I felt a drop in the pressure and my head was flooded with light. A hand gripped my shoulders and hauled me to the surface. I gazed up into infinity. The landscape was vast and varied, but all I could see was the sky. I realised how constricted my life had been in the Bunker, where the only escape was on screen. I felt an intense desire to tear off my mask and drink in the air. But it wasn't the time for suicidal gestures . . . at least not yet.

We trudged over cratered roads to the meeting-point, a cracked concrete pillar, which was incongruously known as the flyover. Sitting on a broken block in the biting wind, I felt a pang of regret for our ergonomic chairs and regulation 22.5 degrees temperature, but that vanished when a gang, a dozen or so strong, emerged from behind the pillar. Although they outnumbered us three to one and were on home ground, I wasn't scared. Despite everything we had been taught about surface people, it was clear that they were no different from us. Physically, of course, they were bulkier, even though we were encased in biosuits and they were wearing skins. Their flesh was darker, not sub-Saharan but tanned. Their faces were more animated than those I was accustomed to: time-life people, as well as avatars. For all their dirt and dishevelment, they exuded a strength and vitality that were most attractive. One man in particular stirred feelings in me that I had supposed existed only in books.

It soon became apparent that the feelings were mutual. After a brief awkwardness, we began talking as frankly as old friends. I listened, horrified yet enthralled, as he described his daily life: the constant threats from hostile tribes, feral dogs, and hazardous waste. One of the gang overheard and teased him. 'Come off it, Arthur. Anyone would think you were trying to turn the girl's head.' He blushed (something else I had encountered only in books), which I now recognise as the moment I fell in love. He spoke of their struggle to build a new world from the ruins of the old, rejecting both the creeds and technologies that had caused so much harm. You might claim to be doing the same but, whereas you burrow like a termite underground, he was willing to suffer, even to die, to preserve freedom.

He invited me home to meet his father. Although I felt sure that he had an ulterior motive, I accepted without hesitation. Perhaps there was something in my blood, as there had been in Sarah's, that drew me to strangers or perhaps – irony of ironies – an unmediated childhood memory had left me with a fascination for surface people. Either way, I quit my companions with the promise to be back by nightfall and walked with Arthur through the rocky wasteland into a wood called the Dean. I was amazed to see so many trees; not lasers or cybernetics, but time-life trees with substance and shadows. Ignoring the risk of bites and rashes, I pulled off my gloves and stroked the bark. Arthur then took my hand, raised it to his lips and kissed each of the fingers in turn.

We reached his hut, where he introduced me to his father who, to my surprise, was blind. 'You have a beautiful voice,' he said. 'It reminds me of someone I knew long ago.'

'Even through the mouthpiece?' I asked, conscious of the distortion.

'She came from the Controlled World too.'

He seemed to know at once why we had come and retreated behind a curtain of skins with such discretion that I felt no embarrassment. Arthur swept a pile of tools off a chair but seemed otherwise unconcerned by the mess.

'I'd offer you something to eat,' he said, 'but I doubt that your stomach could digest it.'

'I'm not hungry,' I replied truthfully. 'I doubled my nutrition before I left.'

He unzipped my biosuit, kissing my neck and shoulders, and caressing my breasts. My flesh thrilled to his touch and I longed to rip off my mask and reciprocate. As if reading my mind, he gently stayed my hand. 'No,' he said. 'No! I won't make love to a corpse.' He traced the contours of my body, circling my stomach to reach my groin. Dazed by pleasure, I raised his head to mine. Unable to kiss him, I willed all my desire into my fingertips and, thankful for once that they were moist, ran them slowly down his throat, across his chest and along his thighs. No sooner had I released his penis than he pulled me towards him and we made love. We made love three times. I hope that you can find it in your heart to feel grateful that your daughter tasted passion before she died.

I laid my head on his chest and closed my eyes.

'We have such a short while together,' he said. 'Don't let's waste it in sleep.' I gazed into the gathering darkness, as rare and wondrous as an unarbited book. 'Our lives are so different . . . so distant,' he said. 'Do you think we'll meet again?' I made no reply, afraid to sound either sentimental or despairing. I wanted to cling to him forever, so that the issue wouldn't arise.

'Tell me about yourself,' I said. 'Everything. I've met your father. What about your mother?' I scanned the hut for signs of a woman's touch. 'Do you have any sisters or brothers?'

'No, to both. Just Pa. My mother came from your world. She died when I was born.'

'What was her name?'

'Sarah. I know . . . I know.' He laughed. 'Now tell me that I've slept with you because I'm searching for my mother.'

'What did she die of?' I asked, unable to share his amusement. 'That's if it's not too painful for you.'

'A virus. Her parents disowned her when they found out that she was pregnant. She came back up here, but her body couldn't cope. There were problems with the birth. She was very weak and caught a bug. I'm not sure what exactly. No one was in any rush to tell me.'

'Did her parents – your grandparents – never make contact?'

'Only to ask Pa to return her body. He agreed. He felt that he owed them that. Once, when I was a kid, he took me down there to meet them. I don't know what he was expecting. Maybe he wanted me to see where I came from? But they threw us out. They set these mechanical dogs on us.'

'The custodians.'

'One leapt at Pa and mauled his eyes.'

'That was what blinded him?'

'Yes. He was in agony, but he picked me up and we managed to get away. My face was covered with blood. His blood. At five, you remember the blood.'

'You were five?' I asked.

'Yes. Why?'

'No reason,' I replied, feeling my flesh creep. 'I must go.'

We barely spoke as we trudged back through the Dean, although our reasons for silence were very different. We reached the flyover, where my companions' ribaldry made Arthur unexpectedly coy, and we parted with no more than a quick hug.

The ribaldry increased as we descended the dizzying ventilation shaft and crawled back through the cramped tunnels. I returned to my dom and, brushing aside my friends' relief, shut myself in my room, where I now write this.

You may argue that I have no proof of Arthur's parentage, and you would be right. There may have been other Sarahs, who ventured up to the Surface World twenty-four years ago; there may have been other fathers, who brought their sons down to visit their grandparents. We shall never know. The only man able to identify me lost his sight on your – that is, on the grandparents' – orders. But to my mind, the evidence is irrefutable.

You may argue that I have committed no crime. Mine

was not the womb that bore him, although the womb that bore him was identical to mine. But I refuse to be reprieved on a technicality. So did some mysterious – not to say, mystical – force lead me to him? After all, even in our depopulated worlds, the odds were heavily stacked against our meeting. Or should we see it as a mere fact of life – not a twist of fate, and certainly not retribution – that two people were drawn to each other, who shared something of a common past and rather more of a genetic inheritance?

I refuse to live in a world of such facts, let alone in a world where such facts have no meaning; where you and your associates are so determined to shield us from tragedy that you even expunge the word from the dictionary; where Father and his associates have substituted novelty for wisdom. Sarah died as a consequence of love, but I shall die of despair, or the closest thing to it that our Controlled World allows. Perhaps at last I am escaping her template.

In a few minutes I shall leave the dom and walk slowly to the Transport Depot. I shall climb back up to the Surface World, making sure to avoid the flyover. This is not one of your arbited stories where love conquers all; I care for Arthur too much to burden him with my guilt. Yet it will comfort me to know that I am close to the one person who has ever wanted me for myself. I shall take off my mask and breathe the air that he breathes, even as it kills me. I shall die alone in the wasteland and trust that my flesh will be devoured by dogs, leaving no trace of my identity – not, whatever you may think, out of spite, but because it is the one way that I can guard against your harvesting my DNA to create another child, the third in the wretched line of Sarahs.

I should also warn you that, to keep you from attempting another cover-up, I am posting copies of this mail to everyone in my address book. I realise, of course, that this runs the risk of a delay mechanism malfunction, enabling someone – not you perhaps, but one of the three thousand other recipients – to activate the custodians to intercept me. That is a risk that I'm willing to take. So, as my finger hovers over *Send*, I shall surrender to the fate in which neither of us believes.

MICHAEL ARDITTI is an acclaimed novelist, short story writer and critic. His novels are *The Celibate* (1993), *Pagan and her Parents* (1996), *Easter* (2000), *Unity* (2005), *A Sea Change* (2006), *The Enemy of the Good* (2009), *Jubilate* (2011), *The Breath of Night* (2013), *Widows and Orphans* (2015), *Of Men and Angels* (2018), *The Anointed* (2020), *The Young Pretender* (2022) and *The Choice* (2023). His previous short story collection is *Good Clean Fun* (2004). He was awarded an Honorary D Litt from the University of Chester and is a Fellow of the Royal Society of Literature.